Steve has been single all his life and lives in the house he bought with his parents, who are now both deceased. Steve has never had much confidence in anything he does; his late mother was the one person who truly believed in him.

Archie
Hope you enjoy
my story

Steve Hetton

I would like to dedicate this book to my parents, who looked after me when I needed looking after, cared for me when I needed to be cared for, and loved me unconditionally.

Steve Pretlove

PRINCE OLIVER AND THE MALEVOLENT DANTE

AUSTIN MACAULEY PUBLISHERS™

LONDON • CAMBRIDGE • NEW YORK • SHARJAH

A CIP catalogue record for this title is available from the British Library.

ISBN 9781528937467 (Paperback)
ISBN 9781528969116 (ePub e-book)

www.austinmacauley.com

First Published (2019)
Austin Macauley Publishers Ltd
25 Canada Square
Canary Wharf
London
E14 5LQ

Chapter 1
Percival's Return

As the branch snapped and fell into the lake, it took with it, the two young boys who had been climbing in the tree. The water shot into the air like an erupting volcano, and the branch drifted across the surface of the lake, carried away by the ever-expanding ripples. Where the boys had fallen, the water was still, its glassy black surface shone in the daylight. The water was icy cold, but not frozen. It was late February. The older of the two boys surfaced, gasping for air as the freezing cold water had taken his breath away. Oliver spun around in the water searching for his younger brother, Nicholas. He was nowhere to be seen. He took a deep breath and dived below the surface, the water was murky, and he could not see anything. He tried searching the bottom of the lake with his hands, he flinched as something moved beneath his fingers. He moved his hand forward once more. There was nothing there but the silt that lay thick on the bottom. He had to surface again for he needed more air. He was losing all feeling in his arms and legs, but, again, he took a large breath and forced himself to dive below the surface of the icy water for the second time. Still, he found nothing. As panic sat in, he had to come up for air once more. Only this time when he surfaced, he spotted his younger brother lying on the bank. He swam towards the bank with great difficulty, his clothes were weighing him down, and with no feeling in his legs, they were no use. Fortunately, he was a strong swimmer and he made it to the bank using just his arms. The next problem Oliver had was hauling himself out of the freezing cold water. He called to Nicholas, there was no response. Through sheer determination, Oliver dragged himself from the lake. His hands were blue with cold, and he tried to stand, but his legs buckled, and so using just his tired and aching arms once more, he pulled himself across the frozen ground. When he finally reached Nicholas, he didn't know if he was dead or alive, but now completely exhausted, Oliver collapsed next to his younger brother, and passed out.

Oliver woke suddenly in a cold sweat. It felt like a dream, for as he opened his eyes looking up at the ceiling, he recognised his bedroom, and he was warm and dry. Only when he looked across at Nicholas's bed, did he realise it hadn't been a dream. The three princesses were sat on side of the bed with their back to Oliver. On the opposite side of Nicholas's bed sat their father, King Richard. The worried look on Richard's face told Oliver all was not well with Nicholas. Oliver tried to sit up in bed but was too weak, and so he lay there listening. The court physician was telling King Richard that the next couple of days would be critical to Nicholas's survival, he must be kept warm, and someone will have to watch over him, all the time.

As the physician left, Richard began to sob, and one by one, all three of the princesses ran past Oliver's bed in tears and left the room. Oliver lay silently in bed and the tears flowed as he listened to his father sobbing. Slowly, the sobbing faded as Oliver once more drifted off to sleep. When Oliver next woke, the room was dark, apart from the glow from the fireplace, and one candle beside Nicholas's bed. A solitary figure sat beside Nicholas's bed, it was their father. He was leaning forward holding Nicholas's hand and praying. Oliver called to his father in a whisper, there was no response. He called louder to his father. This time, King Richard let go of Nicholas's hand and, gently, placed it on the bed. As he left Nicholas's bedside, he picked up the candle, then carrying the candle Richard crossed the room to Oliver's bed. In the glow of the candlelight, Oliver could see the anger and pain in his father's face. "I'm sorry," said Oliver. Richard went to say something, but changed his mind. He knew he might say something he would later regret, and so, he turned his back on Oliver, and retook his position beside Nicholas's bed. In doing so, Oliver felt spurned, and was just as hurt as he would have been if his father had said he blamed him for what had happened. Oliver cried quietly into his pillow and fell asleep.

The next day, Oliver was feeling slightly better and the court physician gave him permission to get out of bed, but was told not to overexert himself. And so, he went and sat next to Nicholas's bed. King Richard had momentarily left Nicholas's bedside and was shocked on his return to see Oliver sitting there. He blamed Oliver for what had happened, and seeing him sat there, while Nicholas was fighting for his life was too much to bear. Anger rose from the pit of his stomach up into his chest. "Get away from him," bellowed Richard. "Haven't you done enough?" Oliver tried to explain what had happened, but Richard was in too much of a rage to listen. Oliver had never seen his father so angry before, and for the first time in his life, he was truly scared. He left Nicholas's bedside, and raced across the room and climbed into his own bed, neither of them spoke another word.

Two more days passed. Oliver was having his meals in his bed, as requested by the court physician. Richard was refusing to eat, as he kept vigil by Nicholas's bed. It was late afternoon when Nicholas finally stirred. Richard had fallen asleep and his head was resting on Nicholas's bed. Nicholas stroked his father's hair as he became aware of his surroundings, then he coughed. Oliver, who had been reading, looked across to see his brother was awake.

"Father, Father," he called, and Richard opened his eyes to feel the small hand stroking his hair. He sat up with a smile on his face, and tears in his eyes. He thought he had lost Nicholas forever.

The first words that Nicholas uttered were, "I'm sorry, I know I should not have climbed that tree. When the branch began to break, Oliver tried to rescue me, but then we fell into the water."

"That's all right," said Richard. "Don't worry about that. Are you hungry?"

"A little," said Nicholas.

Richard crossed the room and opened the door. The guard standing outside was instructed to go to the kitchen and ask for some warm porridge to be sent up. He then crossed the room once more, but this time he went to Oliver's bed. "I'm sorry," said Richard. They both smiled and Richard bent down to embrace his son.

Five weeks had passed since the incident at the lake. Both boys had made a full recovery, and the castle was alive with excitement. Preparations were well underway for the 12th birthday party of Oliver and his three sisters; Alice, Dorothy and

Mary. It had been seven years since they had last seen Percival and Berwyn, the giant white bear. King Richard had received word he was on his way to the castle and was looking forward to seeing his old friend again. So now, on top of everything else that he had to organise, he had to keep Percival's arrival a secret. Every year since that first adventure to find the green-striped zebra, Oliver and his sisters had asked, "When is Percival coming back?" And each year had been a disappointment, especially for Oliver.

Since Percival's first visit to the castle, there had been some dramatic changes. King Richard had a new son, Nicholas. He was now five years old, and he looked just like Oliver did at that age, but when Nicholas was born, tragedy struck, and Queen Elizabeth died three days later. The despair that Richard felt at losing his Queen, made him reject his son. The guilt he felt at wanting another child nearly destroyed him. He was completely withdrawn from family life, and nothing anyone said or did could break him free from his depression. For the first eighteen months of Nicholas's life, Richard ignored his existence. It was the nannies who raised Nicholas, along with the other four children. The three princesses adored their younger brother, it was like having a living doll to play with, until he needed changing. Then it was, "Nanny, Nanny, Nicholas has pooped himself again." And the three princesses would go off and play by themselves. Oliver was not so interested in Nicholas, only because he could not do any of the things Oliver loved to do, like climbing trees, and swimming in the lake, and fighting imaginary dragons. But Oliver would dream of the day when Nicholas was older, then he would show him how to do all the things he loved doing.

Richard's attitude changed towards Nicholas on what would have been Elizabeth's birthday, 13th August. Nicholas was just eighteen months old and he was in the castle gardens with one of the nannies. At eighteen months old, he was quite fast on his feet, and the ageing nanny was not as fast as she used to be. The three princesses were playing down by the lake, it was the middle of summer and very hot. Each had a parasol to protect them from the sun, they were having a tea party with their dolls. The nanny had decided to keep Nicholas away from the lake because of the dangers. Oliver was off somewhere doing his own thing. Nicholas, who had been watching his sisters, suddenly made a dash for it. The nanny, who had been kneeling on a blanket, struggled to get to her feet, her stiff joints meant this was a slow process. By the time she was fully upright, Nicholas was nowhere to be seen. Using her hand to shield her eyes from the brilliantly bright sunshine, she called to the princesses as she limped across the lawn, "Is Nicholas with you?" But before they answered, she could see he was not there with them.

Once again, she called for Nicholas, still no answer. She repeatedly called, with fear and panic building inside herself, she began screaming. "Nicholas, Nicholas where are you?" She was spinning around, looking in every direction, making herself feel dizzy, but he was nowhere to be seen. Her screams were heard from all areas of the garden, the three princesses were the first to reach the nanny, and as she continued to scream for help, they all began to cry. Next to arrive were two of the castle gardeners. What a scene they came across, three princesses bawling their eyes out, and a nanny who was so incoherent, they struggled to work out what was wrong. The two gardeners managed to calm the nanny down, and between sobs learnt that Prince Nicholas was missing. Just then, four castle guards came dashing across the lawn to investigate what all the screaming was about.

One of the gardeners explained, and one guard took control, "King Richard is in the west wing, go find him and inform His Majesty of what has happened." As one of the guards went in search of the King, the others spread out across the lawn calling for the young prince, Nicholas. The guard raced up the castle steps and into the west wing. He found King Richard sitting in front of a portrait of his late wife, Elizabeth.

"Your Majesty," he said. Richard raised a hand, he wanted silence. He always sat alone on her birthday, in silence with his memories. "But, Your Majesty, Prince Nicholas is missing," blurted out the guard. There was no visible response. As Richard sat in front of the portrait of Elizabeth, with his back to the guard, tears filled his eyes and began to stream down his cheeks. He felt guilty over her death, but now he was letting her down once more. He dried his eyes and turned to face the guard.

"Lead the way," he said. As they made their way out of the castle and into the garden, they were greeted by Oliver, who just happened to be holding hands with Nicholas. Richard and the guard were stunned to see Oliver with his younger brother, who was covered in dirt. "Where on earth did you find him?"

"Oh, he was just about to go down a rabbit hole," said Oliver. "I just caught him by the ankle before he could disappear. What's all the screaming for?" he asked.

Richard laughed at the sight of his two sons, and the innocence of youth. "That's nothing for you to worry about," said Richard. He sent the guard to let everyone know that Nicholas had been found and was unharmed. Richard, smiling, bent down and scooped up Nicholas in his arms, who was giggling away totally unaware of the panic he had caused.

Richard then took Oliver by the hand and said, "Why don't we go and play by the lake?" He kissed Nicholas on the cheek, released Oliver's hand, so he could race ahead, and Richard's thoughts went to Elizabeth, but instead of feeling sadness, he felt thankful, for the beautiful gift she had given him, and he made a promise that he would never again abandon any of his children.

The nanny, who had been looking after Nicholas, was in a terrible state. Even after having been told he was safe and unharmed, she could not forgive herself, and decided it was time she left the palace and the care of the young royals to someone more capable of looking after them and keeping them safe. She had a younger sister she could stay with. King Richard made her promise that if she ever needed anything, she would ask for help. And after all the years of loyal service, if ever she wanted to visit, she was always welcome. That was the day that changed everything for Richard, the thought of losing his son on his wife's birthday was just the shock he needed. After his wife had died, he had shown no interest in anything, now he had the rest of his life to live, and to raise his five children.

It was still two days before their birthday and the preparations were in full swing. Richard's sister, Queen Ophelia, and her husband, King Oswald, had arrived early to help with getting everything ready. They had a baby girl of eleven months whom they had named Elizabeth, after asking Richard if this would be acceptable, he had given his blessing and he loved her dearly. The three princesses were happy to look after their younger cousin, which meant her parents could help with the preparations for the big day. Oliver and Nicholas were now inseparable. Now Nicholas was five years old, Oliver had taken him under his wing and shown him all the best hiding places in the castle gardens. Oliver also knew all the secret passageways within the castle like the back of his hand, and now Nicholas knew them also. They would climb trees together, and swim in the lake. Oliver now had a real sword, and had passed on his wooden sword to Nicholas. They would practise sword fighting together, sometimes fighting each other and sometimes fighting alongside each other against a mysterious foe, often a fire-breathing dragon.

Oliver still liked to sneak out at night with a candle to watch the animals come out after dark. This had been something he had been doing since he was five years old. Only now, he had Nicholas to keep him company, but Nicholas could not always keep quiet, and lost interest if the animals didn't show up straight away. And so, Oliver would sometimes go alone, waiting to be sure Nicholas was fast asleep. He would take a lit candle through the secret passage way and make his way across the lawn and into the woods. He climbed the same tree he always had. First on the scene, as always, were the foxes, and as they moved on, the badgers appeared. Nicholas loved watching the badgers, and for some reason, the badgers seemed to love Nicholas. Whenever they appeared, he would climb down from the tree where he had been waiting and they would come to him. Oliver stayed up high in the branches. The older badgers were a bit more cautious, but the young badgers showed no signs of nervousness with Nicholas, and as he sat on the ground, they clambered all over him, licking his face and ears just like a young puppy would, they seemed to realise he posed no threat to them, and so, was accepted. The closest Oliver had to this experience was the time he fell from the tree and landed face to face with one of the adult badgers. He had been five at the time, that seemed so long ago now.

Oliver and Nicholas shared a bedroom, the one with the connecting door to their sisters', the one with the door that led to the hallway with the animal heads mounted on the walls. Oliver no longer played in this hallway, that was now the responsibility of Nicholas to fight those fierce beasts and keep the castle safe. Nicholas seemed even more determined to fight the wild animals than Oliver did at the same age. Maybe this was because

Nicholas had heard so many times of the adventure Oliver had been on, and so played it out down the hallway almost weekly.

With just one day to go before their 12th birthday, the final preparations were well underway. A week ago, there had been snow on the ground, which was not unusual for late March, but that had all melted away and today was the 1st of April, and so this was April fools' day. To keep them out of the way, Queen Ophelia had arranged for the royal children to be taken to the local village. They had not ventured to the village since their mother had died, five years earlier. They were to be dressed as peasants, accompanied by a dozen guards, also dressed as peasants, so as to blend in and not be recognised. The three princesses found this very exciting, as did Nicholas. For this was his first ever venture away from the castle, down to the village. Oliver was not so easily impressed, but wanted to go all the same. They arrived at the outskirts of the village on horseback and left them tied up, with two guards to look after them. As they entered the village, the first thing they noticed was laughter, loud and raucous laughter. Oliver wanted to investigate, alone, and so he stopped and bent down pretending to tie his shoe. One of the guards noticed and stopped also.

"It's all right," said Oliver. "I'll be right with you." The guard turned away to look in the direction the others had gone and when he turned back a second later, Oliver had disappeared.

"Damn that young prince," the guard muttered to himself. "I knew he was up to something."

Oliver had made his way to the main square in the village. There was a crowd of people gathered. Oliver managed to push his way through to the front, where he found himself standing next to a young lad. "What's going on?" he asked.

The young lad looked at him in a suspicious way and said, "What?" He looked Oliver up and down and asked, "Who are you?"

"Oh, I'm Oliver, and you are?"

"Henry," said the young lad.

"So what is going on?" Oliver asked again.

"It's a game called Stag and Hounds. The one in the middle with the blindfold is the stag, that's why he has two sticks held in place by the cloth wrapped and tied around his head. See?"

"Yes, I see," said Oliver. "But what about the others?"

"Well they're the hounds."

"And what is the purpose of this?" asked Oliver.

"It's just a game," said Henry. "Look, who are you?"

"I told you my name is Oliver. So what are they trying to do?" asked Oliver.

"Well, each one has to try and grab one of the sticks from the stag without getting caught, by the stag, watch." And as they stood watching, a young lad ran at the stag. He accidently touched his left leg before he could grab one of the sticks, and before he could get away, the stag spun round and grabbed him with his right hand. The young lad squealed like a pig caught in a trap and everyone burst out laughing.

"Can anyone try?" asked Oliver.

"Of course," said Henry.

And before he could say another word, Oliver stepped forward. Unlike the young lad before him, Oliver took his time. He was stalking the stag just like his father had taught him when they were hunting. The gathered crowd had stopped laughing, they were intrigued by this approach from such a young lad. It was normal for the youngsters to just charge in, but this one, this one was different. Even the stag knew something strange was taking place, he was not used to it being so silent, he even called out, "Is anyone there?"

"We're all here," someone shouted back from the gathered crowd. He started to spin, first one way and then the other, with outstretched arms, but could feel nothing. His breathing was getting faster, he was becoming agitated with anticipation. His movements became more erratic, lurching one way and then the other. All the time Oliver was studying the way the stag was moving, he seemed more mobile when he spun to the right and slightly off balance when turning to the left. After studying the stag, for about five minutes, Oliver knew what he was going to do. Oliver made his approach to the left of the stag and kicked up the loose dirt from the ground. As the stag felt it hitting his leg, he spun to the left and as observed earlier by Oliver, he became unstable. This allowed Oliver to race forward and take a stick from the stag's head before he could regain his balance, everyone in the crowd cheered. Henry was the first to race forward and congratulate Oliver, followed closely by two of the palace guards. As Oliver was led away by the two burly guards, the crowd applauded rapturously. Everyone trying to pat Oliver on the back or shake his hand.

"Bye, Henry," Oliver called as he was led away.

"Bye, Oliver."

Sitting on a rooftop unnoticed because of his invisibility was Dante, the winged fairy. He had spent the last seven years searching for Prince Oliver and could hardly believe that he had finally found him. Now he had to observe and wait for the right moment to steal him away. The crowd was still cheering as Oliver was led away. The stag removed the cloth from his head, it took a few seconds for his eyes to adjust to the light. He caught a glimpse of Oliver before he disappeared into the crowd. He had been undefeated for five years and was not happy to have lost. A young peasant woman approached. "Come on, darling, better luck next year." She placed her hand on his arm and he brushed her off aggressively. "Here, there's no need to be like that," she said. He gave her a disdainful look as he left the square. Seeing his annoyance made the crowd cheer louder. For five years, he had bragged how he was unbeatable, now as he walked away down the street, laughter followed. His annoyance was now becoming anger. *Who was this child and where did he come from*, were the thoughts that ran through his head. He kicked over a bucket of water in his frustration, which angered the woman who was just about to do some washing. She chased him down the street having picked up her broom.

Oliver and the two guards finally caught up with the rest of the royal siblings, they were playing a game of musical chairs. A long row of a dozen chairs were lined up in the middle of the street, an old man playing a flute provided the music. As the music stopped, each chair was sat upon, the person left standing was out of the game. Alice and Mary were already out of the game, but Dorothy and Nicholas were still playing. As the players dwindled, so did the chairs, the music stopped, Nicholas had a seat and so did Dorothy, until another boy pushed her off. She fell to the ground and cut her hand, the young boy who had claimed Dorothy's seat was smiling, but not for long. Oliver raced over and demanded an apology for his sister.

"Why, what's it to you?" the boy snarled.

"How dare you? I should have you horse whipped," said Oliver.

"Why, who do you think you are, a prince or something?" snapped the boy.

With that, Oliver introduced himself, "My name is Prince Oliver and you have just assaulted my sister, Princess Dorothy." At first, the lad thought he was joking, and laughed. Then as he looked beyond Oliver and saw the palace guards dressed as peasants, who were way too clean and easily stood out, the smile disappeared from the boy's face as fast as the colour left his cheeks. He didn't know what to do or what to say, he fell to his knees and apologised, begging for forgiveness. One of the guards bent down and helped Dorothy to her feet.

"I think it's time we went back to the castle," said the guard. Oliver had wanted to hit the young boy for hurting his sister, but Dorothy asked, "Please don't hurt him, Oliver. Can we just go, please?" Oliver unclenched his fist and followed the guard who led Dorothy away. Nicholas reluctantly left the game, he had been having fun and felt sure he was going to win, but he had no choice, it was time to go. The young boy who had pushed Princess Dorothy to the ground was still on his knees, trembling with fear of what they might do to him. He slowly raised his head and watched as the royal party left. Word had spread like wild fire amongst the villagers when Oliver had introduced himself. Now they all lined the streets as the young royals were escorted back to their horses. Everyone wanted to catch a glimpse and see what they looked like, for they hadn't been seen in the village for five years, since their mother had died. Henry had a big smile on his face as he caught sight of Prince Oliver, and Oliver saw Henry smiling and smiled back and gave him a nod of friendship. All this time, Dante sat watching without moving, studying. It was Oliver who he blamed for not getting his wish from the green-striped Zebra but, having seen how big he had grown, Dante had settled on a new target. Until now, he didn't know there was a younger brother, but Nicholas would be far easier to steal away. Dante skipped across the rooftops, watching the royal children being led away. They were now on their ponies heading back to the castle with the guards, totally unaware of being observed. Dante followed them all the way to the castle gates, but for now, didn't go any further, it had taken seven long years to find Oliver, he was in no rush. He knew that at some point, an opportunity to grab Nicholas would present itself.

It was late in the afternoon when they arrived back at the castle. Dorothy's cut hand had now turned purple and was swollen with bruising. The court physician checked Dorothy's hand. "I am sure it is just a bruise, and no broken bones." Richard was not happy when he heard of how this had happened, but Dorothy pleaded with her father not to take any action, after all, it was only a bruise, and the young boy only really pushed her from a chair.

Richard smiled at his daughter. "How like your mother you are," he said. "Alright, if you wish the matter forgotten, so be it."

"Thank you, Father," she said.

"I think you should all go and clean up before supper."

And with that, all five children left the room. Queen Ophelia and her husband, King Oswald, had been sitting just behind Richard as he spoke to his children. Ophelia stood up and placed a hand on her brother's shoulder. "You did the right thing," she said.

While Richard, Ophelia and Oswald waited for the children to return, the conversation turned to the preparation for the birthday party. Ophelia was telling Richard about the cake. "It is magnificent. The bottom three layers are covered in pink and white flowers, made of icing, and the top layer has a prince fighting a green dragon. Between each layer is vanilla cream."

"Excellent," said Richard. "I received news earlier that Percival will be here later today. Without doubt, that will be the biggest surprise." He stopped before going any further, Oliver and Nicholas had entered the room. "Come and join us at the table," he said.

Ophelia asked, "Are you looking forward to tomorrow, Oliver?"

"Yes, I am. I do hope Percival can make it tomorrow. Have you heard anything, Father?" He turned to face his father. "You did invite him, didn't you?"

"Of course, I invited him. Just as you requested, the same as I have done every year, but you know he is not an easy man to get hold of. Always travelling, he could be anywhere." Richard did not like lying to his children but knew the surprise would be worth it, and this was one of those lies that they would forgive him for.

Alice, Dorothy and Mary came into the room, and said, good evening, and sat down at the table. A servant who had been standing at Richard's side was instructed to serve supper. He pulled on a chord which rang a bell in the kitchen to let the servants know supper was to be served. They came into the dining room carrying silver platters. King Richard was served first, followed by King Oswald and Queen Ophelia, and then the children. Baked salmon in an hollandaise sauce, with cream of asparagus spears. Both Oliver and Nicholas looked at each other, and pulled a face. They both hated fish, but they also knew that if they didn't eat it, they wouldn't get any dessert, and so as everyone else was enjoying their meal, the two princes had to force it down. Nicholas had tears running down his face, he hated the taste so much, but he dare not spit it out, that was not the right thing, especially for royal children. He had been told that so many times by his nannies, it was something he would never forget, and so they struggled on. With each mouthful, both princes felt like they wanted to vomit. At last, the plate was empty, and so the plates were removed. They sat quietly waiting, wondering what delight was for dessert. When it was bought to the table, everyone was happy, an apple and pear tart, served with vanilla cream. This was something the two boys could really enjoy.

After everyone had been served, there was a single piece left over. The princes asked their father, "Can we share the last piece?"

Richard answered, "As long as you don't make yourselves sick by eating too much."

"We won't," they said. And so, the servant with the last piece of tart stepped forward, cut it into two and placed each piece onto the plate of the princes. It was gone within seconds.

Richard shook his head and laughed. "I don't know where they put it all."

Ophelia looked at her brother, raised an eyebrow and said, "You must be joking. That is exactly what you used to be like."

"No, I wasn't," he said.

"Oh yes, it was you," replied Ophelia. "And I remember you hated salmon as much as they do now. Only you used to feed it to the dog, when you thought no one was watching." Richard nearly choked on a mouthful of wine when Ophelia made this declaration. Everyone at the table was now laughing at Richard, and when he finished coughing and spluttering, he too could see the funny side of this statement, and joined in the laughter.

They retired to the drawing room and sat around the huge fireplace. Richard wanted to know what else they had been up to that day in the village, and so, Oliver told his story of the stag and hounds game that he had played. They all listened intently leaning in so as not to miss anything, and then the final leap to claim the stick from the stag and everyone was cheering. Richard was so pleased that they had enjoyed themselves, even when Dorothy recounted their game of musical chairs. Richard could see they were having fun. "Alright, children, it's time for bed," said Ophelia. "You have a big day ahead of you tomorrow." And so, they kissed their father good night and went off to their rooms. The three princesses went to their room, they no longer required a nanny to put them to bed. Oliver and Nicholas walked through their sister's room using the adjoining door and went into their bedroom. Oliver did help Nicholas into bed before blowing out the candle, and by the warm glow from the fireplace, Oliver crossed to his bed. As he pulled back the blankets and climbed into bed, they said good night to each other.

"See you in the morning," said Oliver.

Richard had been left alone waiting in the drawing room for news of Percival's arrival. Two guards had been sent to wait by the castle gates, they were to escort Percival to the east wing. This way, they would be far away from the children's bedrooms. Finally, a guard came to the drawing room. "They are here," he said. "They have been taken to the east wing as you instructed."

"Thank you," said Richard. He went immediately to the east wing. Sitting in a chair, warming himself by the log fire was Percival. He was wrapped in a blanket for it was another particularly cold night. As Richard entered, Percival stood up. "Welcome, my old friend," said Richard.

"Your Majesty," said Percival.

"How was your journey?" asked Richard.

"Very cold," said Percival.

"Please sit down," said Richard. "Can I offer you anything to eat?"

"I am not hungry, Your Majesty, but maybe a hot cup of tea."

"Of course," said Richard. He crossed the room to the corner where a chord was hanging and gently pulled, the bell rang in the kitchen. A servant immediately left the kitchen and went to the east wing. He was surprised to see a guard standing outside the door to the sitting room. He knocked once and entered. "We require a pot of tea and two cups," said Richard. "And you have seen nothing."

"Yes, Your Majesty." Shortly afterwards, the servant returned with the tea and cups as requested. "Can I get you anything else, Your Majesty?"

"No, that will be all," said Richard. "And remember, you have seen nothing." Berwyn was lying next to Percival's chair and had not once stirred. "I hope you find the adjoining bedroom comfortable," said Richard.

"This is a lot warmer and far more comfortable than we are used to," said Percival.

"Then I bid you good night," said Richard, having finished his tea.

"Good night, Your Majesty," said Percival.

Oliver and Nicholas woke up early on the 2nd April. It had been a particularly cold night once more. As Oliver pulled open the heavy velvet curtains in his bedroom, his breath was visible in the cold air that was radiating from the frozen window. They had to scrape at the frost that had formed intricate patterns on the inside of the window in order to look out. A heavy frost had settled on the ground, it was totally white, the many trees sparkled like diamonds as the sun dared to show itself above the distant hills, in a pale blue sky with light fluffy clouds that caught the rays of the sun. They glowed a soft pink at the edges, but where the cloud was thicker, this darkened to purple. Oliver stood watching the sunrise for just a few minutes, and in that short time as the clouds parted, a soft yellow winter sun was revealed.

Oliver got dressed and then helped Nicholas. Their clothes had been laid out for them while they were sleeping. This included a thick jumper because of the cold. They joined their sisters at the breakfast table. On a cold day like today, it was porridge for breakfast, but there was also toast and marmalade if they wanted it, and a large pot of steaming hot tea. They all got stuck in, between mouthfuls, they were all talking of their big day. Oliver was saying how he would love for Percival to be there. Mary pointed out to Oliver that he had been saying the same thing for the last seven years, and he hadn't bothered to show up yet, why should this year be any different.

Oliver was left feeling deflated, but he knew she was right, why should this year be any different. Dorothy could see that Oliver was looking dejected, and so attempted to raise his spirits. "I wonder what surprises father will have for us this year."

Nicholas said, "I hope I get a pony."

Mary reminded him, "It's not your birthday."

"But I always get something, and I only want a little pony," said Nicholas. Alice and Dorothy burst out laughing, Mary hated having to share a birthday. Oliver was still staring down at his now cold porridge. A servant entered the room to clear the breakfast table.

"Do you know where our father is?" asked Mary.

"No, princess, I haven't seen the king this morning," answered the servant. "Can I get you anything else?" he asked.

"No," said Mary and she dismissed the servant with a wave of her hand.

"Why do you have to be so rude?" asked Alice.

"I don't know what you mean," said Mary.

"Dismissing him like that, with a wave of your hand."

"Oh that," said Mary. "Well, he is only a servant."

"Yes, and you are only a twelve years old princess."

Mary didn't like being told off by anyone. "You know Mother would not like the way you treat the servants."

"Yes, but she's not here," snapped Mary, and with that last comment, she stomped off out of the room.

Queen Ophelia entered the room as Mary left. "What is wrong with Mary? She just walked passed me in a foul mood."

Alice answered, "Oh that's just Mary being Mary."

"Why? What happened?" enquired Ophelia.

"I told her Mother wouldn't approve of the way she treats the servants, and she got upset."

"You do realise that underneath that tough exterior, Mary misses your mother and is more sensitive than she is willing to let on." Now Alice felt guilty for what she had said to Mary.

Under strict instructions from her brother Richard to keep the children occupied, Ophelia asked, "So who wants to go for a ride?" Nicholas responded eagerly, but Oliver was not enthusiastic. He had moved away from the table to one of the large windows and was staring out into the garden. It was a cloudless sky with a now bright winter sun, which provided little warmth, the frost still covered the ground. Oliver was longing to see Percival and Berwyn again. He had really hoped this was the year they would be back.

Ophelia crossed the room and sat beside Oliver as he continued to stare out of the window. "You never know they may turn up," she said.

He sighed, "I have been waiting for them for so long now. I don't think I will ever see them again." Oliver moved away from his aunt and sat down once more, wanting to be left alone. Drawing his knees to his chest, he rested his chin on top of his knees, and sat quietly staring out into the garden.

She so wanted to tell him they were already here, but didn't want to spoil the surprise. She turned away from Oliver, and facing the other three, she asked, "So do you want to go for a ride?" Nicholas was definitely excited about going for a ride, and raced across the room. He took hold of Ophelia's hand and started to lead her from the room. Alice and Dorothy looked at each other.

"There's nothing else we can do," they said. And so, the four of them headed down to the stables. The three grey ponies that belonged to the princesses were already saddled and waiting. Prince Nicholas was lifted onto the back of the pony that belonged to Mary. Alice and Dorothy just needed a helping hand, as did Ophelia, onto the back of a stunning white mare. She informed the guard that Prince Oliver would not be joining them. As they rode out of the courtyard, the guard turned and led Prince Oliver's pony back into the stables. They set off with Ophelia and two of the castle guards, with instructions to keep them away from the castle until lunchtime. As they rode out of the castle gates, once again, they were being observed. Dante had made himself comfortable sitting in a tree, he spotted Nicholas as he rode on by with two of his sisters, and was thinking maybe today was the day. He was thinking of a plan to separate Nicholas from his sisters. When the two guards and Queen Ophelia appeared, he instantly changed his mind. There would be better opportunities.

Mary had gone back to her room, and out of shear frustration, she had jumped onto the beds of Alice and Dorothy, and pulled them apart. She then went and collapsed onto her own bed, and cried. As she lay there staring at the ceiling, she asked of her mother, "Why did you have to die?"

Ophelia and the three children returned after an exhausting three hours ride. Although the sun was bright, there was still a chill in the air, and where the sun had not shone, the frost lingered in the shadows, winter's icy grip, holding on by its fingertips. Alice and Dorothy dismounted as they reached the stables. Nicholas was riding with one of the guards as he had already fallen asleep, another guard was waiting to greet them. As the guard held the reigns of Nicholas's pony, one guard dismounted. He then took Nicholas from the other guard who dismounted and then took all the ponies into the stable. The guard holding Nicholas followed queen Ophelia through the castle to the boys' bedroom and placed Nicholas on the bed, then left quietly. Oliver hadn't moved in all that time. As Ophelia passed the room where she had left him, she saw Oliver still staring out of the window, in exactly the same position as when she left him there. Only this time, she didn't go and comfort Oliver. Instead, she went and found her brother, Richard. Richard was in the great hall checking everything was in place for the party,

"Richard," said Ophelia. "I think you need to go and have a word with Oliver, he's sitting in the breakfast room."

"Not now," said Richard.

"He's been sitting in the same position for the last three hours just staring out of the window."

"Oh, he will be all right," said Richard.

But Ophelia insisted, "You need to go speak to your son."

And so, Richard reluctantly left the great hall and went to find his eldest son. Oliver was sitting, staring out of the window where Ophelia had said. Richard walked over and sat next to his son. "What's the matter, Oliver?" Richard asked.

"I miss her so much," said Oliver, tears welling up in his eyes, his nose began to run and he used the sleeve of his jumper to wipe under his nose to stop it running into his mouth.

"I miss her too," said Richard. Oliver turned to face his father and they were joined in an emotional embrace.

Richard said to his son, "You know, she is looking down on us always, and she will always be present in our hearts. Each time you talk to her, she will hear you." Oliver wiped the tears from his eyes, and smiled at his father. "You need to go and get changed for your party," said Richard. "And tell the others to get ready as well. I will come and get you when we are ready for you, off you go now."

"Yes, Father." Oliver really didn't feel like he wanted a party, but knew he had to attend. He headed back to his room. Alice, Dorothy and Mary were arguing when Oliver knocked on their door. Alice and Dorothy were not happy when they had returned from their horse ride to find their beds had been ripped apart,

"Father will come for us when everything is ready. You had better get dressed."

"Okay," they said. Oliver walked on through his sister's bedroom and entered his own through the connecting door. The arguing continued as he entered his bedroom. Ophelia was getting Nicholas ready.

"How are you?" she asked.

"I'm fine," lied Oliver.

Ophelia finished getting Nicholas ready. "I think you're needed next door," said Oliver.

"Don't take too long getting changed," she said to Oliver, as she left the room. "Your father will be along shortly. Girls, girls," she said as she entered the bedroom of the three princesses. They stopped shouting immediately. Ophelia walked over to the beds of Alice and Dorothy, turned to face Mary, and asked, "Why?"

"I don't know," she sobbed. "I just get so angry."

Ophelia crossed the room and put her arms around Mary. "It will be all right." Seeing their sister like this reminded Alice and Dorothy of what Ophelia had said earlier, about Mary being more sensitive that she lets on. They both crossed the room to join their aunt in giving their sister a hug.

The banquet tables were all set, laden with food, there was pheasant and peacock, wild boar and venison served with a variety of vegetables and for dessert the beautifully decorated four-tier cake, filled with vanilla cream, between each layer of sponge, all to be served with red wine and ales. The candles which adorned all the walls were lit, as were the candles in the chandeliers, suspended from the ceiling, a warm glow filled the room. There was a roaring fire in the fireplace which sent warmth throughout the great hall. All the entertainment was ready and in place, everyone was waiting. It was time for King Richard to bring his children to their birthday celebration. This was a tradition that Richard and Elizabeth had always done together, but since her untimely death, he had continued to do this on his own. He walked down the long hallway to the bedroom his three daughters shared. He knocked on the door and entered. Standing before him was a vision of beauty, three young girls dressed alike, but oh so different. Mary had grown taller and thin, she had a look about her that made her appear quite aloof. Alice was the shortest and just a little plump. Dorothy was in the middle, both in height and size, with shoulder length dark curly hair, and emerald green eyes, she was the one who most resembled their mother. Richard could not help but smile. Just then, Nicholas raced from the adjoining bedroom he shared with Oliver, and jumped into his father's arms Oliver followed with an assured walk of a young prince.

"Can we go? Can we go now?" pleaded Nicholas excitedly. Richard smiled at all his children, he was so proud of how they had grown up.

"Are we all ready," he asked.

"Yes, Father," they replied.

"Then let's go to the party."

They left the warm bedroom behind. It was late afternoon and had turned chilly once more. The fires were lit in the fireplaces spaced out along the long hallway, candles flickered as they passed by. A look out of the window, and gentle snow was falling once more, being blown about by a strong gusty wind. They arrived at the doors to the great hall, two guards were standing either side of the doorway. Richard instructed them to open the heavy doors, and as they did so. A loud cheer was heard from inside as the royal children entered the hall. Nicholas beamed from ear to ear, he was only five and so loved parties. When the cheering stopped, Richard told his children to go off and enjoy themselves. There were jugglers and stilt walkers, fire breathers and acrobats, musicians and jesters. Nicholas went straight over to the fire breathers, absolutely transfixed. He sat on the floor crossed legged and watched, as they placed the burning sticks up to their mouths and blew, the flames shot high in the air. Nicholas was on his feet jumping for joy. The three princesses went over to the musicians. There were other members of the nobility already dancing, and they readily joined in, they all seemed perfectly happy. Only Oliver was left wandering aimlessly around the great hall. There was a heavy velvet curtain hanging in one corner that wasn't normally there, but when Oliver tried to approach, two guards standing in front of the curtains blocked his way.

"Sorry, Prince Oliver," said one of the guards. "We are under strict orders, no one can go back there." Normally when Oliver was told he could not do something, he went ahead and did it anyway, but this time, he just walked away. Both guards looked at each other, they knew this was not normal behaviour for the young prince. As they watched him walk away, they retook their positions. Oliver sat down, alone. Ophelia, Richard's sister, was his dance partner, she had been watching Oliver as he moved around the room. She pointed out to Richard that Oliver was still unhappy.

Richard said, "I think it's time to bring in the guest of honour." Ophelia agreed. Richard raised a hand and on seeing the signal, the musicians stopped playing, everyone had stopped dancing, the fire breathers ceased, the jesters fell quite, the tumblers and stilt walkers had all come to a standstill, not knowing what was going on. Richard called for all his children to join him. Alice, Dorothy and Mary walked across the room, Nicholas wanted to stay with the fire breathers, but again was called by Richard and so reluctantly left them. Oliver stayed sitting alone.

Ophelia walked over to Oliver, placed a hand on his right shoulder and said, "Please come join your father." He slowly got to his feet and they silently walked across the room. It was dead silent and all eyes were upon them, this only helped to make Oliver feel worse than ever. They all lined up in front of their father, he told them to turn around. As they did, they were now facing the heavy velvet curtain, with the two guards standing in front of the curtains. Richard called for the curtains to be opened, everyone in the hall stood in silence, not knowing what to expect. Oliver was so not interested, he was looking down at the floor.

It was Dorothy who called out first as she raced forward and flung her arms around his neck. "It's Percival," she cried. She was closely followed by her sisters. Because Oliver, who had been looking at the floor, was the slowest to react, he raised his head but could barely make out Percival from beneath his three sisters, but there stood Berwyn, the giant white bear. Nicholas had already crossed the hall halfway and stopped in front of Berwyn.

Oliver walked up behind Nicholas and bent down, he whispered in Nicholas's ear, "Would you like to meet him?" he asked. Nicholas nodded. Oliver took his younger brother by the hand, they started to walk forward. Nicholas was nervous, but with encouragement from Oliver, they walked up to Berwyn. Berwyn lowered his head and Oliver picked up Nicholas so as to stroke the top of the giant bears head, his fur was soft to touch and instantly, the nerves Nicholas had felt disappeared.

Having been smothered by the three princesses, Percival was happy when they moved over to greet Berwyn. This left the way clear for Oliver to finally greet his old friend. Tears of happiness had welled up in Oliver's eyes and were now streaming down his face. He didn't care who saw, he threw his arms around Percival, and said, "I have waited so long for you to return." The embrace they shared seemed to last forever, then Oliver remembered. "I have someone else who wants to meet you." Nicholas was sat on the floor stroking Berwyn's giant feet. "Nicholas, come over here." He raced to his brother's side. "Nicholas, I would like you to meet Percival, the man who helped me find my voice."

Percival smiled at Nicholas, and asked, "How are you, young Prince?" Nicholas was nervous and laughed, but did not reply. He simply turned away and ran back to Berwyn, totally in awe of the giant white bear.

Richard had crossed the room and was standing next to Oliver. He greeted his old friend. "So when did you arrive?" asked Oliver.

"They arrived yesterday," said Richard. "After you had all gone to bed."

"I cannot believe how much you have grown," said Percival.

"Twelve years old and almost as tall as his father," said Richard.

It was time to eat, they took their places at the table and the food was served, the wine and ales flowed, the children had freshly squeezed lemonade, although Oliver did manage to get hold of a glass of red wine, when no one was looking. Just one sip left him wondering why anybody would want to drink that. It was horrible, he quickly drank some lemonade to remove the taste of wine. At the end of the meal, the cake was bought in and placed on the table in front of King Richard. They were all impressed with the decorations on the cake, the icing flowers on the lower tier looked so real and, as for the dragon which adorned the top layer, just perfect, and when they ate it, they all agreed it tasted as good as it looked.

Nicholas was the first of the royal children to become tired. Queen Ophelia said, "I expect he's exhausted from the horse ride earlier today. I will put him to bed." She approached one of the guards and asked for his assistance. The guard picked Nicholas up and carried him down the hallway to his bedroom. Ophelia opened the bedroom door, and as they stepped into the bedroom, the warmth from the fire filled the room. The guard carried Nicholas across the room and placed him onto his bed. "Thank you," said Ophelia. "I can manage now."

Having put Nicholas to bed, Ophelia had returned to the great hall, the celebrations were in full swing. Alice and Dorothy were having a go at stilt walking, Mary refused, saying it was common to do such a thing. Alice and Dorothy didn't care what Mary thought; they were having the best time ever, even when they fell, it was into the arms of the stilt walking young men. Richard was watching closely. Ophelia tapped him on the shoulder, and reminded him that they are growing up. He smiled, and said, "I know." Mary had decided to take herself to bed. Only after she had gone did Richard realise that he hadn't given them their birthday present.

Ophelia reassured him, "There's another day tomorrow. Look at how much fun they are having." And she was right, the two princesses were having so much fun, the thought of presents had gone out of their heads completely, and as for Oliver, he had received the only thing he had been hoping for, Percival and Berwyn.

The night finally came to an end. It was gone midnight before everyone was in bed. Oliver lay in his bed, looking at the ceiling, he was so happy. He spoke to his mother before going to sleep, telling her of everything that had happened that day, and as he closed his eyes, he whispered, "Goodnight, Mother."

Chapter 2
Percival's Tale

Oliver was the first of the young royals to awaken the next morning. He crossed the bedroom to the selection of clean clothes that had been left out for him on the chair by the fire. As he removed his nightshirt, he shivered, but as soon as he pulled on a clean vest, the warmth enveloped his body like a warm blanket. As he pulled on his trousers, they felt like a warm glove. He quickly put on the rest of his clothes, so now the whole of his body was comfortably warm. Nicholas was still fast asleep. Oliver left the bedroom, using the door that led to the hallway, not wanting to disturb his sisters. As the door clicked shut, Nicholas awoke, still excited from the party. He was eager not to miss anything, and wanted to see Berwyn again. He raced across the room and got dressed quickly. Instead of using the door that Oliver had, Nicholas opened the adjoining door to his sisters' bedroom. They were just waking up themselves. In his excitement as he dashed across the room, he shouted, "Morning," and was gone. The three princesses got out of bed, thankful for the warm fire in their room, they dressed quickly and made their way down to breakfast.

Seated around the table were King Richard, King Oswald and Queen Ophelia, all five royal children and Percival, Berwyn was lying at Percival's feet as always. Percival had a new tale to tell, and so, when everyone had finished breakfast, Percival stood where everyone could see him, and he began, "There was once a wicked fairy, who believed he had been unjustly treated. Seeking revenge on his betrayers, he made a plan; he dreamt of untold wealth and power, and to achieve his aim, he would kidnap a royal child and hold that child for a king's ransom." Percival turned to Richard, "I am sure you recall from our first adventure, the winged fairy called Dante." Richard nodded in acknowledgement. "But are you aware of what happened to him?"

"Come to think of it," said Richard, "I have not given him a second thought since we parted. Why? What has he been up to?"

"He was not happy with the way things turned out, Your Majesty. After Oliver had seen the green-striped zebra, Dante had approached the pool and could also see the zebra. He demanded a wish, and a wish he got."

"And what did he wish for?" asked Richard, enquiringly.

"He wished to be sat upon a pile of gold."

"So, why was he not happy with this outcome?" asked Richard.

"Because he made a selfish wish to be sat upon a pile of gold, and the green-striped zebra placed him upon a pile of golden sand."

Richard roared with laughter, slapped his thigh, rocked back on his chair so the front two legs lifted off the floor, he nearly fell from the chair to the floor. Only the guard standing close by caught the chair and raised it back onto all four legs. Richard was laughing so much, he had tears in his eyes and an ache in his side, everyone was now laughing, everyone except Percival. He patiently waited for them to stop. Oliver who had been looking at his father turned to face Percival. He stopped laughing straight away. He could tell from the expression on Percival's face that something was troubling him. Oliver turned back to King Richard. "Father," he said.

And with that, Richard looked first at his son, and then followed his gaze back to Percival. "Sorry about that," he said, regaining his composure. "Please carry on."

"Dante's lust for gold has not waned, Your Majesty. In fact, it has grown stronger. Dante blames you for not getting his wish from the green-striped zebra. In his warped mind, he has come to believe that because Oliver got his wish, the zebra did not grant his."

"Well, Dante is more a fool than I thought he was," said Richard.

"I agree," said Percival. "But a dangerous fool, nonetheless."

"So, do we know what he is up to?"

"He still has the desire for gold, that we know for sure. But what he is up to, no, we do not know. I am concerned for Oliver's safety," said Percival.

But before he could say anymore, Richard stood up and said, "I think we should leave it there. We can talk later." Percival nodded and sat down once more. Breakfast was finished in silence. Richard had stopped Percival from going any further because he felt this was a discussion that should be held between grown-ups, without the children present.

After breakfast, Percival and Berwyn had left the room. They had gone for a walk in the palace gardens. Oliver caught up with them down by the frozen lake, their breath visible in the cold morning air, where the wind had blown the snow. In places, the grass was bare, while in other places, it had been blown into drifts of several inches deep. "Do you remember what happened the last time we were here?" said Percival.

Oliver shook his head. "No."

"You were just five years old, and fell asleep. I placed you onto Berwyn's back who carried you all the way around the lake until we met your father."

"What are you afraid of, Percival?" asked Oliver.

Percival lied, "I'm not afraid of anything."

"Why are you concerned for my safety?" But, before this conversation could go any further, they were interrupted by a very excitable Nicholas. He had raced across the lawn to catch up with them, the snowy conditions made this more difficult than normal.

As he slipped his way across the ground. "Hey, wait for me," he shouted. They stopped walking, he caught up with them but was now out of breath, and breathing heavily. His breath in the cold air consumed his head like his own personal fog. Berwyn lowered his head and Oliver placed Nicholas onto his back, just behind his head.

"Now hold on," said Percival, and Berwyn stood up, onto all four feet. Nicholas was now sitting higher than on any pony he had ever ridden. The thick fur of Berwyn's coat helped to keep Nicholas's hands warm as he sank them deep into the thick fur to hold on. The conversation between Percival and Oliver had changed, they were now talking of last night's festivities, and this continued all the way around the frozen lake. Again, they were observed by Dante, but this time, it was the presence of Berwyn that stopped him from trying anything.

Alice, Dorothy and Mary were sitting at the breakfast table, only their aunt Ophelia was present. The silence was broken when Mary asked, "Do you know where our father has gone?

Ophelia took no notice of the tone Mary had used, and simply answered, "I have no idea where your father is."

Mary was obviously in one of her moods. "You do realise he didn't even give us a birthday present," she ranted, to everyone present.

"Oh, Mary, stop complaining," said Alice. "Look at that wonderful party we had. Was that not enough?"

"You must be joking," said Mary, and then she added spitefully, "I saw you two cavorting with the young stilts men, how disgusting."

"Now that is quite enough," said Queen Ophelia. "It was a party, everyone was there to enjoy themselves, and nothing untoward happened." Mary had turned red in the face, she had been told off and knew she dare not reply, and so she stomped her way out of the room like a spoilt child. Alice and Dorothy both laughed as Mary left the room. They glanced across to where their aunt was sitting, she was not laughing. They tried their best to stifle their laughter, but they couldn't help it and their laughter was infectious, and soon, Ophelia was laughing also, but, she quickly composed herself.

"Now, girls," she said. "It is not gracious to laugh at your sister like that. I know your father has a present for each of you, but with all the festivities going on yesterday, he just forgot to give them to you."

"Oh that's fine," said Dorothy and Alice. "We don't need anything, we only wish our mother could have been there with us. Can we be excused?" they asked.

"Of course," said Ophelia, and with that the two young princesses left Ophelia on her own. They went into the sitting room that had the portrait of their mother. Mary was already there. As they entered, she turned to face them and they could see she had been crying. They ran across the room and hugged their sister, and so, they sat on the sofa facing their mother and began to recount in great detail the events of the night before.

Richard stood silently in the doorway and listened, this was their time to be with their mother.

Chapter 3
Oliver Disappears

Next morning in one of the sitting rooms, Richard and Percival were speaking of Dante and what possible threat he posed. "He blames you and Oliver for not getting his wish. If he is thinking of claiming a king's ransom, it seems to me that it will be Oliver he tries to kidnap."

"That seems a reasonable assumption," said Richard. "So what can we do?"

"I would suggest you send out a search party and try to find Dante, before he strikes." Percival had laid out a map and was indicating the last known location of Dante. "I would suggest sending a party of guards there." They left the sitting room, leaving the map spread open on the table, and they headed off to the guards' quarters where Richard selected ten guards to go in search of Dante. Stephen the scribe had requested to go along, his request was granted. Oliver knew his father was meeting with Percival in the sitting room, and had been hiding in the secret passageway that opened into that room. This was the easiest way to find anything out. While Richard and Percival had gone to the guards' quarters, Oliver had slipped into the sitting room from the secret passageway in which he had been hiding. He was studying the map, and noted where Percival had said was Dante's last known location.

Suddenly, footsteps, he moved quickly, silently across the room and slipped back inside the secret passageway, just as Richard returned to the sitting room with all the guards he had selected to go in search of Dante. He showed them the map and the last known location of Dante. "This is where you need to start your search." Percival handed the head guard a copy of the map. "It will take a couple of days to get together the supplies," said Richard.

The two days passed quickly. As soon as the guards had eaten breakfast, ten horses were waiting in the courtyard. Stephen had volunteered to drive the wagon, loaded with supplies. They said their goodbyes and left. Oliver had made up his mind that he was going to follow, but, on his way to the stables, he was joined by Nicholas. "Where are you going?" he asked.

"I'm going for a ride," said Oliver.

"Can I come?" asked Nicholas.

"No," said Oliver. "I wish to be by myself."

"I bet I know where you are going," said Nicholas.

"Keep your voice down," snapped Oliver.

"Please let me come," pleaded Nicholas.

"Don't be daft, you are only a baby," said Oliver.

"But I want to come with you."

"Well, you can't, it's too dangerous," he said.

"If you don't let me go with you, I will tell father what you are up to." Oliver felt trapped, he knew he couldn't take Nicholas with him, so what could he do, he sat down to think. Nicholas sat on the seat opposite his brother, and mimicked his every move.

"Would you like to play hide and seek?" asked Oliver.

"Only if I can hide first," said Nicholas.

Perfect, thought Oliver. "Alright, I will count to one hundred." And so, Oliver put his hands over his eyes as Nicholas raced out of the room. This was Oliver's big chance to sneak away. Little did he know, Nicholas had chosen the stables for his hiding place. He had climbed a ladder and was hiding behind some bales of hay. He watched as Oliver entered the stables. Fully expecting to be found any minute, he ducked down behind the bales of hay, and waited. He could hear Oliver moving about and so dared to take a look. When, to his surprise, Oliver started to put a saddle on one of the horses, and then the reigns. Nicholas realised he had been tricked.

"Hey, wait for me," he called, as Oliver rode from the stables. He looked back over his shoulder, and saw Nicholas standing in the doorway to the stables, he began to cry. Oliver faced forward once more and galloped off into the distance. Nicholas was left crying, he couldn't understand why his brother would not take him to the village with him.

A short while later, Mary found Nicholas crying inside the stables. "What's the matter, Nicholas, why are you crying?" she asked.

"Oliver wouldn't take me riding with him," he sobbed.

"Come on, I'll go riding with you." She dried his eyes and he helped Mary as best he could, with the saddle and reigns. Soon, they were out in the sunshine. It was still a bit chilly for early April. Mary had hold of Nicholas's reigns as well as her own, and so the two rode side by side. This was the first time he had done this alone with his big sister. She seemed happier than normal.

"Why are you so grumpy?" he asked.

"Oh thanks," said Mary, as she laughed, and then she thought. "I think it's to do with losing our mother. Nothing is the same any more, I think of her all the time, and it makes me sad, but, it's different for you, because you never knew her."

"What was she like?"

Mary was taken aback, for Nicholas had never asked her before about their mother. Mary told Nicholas how beautiful and kind their mother had been, and generous to everyone. Nicholas was smiling, and so Mary asked, "Why are you smiling?"

"I think I would have liked her," said Nicholas. "She sounds lovely."

"She was," said Mary. It started to snow, lightly. "We had better head back."

"What about Oliver?" said Nicholas.

"He will be alright," said Mary, and so they rode back to the castle.

Later that evening when everyone was seated at the dining table, did it become apparent that Oliver was not present. King Richard asked, "Does anyone know where Oliver is?"

Mary spoke, "He went riding earlier today, and upset Nicholas because he wouldn't take him with him."

"Have you seen him since?" asked Richard.

"No," said Mary. "Why, should I?"

Richard then asked everyone present at the table, "Has anyone seen Oliver?"

Everyone said, "No."

Richard turned on Mary. "Why didn't you say something earlier?" he raged.

"Why, what's wrong?" asked Mary. Everyone at the table was stunned by the way Richard spoke to Mary. She was feeling hurt and tearful. Richard realised he had snapped at Mary.

"No, sorry," he said. "Forgive me, Mary, none of this is your fault." Richard looked down the table at Percival, stood up and walked out of the room, Percival followed, and Berwyn as always followed Percival. They went to another sitting room and as Percival, followed by Berwyn, entered. Richard closed the door.

"You are worried about Oliver," said Percival.

"Yes, I am," said Richard. "You know what Oliver is like, if he heard us talking about Dante…"

"You are worried he might have gone looking for him," said Percival.

"It's dark out and it's snowing, we can't go looking for him tonight," said Richard.

"You know Oliver is smart, he will have found somewhere safe and warm for the night," said Percival. "And if he hasn't returned in the morning, we will go searching for him then." Richard knew what Percival was saying was correct, but it didn't stop him from worrying.

Having left so soon after the guards, Oliver had managed to pick up their trail easily. They had set up camp overnight in a clearing in the forest, they had a huge fire for warmth, and plenty of blankets. Oliver had found a hollow tree, and climbed inside, he dare not light a fire for fear of giving himself away. It was a long freezing cold night, with no sleep, for him.

At first light, Richard had gone to check in Oliver's bedroom, just in case he had come back overnight. He hadn't returned as hoped. Richard made his way to Percival's room. He was about to knock on the door when Percival opened it. "Good morning, Your Majesty. Did Oliver return last night?"

"Good morning, Percival, no he did not." Although Richard was eager to set off, it was decided they must have breakfast, scrambled egg and bacon had been prepared. Percival helped himself and poured out a large mug of piping hot tea, Richard declined. As soon as they had finished eating, Richard was out of his chair and followed by Percival, they made their way to the stables. Two horses had been saddled and were ready to go, Berwyn followed behind. Richard was leading the way, and they were riding in silence, when he suddenly broke the ice, by saying, "He must have gone in search of the guards."

"It would seem so, Your Majesty," said Percival. Richard didn't bother looking for any tracks, for they knew the direction the guards were heading.

Oliver had spent a freezing cold night with no sleep, feeling chilled to the bone he was thinking of how he had never felt so cold in all his life. The temptation to catch up with the guards was almost irresistible, and he was hungry. He had left the castle so quickly the day before, he hadn't thought of needing anything to eat, and he had no money either, but, he could not join up with the guards yet, for he knew they would take him straight back home. He did, however, have a knife. As he rode along, he was thinking, he would have to catch something to eat. With these thoughts running through his head, he rounded a bend in the forest road. The forest opened out into open countryside and in the distance, was a farmhouse, with smoke billowing from its chimney. Oliver watched as the guards had taken a road which turned away from the farmhouse, but Oliver was so hungry he decided on the farmhouse and a chance of something to eat, he could catch up with the guards later. He galloped towards the farmhouse, and slowed to a trot as he approached. Standing in the snow with an armful of chopped wood was a familiar face, it was Henry, the young boy from the village whom Oliver had met the other day.

"Good morning," said Oliver. "Do you live here?"

"Yes," said Henry.

"I'm starving," said Oliver. "Do you have any food you can spare?"

"You wait here and I'll go and have a look." Henry came back a moment later with a piece of cheese and a chunk of bread. "That's all I could get," he said.

"That's fine, said Oliver, grateful for any morsel of food, he ate it quickly, "could I have a drink of water?" he asked. Henry went back to the farmhouse to get some water, and returned shortly, with a mug of water in one hand, and an old grey haired man carrying a pitchfork behind him.

"Who are you?" the old man shouted. "What do you want?" Henry shook his head slightly, Oliver noticed and took this as a warning, before he said anything. The old man clipped Henry across the back of his head. "Why are you giving away the only food we have to a stranger?" Tears welled up in Henry's eyes as the old man hit him a second time.

"Stop that," shouted Oliver. "Leave him alone."

"Who's going to stop me?" said the old man.

"I will," replied Oliver.

The old man laughed. "You? You're only a boy." He lunged at Oliver's horse with his pitchfork, the horse rose in the air onto his hind legs, with his front legs flailing in the air, the old man took a step backwards. Oliver sat firm. Now it was Henry telling his father to leave Oliver alone. This got him another clip around the ear, that was enough. Oliver rode his horse straight at the old man and knocked him over. He lay on the ground covered in snow, screaming and cursing, too drunk to stand up. Oliver moved his horse alongside Henry.

"Give me your hand," he said. He leant down as Henry raised an arm, and pulled him onto the back of his horse. They galloped off into the distance, all they could hear was Henry's father cursing them both as they disappeared from view. "Is that really your dad?" asked Oliver.

"Mum died about two years ago. Since then I have had to do everything, he just drinks all the time. But, at least, when he is drunk, he falls asleep and leaves me alone. It's when he's awake he can be a handful." Oliver had not intended to take Henry with him, but as Henry pointed out, he could not go back now. "So where are we going?" asked Henry.

"I will drop you off at the next village," said Oliver.

"No," said Henry. "I want to come with you."

"You can't," said Oliver. "It's too dangerous." They had been travelling all day, and hadn't caught up with the guards. It was beginning to get dark and the chill of night was falling around them. They dismounted Oliver's horse and secured it for the night. Then they proceeded to gather wood to make a fire for warmth. As they sat around the fire, Oliver told Henry all about Dante, and the green-striped zebra. Henry sat without making a sound all the time Oliver was speaking, but he was wide eyed in amazement, and grinning from ear to ear.

"That sounds amazing, you must let me come with you."

"Have you not been listening? It's way too dangerous," said Oliver.

"And I told you I have nowhere else to go," said Henry. They had reached a stalemate, Oliver conceded, it might be better to have a companion with him rather than going on alone.

Chapter 4
Guards on Thin Ice

At first light, the guards had moved on. It was chilly but dry, the forest canopy had kept the frost at bay, but on leaving the forest, the ground was frozen and covered in a thick white frost. It began to snow, softly at first, but within a matter of minutes, the weather had changed considerably. The wind had picked up and the snow was falling heavily, and visibility was compromised. As they shielded their eyes with one hand and held the reigns of their horses with the other, they were walking in single file, as this was the best way of not getting separated. The guards led the way and Stephen was driving the wagon at the rear. With snow falling heavily onto frozen ground, it was building up quickly. Within an hour, there was four inches of snow. The horses were able to cope with the conditions without too much difficulty, but for the wagon, it had become increasingly difficult. Not only was the depth of snow making it slow going for Stephen, but hidden beneath the snow was an array of obstacles to overcome. Stephen, driving the wagon, had become stuck, the wagon had tilted to one side. It was the front right wheel that had become stuck, he called to the guards, no one came. He called again, with howling winds and poor visibility, they had disappeared. He had dropped back further than he had realised. He shook the reigns once more, the two horses pulled together, but nothing moved. He called again, still no one came. Seconds seemed like minutes, and minutes felt like hours. Then he heard a voice, "Do you need any help?" He turned and looked over his shoulder. At first, all he could see was a shadow approaching through the curtain of snow. As it got closer, a horse's head appeared, then a young boy riding the horse, it was Prince Oliver.

As he dismounted his horse, another boy was revealed. "What are you doing here?" said Stephen.

"Offering to help you," said Oliver.

"It's stuck and won't move," said Stephen. Oliver walked to the front right wheel to have a closer look. The strong wind was blowing the snow right into his face, his hands had become so cold he could barely feel them. There was nothing they could do in these freezing conditions. They decided to unhitch the horses, this was made all the more difficult with frozen fingers. Oliver introduced Henry to Stephen, he then suggested Stephen could ride one of the horses and Henry the other. Oliver remounted his own horse, with no one in sight and no tracks to follow, for the heavily falling snow had erased any tracks, all they could do was look for some shelter.

Ahead, the guards moved forward. Unaware that Stephen and the wagon had been left behind. With the unrelenting snow came a strong wind, the snow was now being blown into banks of deeper snow. The guard leading the way discovered this when his horse sank into snow up to its stomach. "Stop," he yelled at the top of his voice. The following guards stopped.

The guard who had been second in line shouted, "Are you all right?" All he could make out was a blurred mass in the snow.

The lead guard shouted back what had happened, "The snow is deeper here. My horse is stuck, we need help to get out. Throw me a rope. When I tell you to pull, pull."

The second guard tied a rope to his saddle and threw the rope in the direction of the blurred mass. "Have you got it?" he called.

"No," came the reply. He pulled the rope back, and threw it once more in the direction of the guard's voice.

"Do you have it this time?"

Again, "No," was the answer.

Getting frustrated with himself, he threw it again. "Got it!" shouted the first guard, with trembling fingers so frozen, that felt as though they might break at any minute, he tied the rope around the horses head. He was lying on the ground, he had tried to move some of the snow with his bare hands to release the horse, but as he tried to scoop the snow away from the horse's legs, the horse began to struggle and this caused the snow to fall back into the hole. He steadied his horse once more. Again, he tried clearing some of the snow from around the horse's body, and at the same time, he called for the guards to pull gently on the rope. Inch by inch, they slowly pulled on the rope, with gentle persuasion and without the weight of the guard on his back, the horse was eventually pulled clear of the snow bank. The guard rolled onto his back and breathed a sigh of relief. He lay there with bare hands which had become frozen, both he and his horse were exhausted from the exertion of escaping the deep snow. As the other guards tried to pull him to his feet, he screamed in pain. His hands so cold were painful when gripped, they released his hands and grabbed him by the arms, raising him to his feet the other guards stood together. The snow had eased off, only a few flakes fell gently from a dark grey sky. It was only now as they looked around that they realised Stephen and the wagon were missing. They looked back the way they had come, no sign of Stephen anywhere. They looked in all directions, Stephen was nowhere to be seen. But in the distance, it looked like a farmhouse. They made the decision to head for that, they needed somewhere to rest, and Stephen might already have found his way there.

They moved forward slowly. They did not want to find another snow bank. This time, one of the guards was in front but on foot. He used a long piece of wood they had uncovered when freeing the horse from the snow, he used it to test how deep the snow was. Luckily, with no more deep snow, they made it to the farmhouse. Sadly, it was not what they had hoped for, instead of finding a cosy and warm sanctuary from the snow, they found an abandoned house, with hardly any roof and one wall missing. Still, at least, this meant there were plenty of timbers for making a nice warm fire, but with no wagon they had no blankets and no food.

Stephen, Oliver and Henry had a dilemma of their own. With no snow falling, they could see clearly, and there was no one in sight. All around was an empty open expanse of white snow, except to the far right where they could see on the horizon, a dark line. They couldn't tell if this was made by a row of trees or maybe a row of houses, or maybe a village, but with no other choice, that was the way they decided to head. They slowly crossed the snowy landscape, it started to snow again. Stephen hoped and prayed it would not be as bad as before. He got his wish, and as they got closer they could make out a farmhouse, with smoke billowing into the sky from the chimney. This was a wonderful sight, for they knew it meant shelter and warmth from the freezing conditions they had endured all day. They could only hope that the owner of the farmhouse would be hospitable. They dismounted their horses, and led them into the barn and tied them up. They then walked across the yard to the farmhouse and knocked on the door. It was opened by a small woman who ushered them inside. "Hurry up," she said. "Must keep the cold out." When all three were inside, she quickly shut the door. "What were you doing out there?" she asked.

"We got lost from our friends when the snow came down. Have you seen them?"

"I haven't seen anyone for over a week. Where have you come from?" she asked.

Stephen went to the window and pointed in the direction they had crossed the snowfield. "Good god, you were lucky," she said.

"Why is that?" asked Oliver.

"That's what's known as 'dead man's lake'. That is, if your friends tried crossing that, you may never see them again." They all looked at each other worryingly. "Come and sit by the fire. I was just about to have some stew. You can't do anything tonight, not now, it's started snowing again. Come, have some stew and get warm. There's plenty to go round. I always make enough to last a few days."

"We have three horses. I placed them in your barn."

"That's alright, we will tend to them after you've had something to eat," said the old woman.

King Richard had known the route the guards would take, but having started out a day later, they were someway behind. As night fell, they had reached the edge of the forest. In front of them lay nothing but a field of white snow. Richard wanted to keep going, but Percival stopped him. "Your Majesty," he said. "All is not what it seems."

"What do you mean?" asked Richard.

"What do you see?" said Percival.

"A field covered in snow," replied Richard.

"Underneath the snow is a lake," said Percival. "Known as, 'dead man's lake'. It is notorious for its snow cover, many a traveller has passed this way in winter unaware of the danger, and succumbed to its perils. It is getting dark and snowing once more. I suggest we should stay tonight on the edge of the forest.

This will provide some shelter, better than being out in the open." Richard agreed, and so, they started a fire and settled down for the night. Berwyn with his thick coat was accustomed to surviving in these conditions.

The guards had huddled together in their dilapidated farmhouse trying to stay warm overnight, and in the morning, the fire was just a pile of smoking embers. One by one, the guards were waking up. Finally, when they were all awake, the lead guard asked, "Is everyone alright?"

"Yes," was the reply. The two guards who had led the way across the snowfield, George and Robert, stood up and stretched their tired limbs. Their joints were stiff with the cold, they stepped away from the dilapidated farmhouse. The snow had stopped, but the temperature had fallen. The surface of the snow sparkled in a clear blue sky. As they stood looking out over the snowfield, slowly, one by one, they were joined by the other guards.

"So, what do we do now?" asked one of the guards.

George and Robert looked at each other. "There's only one thing we can do. Go back, and look for Stephen and the wagon."

"Well, let's not waste any time," said Robert. And with that, they all mounted their horses and started out across the snowfield once more, blissfully unaware of the hidden 'dead man's lake'.

Richard and Percival had also woken, and Berwyn was not in sight. Percival reassured Richard, "He has gone to feed, he will find us." They left the forest once more and stopped to look at the vast emptiness before them. Berwyn reappeared, as Percival knew he would.

"So how do we get around the lake?" asked Richard.

"Berwyn will lead us," said Percival. "Berwyn can smell the water beneath the ice." And so, they set off.

From the opposite side of the lake, the guards were on the move. Without snow falling, visibility was better, the problem now was the reflecting brightness of the sun off the snowy surface, shining in their eyes.

After a couple of hours, with Berwyn leading the way, Richard and Percival came across the abandoned wagon. Luckily, it had not got as far as the frozen lake. The front wheel had just got wedged into a shallow hole, it was the packed snow around the wheel that made it difficult to release, but with

Berwyn's size, he pulled the wagon free. A quick check of the surrounding area revealed no bodies. "Berwyn would find them under the snow if they were here."

"That's a relief," said Richard. Looking out over the snowfield, something caught Percival's eye.

"Look," he said, as he pointed towards something moving across the snow, covered lake. They stood and watched, at first unable to make out what they were looking at, but as they approached, Richard could see it was his guards. He called to them, and began to wave his arms in the air above his head, trying desperately to catch their attention. Percival urged him to stop, but it was too late. The guards had seen some one waving, thinking it was Stephen with the wagon, they altered their course. They were now heading straight across the centre of the lake. Berwyn did not want to move forwards.

Percival warned Richard, "We must be at the edge of the lake."

They watched the guards approach with baited breath. They were only twenty feet away. "Good morning, Your Majesty," said Robert. Without warning, there was a loud cracking noise as the ice broke, all the guards and their horses fell into the freezing water. Richard and Percival stood helpless, with panicked horses struggling to get clear of the freezing water, and guards fighting to stay above the ice. The screams rang out over the frozen lake.

Richard came to his senses, there was some rope in the wagon, he tied one end around Berwyn's neck, and threw the other end towards the guards. "Grab hold," he shouted. One by one, the guards grabbed hold, pulling their friends toward the rope. Percival got Berwyn to back up, and as he did so, pulled the guards free from the lake. All but one of the horses had scrambled free, and one of the guards was last seen trying desperately to save his horse before they both disappeared beneath the ice. There was nothing more that could be done to save them. Now they had to concentrate on those they had pulled from the freezing water. Richard began to break up the wagon for firewood, all the guards had to strip out of their wet clothes, wrap themselves in blankets from the wagon, and sit around the fire. They were freezing cold, all huddled together. Percival got Berwyn to lay behind them, the warmth generated from the giant bear's body helped to warm the guards. Happy to be alive, looking around the group of men, Percival asked, "Where is Stephen?"

"We got separated in that blinding snow storm yesterday, that's why we came back today." Robert then asked, "Your Majesty, why are you here?" Richard then told them of Oliver going missing.

"We have not seen him," said Robert.

"We will head home," said Richard. "We will hopefully find him there all safe and warm back at the castle." Or at least, that was what he hoped.

Chapter 5
Dante's Quest for Gold

Sitting around the campfire that evening, the guards were once more fully dressed in dry clothes. They had moved back into the forest as they were heading home. Percival addressed King Richard and the guards, "I know more about Dante's movements than I originally let on. Having failed to get any gold seven years before, Dante had been left seething upon a pile of golden sand. He had made his way back to the Matsuba kingdom and requested an audience with Ossirus, which had been granted. When Dante met with Ossirus, he demanded gold, as payment for his help in reclaiming the Matsuba kingdom, Ossirus refused. Dante became more threatening and so Ossirus had him escorted from his kingdom, never to be allowed back. Dante blamed all his misfortune on you, King Richard, and Prince Oliver. He vowed that he would one day get the gold he deserved, and revenge for the humiliation he felt. Dante made it off the island of Colossus, and travelled east. He met with a high priest in a mountainous village that was said to be made of gold, but this was not the case. It was only the sunlight on the lake below the village that reflected the golden light of the sun as it set that lit up the village, making it appear as if it was made of gold. It is said he left the village, still travelling east. He came upon a kingdom ruled by seven sisters. They were fascinated by his appearance, for they had never seen a winged fairy before and he was invited to stay. But as they got to know him, his greed for gold became apparent. Over the years, the sisters had many suitors, and although they had never married, they had a wealth of treasures which had been given as gifts. Athena, the youngest of the sisters, had made the mistake of showing these treasures to Dante, but her sisters were not as gullible. Once again, he was escorted from their kingdom and told never to return, under the penalty of death. While he continued to travel from one kingdom to the next, in his search for gold, it is said he found a sorcerer, with a book of magic. The sorcerer is said to have been over three hundred years old, and very tired. He had wanted to pass on his book of magic, but, only to someone who was worthy of its power. Dante befriended the old sorcerer, and the night before he died, he gave Dante his book of magic. But to Dante's horror, when he opened the book, it was an ancient language that Dante did not recognise. His first inclination was to throw the book away, believing it to be useless, but something stopped him. Instead, he now went in search of someone who could teach him how to read the text in the book. After a long search, he eventually found a monastery that would take in travellers who had lost their way. Writings on the walls of the monastery were written in the same text as the book in Dante's possession. Once again, he made friends with the older members of the monastery, he showed an interest in the text on the walls and was eager to learn the ancient language. Nobody knows for sure how long he stayed, long enough to learn the language, but, it turned out, it wasn't a book of magic, but a book of medicine. Dante remembered the stories the old man had told him of saving lives that were beyond saving, this was why people had thought him a sorcerer, and his book a book of magic. All this time, he had wasted on this book, but for some reason, he still never threw it away. Now he had learnt to read the text in the book he left the monastery, still searching for his pot of gold.

At some point on his travels, he was captured and sentenced to be beheaded. But before this happened, the wife of the emperor was screaming in pain, she was having difficulty in childbirth, and no one it seemed could help her. Dante offered to help, the emperor was worried he might lose both his wife and unborn child. Dante claimed he could save them both. The emperor was so desperate, he agreed to let Dante try.

"Succeed, and you can have anything your heart desires, fail, and you lose your head."

Dante asked for his book which had been taken from him, he told them it was a book of magic. If he failed, he would be no worse off than he was, but if he succeeded… He opened the book and found the page for childbirth, read the section on child birth difficulties and how to overcome them. So, he read from the page what he needed, and when this was bought to him he told everyone they had to leave. And so, Dante performed his magic, the child was born and the mother survived. Believing it to be the work of magic, the emperor gave Dante what he wanted, a cart loaded with gold. But Dante was foolish, instead of hiding the gold on his cart, he wanted everyone to see what wealth he had. It wasn't long before word reached a group of thieves, that a winged fairy had a cart loaded with gold. For several days, they followed him, they had heard of the book of magic that he possessed and so were wary. Then one day, he had stopped by a pool of water and was lying on the grass resting. The thieves had gathered, Dante was blissfully unaware of their presence. He was talking to himself, how clever of him to save the emperor's wife and tell him it was magic, when it wasn't. Upon hearing this, the thieves attacked, they robbed Dante of his cart loaded with gold, and left him with nothing but his clothes he wore.

Then it is said that Dante found himself in the black forest."

"Why the black forest?" asked Richard.

"It sits beneath a volcano, and when the volcano erupts and sends up black smoke and ash, it rains down on the forest, hence the name."

"Is the forest dead, covered in all that ash?"

"No, Your Majesty. It is very much alive. When the rains come and wash the ash from the trees and plants, they grow incredibly fast. For the ash makes the land extremely fertile. It is here that Dante is said to have found the black unicorn."

"And is it black, or just covered in ash?"

"No, it is said to be black. On his travels, Dante had learned of the black unicorn, and the legend that surrounds it. Anyone who can tame the black unicorn will have great power. Having been robbed of his gold, Dante now wanted power to gain his wealth. Dante managed to get the black unicorn under his spell, using the hypnotic qualities of a purple rose. When Dante rode the black unicorn out of the black forest, it is said that people fell to their knees and prayed to the gods, such was the legend that surrounds the black unicorn, fighting men offered their services to Dante, believing him invincible. As he crossed the lands, more and more men joined his growing army, and each new kingdom he came across paid homage to the black unicorn god, the name he was given, the name he then used.

His downfall came when he discovered a kingdom in the mountains of the east, where three brothers ruled together, side by side. They refused to pay homage, and so Dante ordered an attack but things didn't go to plan. Hundreds of archers were hidden behind the wall that circled the kingdom. When the arrows rained down upon Dante's army, many lives were lost. Again and again, he ordered another wave of men to attack, and each time his men were cut down by arrows. His army began to get unsettled, they wanted him to use the power of the black unicorn. It is said that when the black unicorn raised onto its back legs that fire balls from heaven rained down on the earth, and that when the black unicorn crashed down again onto four feet, that the earth trembles and splits. But Dante knew this was not true, he knew the black unicorn would rise up onto his back legs when the volcano erupted. It was the volcano that sent fireballs into the sky that rained down onto the earth, and Dante knew also that it was not the black unicorn that made the earth tremble and split, but again it was caused by the volcano, that stood next to the black forest, where the unicorn lived. Finally, Dante was hit by an arrow and bled. He fell from the black unicorn which then ran off. His army realised he was not invincible, and abandoned Dante, leaving him to crawl away to safety, and escape."

"We must get back to the castle as soon as possible," said Richard. "And pray that Oliver is there."

Chapter 6
Oliver's Big Fall

Oliver, Henry and Stephen had woken the next day to find a hearty breakfast waiting for them on the stove. "Good morning," the old woman said. "How did you sleep?"

"Surprisingly well," said Oliver.

"That's because you were exhausted," she said. "Come, have some breakfast, there's plenty to go around."

"Thank you," said Oliver. Stephen and Henry followed Oliver to the table.

"Help yourselves. Would you like some tea?"

"Yes, please," they all answered.

While they sat at the table eating, Oliver asked, "How long have you lived here?"

"I've lived here all my life," said the old woman. "Born upstairs I was. Lived in this house now for, forty-nine years. Ten years since my parents died, been on my own ever since."

"Do you not find it lonely?" asked Henry.

"Don't have time to be lonely, lad, too much to do. There's always something that needs fixing. Go to the village once a week for provisions, that keeps me going."

"How do you get your money to survive?"

"Nosey little bugger, aren't you?"

"Sorry," said Henry.

"That's alright, you wouldn't believe me if I told you," she said.

"Go on," said Henry. "Tell us."

She sat forward and placed her withered hands on the table, a big grin on her face revealed broken yellow teeth, her eyes bulged and for the first time, they noticed a large boil on the end of her nose. "I have a way of draining the lake," she said, looking at each one in turn, with a wicked glint in her eyes. "Each spring,

I drain the lake and check the bodies of any victims who have drowned in the lake over winter."

"What do you check them for," asked Henry.

She sat upright in her chair and laughed an old woman's cackle. "Valuables and money, of course."

"But that's stealing," said Oliver.

"I won't tell them if you don't," said the old woman, and she laughed again. She went on, "Throughout the year, as it rains, it fills the lake once more, ready for the following winter. I keep a lantern lit to encourage travellers in need of safe refuge from the winter storms, this helps to attract them across the lake." Henry thought she looked mad as she stared from one to the other.

Stephen said to Oliver, "She's pulling your leg."

"Am I now?" she replied. "Can you be sure?" She rocked back in her chair and laughed for a third time. None of them were sure if she was making this up or whether she was telling the truth, but, this made them feel uneasy.

"I think we should go back and have a look at the wagon."

"I wouldn't bother," she said. "It's gone."

"What do you mean it's gone?"

"I checked already."

"What do you mean already?"

"Gentlemen, you have slept for over a day, you arrived Thursday night, but this is Saturday morning."

They looked at each other. "Is that possible?" Oliver asked.

"As I said, you were exhausted."

They no longer felt safe in the company of the old woman, and decided to leave. If it was true and the wagon had disappeared, there was no point in going back. They made their decision, even if it was there, they probably wouldn't be able to move it. They had finished their breakfast, and decided it was time to leave. Oliver thanked the old woman for her hospitality and they said goodbye. She wished them a safe journey as she watched them ride away. Henry looked back once, and immediately wished he hadn't. The look the old woman had on her face as she stood in the doorway of the farmhouse sent a chill down his spine. Smiling, revealing yellow teeth, she reminded him of a witch from a story told by his mother when he was just a young boy. He quickly turned away. They travelled all morning across open countryside that was covered in snow, the thought of 'dead man's lake' made them more cautious than before, and so progress was slow. The wind had picked up and snow was falling once more. They continued to travel in these conditions for over a week, unable to return home, even if they wanted to, for they were lost. Then one day, they came to a shallow river that was not frozen, but they could not see what was on the other side because of the falling snow, they decided to cross.

Although the river was shallow, it was a lot wider than they had realised. With the snow blinding them from their destination, they were wondering if it had been wise to try and cross the river in the first place. However, when they looked back, they realised they could no longer see the bank from which they had set out, and so they pressed on, with the bitterly cold wind biting at their fingers and their faces. Henry was so cold, he nearly fell from his horse. Oliver riding next to Henry was able to keep him from falling. Slowly, the horses walked on. When finally they reached the other side, they left the river and stepped out onto a grass bank. The snow had stopped, after shaking the snow from their hair and clothes, they slowly realised there was no snow, anywhere. The wind had also stopped, and yes, there was warmth.

"Where are we?" asked Henry.

"I have no idea," said Oliver. Their fingers and toes were slowly coming back to life in the warm sunshine, and they dismounted their horses. All they could see before them was green grass, blue sky and a bright yellow sun. Exhausted, they lay on the ground. Soaking up the warm sunshine had never felt so good before, watching fluffy white clouds sailing by, when suddenly a second sun appeared, bright blue. At first, Oliver thought he was imagining it, but soon became aware that Stephen and Henry had spotted it as well. And yet, before anyone could speak, yet a third sun appeared, this time bright pink. Oliver sat up so quickly, he made himself dizzy.

"Did you see that?" he asked, and when there was no response, he looked across at Henry and Stephen. The look of surprise on their faces told him the answer to his question.

"Where are we?" said Henry. "What strange place is this?"

"I think we should investigate," said Oliver. And so, he stood up, yet when he turned around and looked behind them, all he could see was a wall of stone.

"But where's the river and the snow?" he said. Henry and Stephen had gotten to their feet, and were standing either side of Oliver, in total disbelief, they stared at the wall.

"This is very strange," said Stephen. He stepped forward and placed his hands on the wall, testing it, to see if it was real. It felt cold to touch and solid, he walked along with his hands touching the wall searching, hoping for a doorway, but nothing.

"What do you think we should do?" he asked Oliver.

"For now, I think we should stay here, it's dry and warm, and we can rest before going any further." This seemed like a good idea, and so they lay on the grass, looking up at three suns in the sky above, wondering, and it wasn't long before they had all fallen asleep.

Oliver was woken suddenly by something sitting on his chest. He was startled to wake up face to face with some strange animal staring back at him. He brushed it aside and sat up quickly. All he could see was the rear end of a rabbit scurrying away. He woke Henry and Stephen, but before he could tell them what had happened, from nowhere, they were surrounded by rabbits, or what looked like rabbits at first glance, but they had antlers like a deer, only smaller, and then they heard a voice.

"Did you hear that?" asked Oliver.

"I did," said Stephen and Henry nodded. "But where did it come from?"

The rabbits moved closer. This time, the voice was clearer, "Who are you?"

The three of them looked at each other puzzled by what was going on. "Where did that voice come from?" said Oliver. Stephen looked closer at the rabbit nearest to him.

"Well, what are you looking at?" Stephen jumped back in amazement, and fell over. Oliver bent down to help Stephen back onto his feet.

"Are you all right?"

"It's the rabbit, the rabbit's talking."

Then they heard laughter. "He thinks the rabbit can talk."

"Who said that?" demanded Oliver.

One of the rabbits hopped forward, and a tiny creature that looked like it was made of sticks sitting on the back of the rabbit said, "We are pixies. My name is Oscar, and this is Tosca."

"And my name is Bert." Henry sniggered.

"Now, who are you?"

"My name is Oliver, and these are my friends, Henry and Stephen. Where are we?" he asked.

"Why, you're in the kingdom of the rainbow fairy."

"I've never heard of it," said Oliver.

"I should hope not," said Oscar. "It's enchanted to stop strangers from finding it."

"How did you find it?" asked Tosca.

"It was snowing hard and we just crossed a river, and here we are," said Oliver.

"Well, you best turn around and cross the river again, and leave. Goodbye," said Bert.

"But we can't leave," said Oliver.

"And why is that," said Tosca.

"Well, look," said Oliver, as he pointed behind them. "There is no river, only a solid wall."

"Oh, dear," said Oscar. "You know what that means?" "What?" asked Henry.

"She knows you're here," said Bert.

"Who's she?" said Henry.

"Cressida, the rainbow fairy, of course." Quick as a flash, the rabbits and the pixies were gone, looming in the distance a large shadowy figure had appeared. With the three suns behind it, the shadowy figure revealed no features, but because of the yellow, blue and pink suns, it was surrounded by a strange but beautiful glow. They stood mesmerised by the beautiful sight before them. As it got closer, they could see it looked female, standing about 6 feet tall, wearing a long robe which brushed the ground as she walked. It was patterned in various shades of blue, she wore a tall hat decorated in the same colours and pattern, with flaming red hair. She had pale pink skin and purple lips, her ears were long thin and pointed. They lay horizontally from the sides of her head, she had pale blue eyes and a long thin nose. She carried in her left hand a long thin staff patterned in white, red and black. It drooped down behind her head, the top half of the staff was covered in green leaves. It also had growing in small clumps, berries and flowers in a multitude of bright colours that glittered in the sunlight. She walked straight up to the three young men, smiled, revealing perfectly white teeth, and said, "Hello." Her voice had a musical quality to it, and they immediately felt at ease. As they watched, she placed the staff into the ground, and as she did, roots appeared and sank into the ground, she removed her hand, it stood alone.

"My name is Eleanor," she said. The musical quality of her voice made it sound like she was singing.

"Hello," said Oliver. "My name is…"

"I know who you are," she said. "Welcome, Prince Oliver."

And then, she turned and welcomed both Henry and Stephen. "But how do you know who we are?"

"I know many things," said Eleanor. "I know you crossed the river in the snow but now cannot go back the same way. I know you want to get back. What I don't know is why you came here in the first place?"

"We didn't mean to come here. We didn't know this place existed, we were just trying to escape the storm." Eleanor walked around them slowly, in each turn she placed a hand on their left shoulder and ran her hand across their back to their right shoulder. She then traced her finger down their spine, repeating this three times. She walked back to the front, all the while the three boys stood silently watching.

"I know you are telling the truth," said Eleanor.

"Can you help us?" asked Oliver.

"I can point you in the right direction," said Eleanor. And with that, she approached her staff and as she placed her fingers around the slim trunk, the roots were withdrawn from the ground and Eleanor lifted it into the air. "Follow me," she said.

Oliver, Henry and Stephen had mounted their horses and were following behind Eleanor. Henry whispered to Oliver, "Do you think we can trust her?"

"What choice do we have?" said Oliver.

"You can trust me," said Eleanor.

Stephen glanced across at Henry and Oliver. "How is that possible, she must be thirty feet away?"

"I cannot only hear your words, but I can also hear your thoughts," she said. Henry doubted this, and thought so. "I know you don't believe me, Henry," she said. Eleanor turned to Oliver. "Please think of someone back home." Straight away, Oliver thought of his siblings. "You have a brother and three sisters," said Eleanor. Oliver, Henry and Stephen looked at each other in amazement, and before anyone said anything, she named them, "Nicholas, Alice, Dorothy and Mary."

"How do you do that?" asked Stephen.

"I don't know how I do it, I just know that I can," said Eleanor. As they followed Eleanor across the grass, they kept catching glimpses of rabbits with tiny antlers being ridden by pixies. "Don't worry about them," said Eleanor. "They will cause you no harm."

This prompted Stephen to ask, "Is there anything here we do need to worry about?"

"Of course," said Eleanor, "There are always dangers when travelling through an enchanted forest."

"Why didn't you tell us?"

"Because you didn't ask me," said Eleanor.

"But you can hear our thoughts," said Oliver.

"Yes," said Eleanor. "And not one of you had thought to ask if there were any dangers." She stopped suddenly. "Come, look," she said. They all dismounted their horses and walked up and stood alongside Eleanor. They were high up on a hill, with no visible means of getting down. "This is the kingdom of the rainbow fairy," she said. As far as the eye could see, there were trees the colours of the rainbow. She pointed to something that shone in the distance. "That is the crystal palace, home of the rainbow fairy," said Eleanor. "She can help you return home."

"But how do we get down there?" asked Oliver.

"Take a leap of faith," said Eleanor. And before anyone could ask what she meant by that, she jumped off the hilltop and disappeared out of sight.

The three of them looked at each other. "If you think I'm going to jump off this hill, you must be mad," said Henry.

Stephen looked at Oliver. "Can we really trust her?" Stephen asked.

Oliver said, "There's one way to find out." And with that, Oliver raced forward and jumped off the hilltop. He began to spin through the air. Instinctively, he put his arms out to the sides and this stopped the spinning, and he found himself gently floating towards the ground. He landed softly on his feet, he was exhilarated, he turned and looked up. It was so high he could not see the top, but, what would the others do, would they follow his example and jump, or would he have to go on alone.

Stephen and Henry were arguing over what to do. Stephen said that they had to jump but Henry was adamant, he would not.

"And what about the horses?" he asked. Stephen felt he had no option but to follow the lead of Prince Oliver, and so, he jumped. Immediately, he started to spin, everything was a blur, he felt sick, and felt sure he was going to die, he passed out. Oliver was still standing at the bottom looking up, a small black spot had appeared. As Oliver watched it approach, it grew larger, falling faster than he had, and spinning violently. Oliver was worried for he could see it was one of his friends, he abruptly stopped two feet above the ground, and then gently descended. Oliver ran over to Stephen who was lying face down on the ground, not sure whether he was alive or not. Oliver rolled him over and as he did so Stephen opened his eyes. Oliver lifted Stephen's upper body from the ground and embraced him, so relieved that he was alive. Stephen struggled to break free from Oliver's arms, pushed him to one side and then, threw up on the ground.

"Feeling better?" asked Oliver.

"A little," said Stephen.

Oliver then asked Stephen about Henry. Stephen said, "Henry won't jump, he thinks there must be another way down, and he will bring the horses." Stephen was on his hands and knees taking deep breaths.

"How are you feeling now?" asked Oliver.

"I feel as though I could throw up any minute, my stomach still feels as though it is being tossed back and forth, and my head is still spinning," said Stephen. "Have you had a look around yet?" he asked Oliver.

"No, not yet." Oliver stood up and gave Stephen his hand and pulled him to his feet. He felt a bit unstable at first, his legs were still a bit shaky, and his head still felt as though it was spinning.

"There's obviously magic here," said Stephen. "Or we would both be dead."

"I wonder where Eleanor went," said Oliver.

"Look over there," a tall figure wearing a robe of blue was just visible in the distance, Stephen called, "Eleanor," just as she disappeared out of sight. "Do you suppose we should follow her?" said Stephen.

"If she wanted us to follow her, why didn't she wait," said Oliver. Before they took a step, Oscar, Tosca and Bert appeared riding their rabbits. "How did you get down here?" asked Oliver.

"We used the pathway, of course."

"You mean you didn't jump?"

"Hell no, we're not stupid," said Tosca.

Before any more questions could be asked, there was Henry with the horses. "I told you there had to be another way down," he said, with a big grin. They all laughed, thankful they had all made it down safely. It was getting late in the day, they decided to make camp for the night, and so they made a small fire and settled down. They each lay on their backs looking up at the sky, Oliver and Henry had closed their eyes, but Stephen was lying awake, and as he watched, the strangest thing happened, the three suns slowly merged together and created a purple moon. He wanted to share this with the others but as he sat up and looked across, he could see they were both sleeping and so he lay back down amazed at what he had just witnessed, and slowly he drifted off to sleep.

Chapter 7
Richard's Return

It was late at night when King Richard and Percival had returned to the castle along with the guards. Their journey back home had been made easier, for the closer they got home, the snow had melted. Their arrival was unexpected, and only when they entered the courtyard and Richard rang the bell did anyone appear. One of the castle guards came to investigate who had rang the bell at this late hour, "Your Majesty," he said. "We were not expecting you." Richard and Percival dismounted their horses, without saying a word, and handed the reins to the guard, he led the two horses into the stables. Richard and Percival entered the castle, followed by Berwyn.

The first person inside the castle they met was the cook who had not been sleeping, and had heard the bell. "Your Majesty," said the cook.

"Can you cook something for a dozen hungry men?" asked Richard.

"I can make a giant omelette that won't take long," said the cook.

"Perfect," said Richard. "I will let the men know."

The other guards had dismounted and led their own horses into the stables. Only now as the guard from the castle greeted his friends, did he ask, "Where is Arthur?" With heads hanging low, none of the guards wanted to be the one to tell Gregor that his younger brother Arthur had perished in the frozen lake. Again he asked the question, "Where is Arthur?" The fact no one would answer his question allowed Gregor to realise that it was not good news. "How did it happen?" he asked. Still no one answered.

Finally, Robert stepped forward, "I'm sorry, Gregor, there was nothing we could do, it happened so fast, we were all fighting for our lives." Gregor ran out of the stables and in the courtyard, fell to his knees and began to sob. Robert followed Gregor into the courtyard, the rest of the guards stood and watched as Robert tried to comfort Gregor.

Gregor blamed himself. "He should never have gone," said Gregor. "It should have been me."

"You cannot blame yourself for this," said Robert. "It was an unfortunate accident." Gregor was inconsolable, he broke away from Robert's embrace and headed towards the guards' quarters. He went, and lay on what had been Arthur's bed and cried into the pillow. The guards who had been sleeping woke up and wanted to know why Gregor was crying. They looked across the room at Gregor, and then it dawned on them that something had happened to Arthur. They decided not to ask Gregor tonight, and so they lay down and left him alone. It was an uncomfortable feeling lying there, listening to their friend crying but eventually they fell asleep. Richard had sent one of the castle servants to let the guards know that food was being prepared. They followed the servant back to the dining room.

Richard and Percival were already sitting at the table. "Please join us," said Richard. They each took a seat around the dining table, no one spoke. There were two plates piled high with bread one at each end of the table. Shortly after the guards had arrived at the table, servants entered with plates of bacon and omelette. This was eagerly received along with the bread, all washed down with a hot cup of tea. When finished, the guards asked to be excused, and Richard said goodnight. Richard made his way to the bedroom that Oliver and Nicholas shared. He wanted to go in and check to see if Oliver was there but didn't want to wake Nicholas. He placed his hand on the handle to open the door, but stopped. If Oliver wasn't there, there was nothing he could do, not this late. So he removed his hand from the handle and slowly made his way back to his bedroom.

Richard told himself after a good night's sleep he would feel refreshed, but it was a troubled night without sleep. Richard had tossed and turned all night. Finally, dawn had arrived. It was early but he was desperate to find out if Oliver had returned home in his absence. He did not want to disturb his daughters, and so instead of crossing through their room and using the adjoining door, Richard used the hallway that led directly to the boys' bedroom. He slowly turned the door handle and made not a sound. He opened it enough to slip inside. There was a warm glow coming from the fireplace, he quietly crept across the room, passed Nicholas's bed and as he reached Oliver's bed, his heart sank, the bed was empty. He let out a gasp and placed his hand over his mouth. Tears welled up in his eyes. He turned to leave the bedroom and as he did, he was caught by surprise. Nicholas was awake, he launched himself from his bed into his father's arms. Richard was happy to see Nicholas, and this briefly helped him to not think about Oliver, but it did not last. He told Nicholas it was too early to get up and so made him go back to bed. Richard left the bedroom distressed, he made his way to the sitting room with the portrait of Elizabeth hanging on the wall. He sat on a chair facing the picture, with his head in his hands. Once more, he felt as though he had broken his promise to Elizabeth, his promise to never again abandon one of their children, and yet, here he was once again with Oliver missing.

Richard had no idea how long he sat there in front of the portrait of his late wife. It was only when Dorothy walking past, heard some sobbing and came to investigate, that she found him sitting in the chair with his head in his hands. He looked up as she approached, she could see his eyes were red from all the crying he had done. She knelt down beside her father but said nothing. She knew that if he was this upset, he hadn't found Oliver, but had returned to find Oliver was not here either. No words were necessary, they just sat quietly taking comfort from each other.

Slowly, the castle started to come alive, servants were on the move, first to wake as always, they started their chores. Percival and Berwyn had found Richard and Dorothy in the sitting room. "Come in and join us," said Richard. Percival entered the room and sat on a chair opposite Richard, Berwyn lay at his feet as always.

"I take it Oliver did not come home," said Percival.

"No," said Richard.

"So, what do you intend to do next?" asked Percival.

Struggling with his conscience, Richard answered, "I don't know. If I go looking for Oliver again, I abandon my children here at the castle, and if I don't go looking for Oliver, then I have abandoned him."

"It's a tough decision, Your Majesty, and one that only you can make," said Percival.

"But if I go looking for Oliver and something happens to me, then all my children will lose a father. If I stay and something happens to Oliver, I lose just one child."

"This is true," said Percival.

This was the hardest decision Richard had ever made. He looked at Dorothy, but he decided he had to stay with his children and put his trust in the guards to find his son. Percival said, "I will go with them, Your Majesty."

"Thank you, Percival, that makes me feel more hopeful, knowing you and Berwyn will continue to look for Oliver." Richard went to the guards' quarters, he found Gregor. He took him to one side and said, "I am deeply sorry for your loss. Arthur was a brave man and will never be forgotten."

Gregor struggled not to cry in front of everyone and Richard led him into the castle where they could be alone. "How did he die?" asked Gregor.

"Are you sure you want to know?" said Richard.

"Please tell me," said Gregor. And so they sat opposite each other in front of a roaring fire, and Richard told Gregor how his younger brother had died. Gregor cried uncontrollably. When able to speak once more, Gregor told King Richard how when they were children they had been playing on a frozen lake, when he had fallen through the ice and it was Arthur who had saved his life. To think that Arthur had died that way, and he had not been present to try and save his brother was heart breaking. Richard struggled to hold back the tears as he tried to comfort Gregor as best he could, eventually, leaving him alone.

"Take as much time as you need," said Richard.

Nicholas was awake once more and raced into his sisters' bedroom. "Father's back, Father's back!" he shouted.

Alice and Mary woke up. "Go away," said Mary. But Alice had sat up in bed and realised that Dorothy was not in her bed. This prompted Alice to get dressed, she followed Nicholas back into his bedroom and helped him to get dressed. Then, they went together in search of Dorothy. As they left the bedroom, Dorothy appeared.

"Is it true?" asked Alice. "Is father back?"

"Yes, he is back," said Dorothy.

"And Oliver?" said Alice. Dorothy had dropped her head to face the floor and shook her head. Alice burst into tears and Dorothy stepped forward to hug her sister. Nicholas didn't understand what all the crying was for, he let go of Alice's hand and went in search of his father.

Richard had gone back to the guards' quarters, he told them of his decision to stay behind. He was no longer interested in Dante, his only concern was in finding Prince Oliver. He asked for six volunteers. The first to volunteer was Gregor. Richard was unaware that Gregor had followed him back.

"Thank you," said Richard. Immediately, five more hands were in the air. "Come with me." He took them to the dining room where Percival was waiting. Three of the six guards present had been part of the first group, one of these was Robert, the head guard, Gregor and two other new guards made up the six.

"This time, there would be no wagon, they would each have their own blankets to carry, with bows and arrows supplied for hunting. Each guard would have their own knife and sword, they would also be provided with some money. Does anyone have any questions?" asked Richard.

"How long do you want us to keep looking?" asked Gregor.

"Until you find my son," said Richard. As the six guards left, Richard watched from the castle steps. Percival and Berwyn followed at the rear.

"We will find him," said Percival.

Chapter 8
Dante the Sneak Thief

All the time Richard had been away, Dante had been observing the castle, watching the daily routine of the guards. He had used his invisibility to get close to the castle and peer inside the windows to discover which was Nicholas's bedroom, the fact that Richard had come back did not deter Dante from his plan. In fact, it excited him to think he would steal Nicholas right from under Richard's nose. With Percival gone and Berwyn too, Dante waited until night. As the guards did their last walk around the castle, he knew this was his chance. As they headed back to their quarters, he made himself invisible and followed. They entered the door to the castle, and he slipped inside. This was then locked and bolted, and from there, they turned right down the hallway that led to their quarters. The guards' quarters consisted of thirty ordinary beds, in three rows of ten. There was a huge fire at the far end of the room, and each bed had a small table next to it with a candle on each. Only a few of the candles were still lit, this provided a warm glow. As the guards got ready for bed, Dante waited. In Robert's absence, Phillip took on the responsibilities of the head guard. He had locked and bolted the door, and was in charge of the key and had placed it on the small table besides his bed. All Dante had to do was wait for Phillip to go to sleep and then he would steal the key. It seemed simple enough and it wasn't long before all the guards were sleeping, and Dante moved silently and picked up the key from the small table besides Phillips bed. Just as Dante had placed his hand upon the key, Phillip rolled over in bed, and his muscular arm stretched out and his large hand fell upon Dante's as he grasped the key. Dante froze, but Phillip was still asleep, and eventually, he rolled back and released Dante's hand. Dante breathed a sigh of relief. He then made his way out of the guards' quarters and back into the main castle. He knew where he was going. After climbing the stairs, he quietly walked down the hallway that led to Nicholas's bedroom. The animal heads mounted on the wall sent a chill down Dante's spine, but this reassured him this was the right door. He slowly turned the handle and pushed the door open. The fire that was lit provided just enough light for Dante to make out the two beds that dominated the room on one side. He crept into the room and approached the first bed, this one was empty. "So this one must belong to Oliver," he said to himself. Silently, he made his way to the second bed, fully expecting to find Nicholas, but this bed was also empty. He couldn't understand. *What is going on,* he thought. While he was deciding what to do, to his surprise, a picture on the wall opened and from behind the picture stepped Nicholas, carrying a candle. He had been down to the kitchen and came back eating a thick slice of bread covered in butter. As the picture on the wall had swung open, Dante had ducked down behind one of the fireside chairs. He watched as Nicholas climbed into bed and blew out his candle. Nicholas finished eating his slice of bread by the glow from the fire, unaware of the presence of Dante. When finished, he lay down and pulled the covers of his bed up around his neck. Only now did Dante come out from behind the chair. He carried a small pouch that was suspended from the belt around his waist. He opened the pouch and poured into the palm of his hand a small amount of black dust, sleeping dust. He approached Nicholas's bed and placed the dust on the pillow beneath Nicholas's nose. As he inhaled, the black dust was drawn into his nose, Dante knew this was the moment he had been waiting for. He pulled back the covers and lifted Nicholas's limp body from the bed. He left behind a small piece of paper addressed to Richard. He quickly made his way through the castle to the main door. He placed Nicholas on the floor so he could unbolt the door and use the key to open the lock. He then pushed the door open and gathered Nicholas up in his arms. As he walked down the pathway leading away from the castle, he could not help but smile to himself. *Imagine their surprise when they realise that Nicholas has been taken,* he thought.

Dante merrily walked through the castle gates carrying Nicholas and headed towards the nearby forest where Richard liked to go hunting. With Nicholas being only five, he was not very heavy and so Dante who could only fly short distances was able to fly up into the trees. This meant there would be no trail on the ground to follow. Dante skipped his way through the forest from branch to branch. He had already found a large tree that had a hole in its side, which he had made big enough for a small child to be hidden, the hole was about fifty feet above the ground, ivy wrapped itself around the tree trunk and the branches fully covered in leaves meant the hole was completely hidden from the ground below. Dante had a limited supply of black dust sleeping powder, it was made from a very rare mushroom that had to be dried and then ground down to make the dust, although each dose would keep Nicholas asleep for about a week.

Next morning, Richard woke early as usual, just as someone started knocking on his bedroom door. "Come in," he shouted, as he sat up in bed.

One of the guards entered the room, it was Phillip. "Your Majesty, when I woke up this morning, I realised the key that locked the main door of the castle was missing."

"Missing? What do you mean missing?" said Richard.

"I placed it on the side table next to my bed, just as I do every night, and this morning, it was missing."

"Could you have knocked it off the table whist sleeping?" asked Richard.

"I already thought of that, and so I checked under the table and under my bed, it is not there."

Richard was now getting worried. "Is anything else missing?" he asked.

"We found the main door was open, but so far, everything seems to be in place."

"I will get dressed and join the search," said Richard. "Wait for me outside."

"Yes, Your Majesty," said Phillip.

Within a couple of minutes, Richard opened the door. In a hurry, he had only put on trousers and boots. "Right, where have you checked so far?"

"We have completed a search of downstairs and can find nothing missing, we are about to start searching upstairs."

"Oh my God," said Richard.

"What is it?" asked Phillip, as Richard raced up the stairs. But Richard wasn't listening, he was running along the hallway as quickly as he could. Guards had to step aside to let Richard past. One of the guards was not quick enough to move out of the way and got shoved to the floor, but Richard didn't stop. All eyes were now following Richard along the hallway, he had reached the door to the princess's bedroom, and burst in, the doors flew open and crashed against the wall. The three princesses woke up frightened, until they realised that it was their father who had burst through the door. He looked around the room and satisfying himself all three of his daughters were there, he raced to the adjoining door that led to the boys' bedroom. He flung this door open and entered, followed by the guards. Richard lit a candle and then another. Both beds were empty, his heart sank in his chest.

"Search the castle again," Richard shouted. "Nicholas is missing, check the secret passageways." As the guards retreated from the room, Richard slumped onto one of the fireside chairs. Having heard Nicholas was missing, the three princesses raced from their adjoining bedroom to find their father in tears. "This cannot be happening," he said. Dorothy went to get a blanket from Nicholas's bed to wrap around her father's bare shoulders. As she pulled the blanket from the bed, a piece of paper fell to the floor. She picked it up and could see it had her father's name on it. She went to her father with the blanket and showed him the piece of paper. It was only a small piece of paper that had been folded over. He opened the paper and found a message inside,

'Your Majesty, for ten thousand gold coins, I will return your son, but find us first you must. In a land you have never seen, a kingdom like no other, and a valley of tall green trees, I will be waiting. Dante'

Richard raced from the bedroom and ran down the hallway. At the top of the stairs, he called for Phillip. Phillip heard the call and came from the great hall. At the bottom of the stairs, he looked up and could see Richard looking down. "Gather all your men in the great hall, I will be down once I have finished getting dressed."

"Yes, Your Majesty," said Phillip. When Richard finally appeared in the great hall, all of the castle guards were waiting. King Richard told them of the note that had been found. There was an audible gasp that went around the room. "Does anyone know of a kingdom like no other?"

They all looked at each other. "No, Your Majesty, none of us know of such a place," said Phillip.

"I didn't think so," said Richard. "I don't know of such a place either. If only Percival was here, he might have some idea of where this place is." Richard selected two guards to find Percival and bring him back, now all he could do was wait.

Chapter 9
The Rainbow Cloud

Oliver was first to wake the next morning. He sat up and looked over at Henry and Stephen, they were both fast asleep, and so he lay back down on the grass facing up at the sky. Oliver lay gazing at what he thought was just a purple moon, and, as if this wasn't strange enough, he was surprised to see the moon slowly expand sideways. He watched in awe as it expanded to the right, when suddenly on the left side, a yellow glow appeared. Firstly, just a small thin line of yellow, then gradually it grew and grew. Oliver realised this was the yellow sun, it was like watching it being reborn. Now with the yellow sun fully exposed, the mass continued to drift to the right and began to separate once more. A blue line appeared, and as the pink sun drifted away, it became paler. Finally, all three suns were in the sky once more. Watching this helped to remind Oliver where they were. Henry began to stir and finally, Stephen was awake. Now all three were sitting up. Oliver told them what he had just witnessed. It wasn't that they didn't believe him, it was just hard to imagine what it must have looked like. Stephen then told Oliver that he had seen the three suns merge the night before to create the purple moon. Then another strange thing happened, a large white cloud was slowly drifting across the sky, and as it passed over the three suns, the colours combined to transform the fluffy white cloud into a multi-coloured cloud that resembled the colours of a rainbow. "Oh my," said Stephen.

"No one will ever believe us," said Henry.

"Good morning," said Eleanor. They were taken by surprise, they were so enthralled by the sight in the sky that not one of them had seen Eleanor approach.

"Good morning," said Oliver. "We were just watching the cloud pass over the sun."

"Why?" asked Eleanor.

"We have never seen anything like it before," said Stephen. Eleanor looked at them with a puzzled expression. Oliver didn't understand why she looked at them this way, but then it dawned on Stephen. "We only have one sun where we come from," he said.

"How strange," said Eleanor, and she turned to walk away.

"Please wait," called Oliver. "Can you show us the way to the rainbow fairy's palace?"

"Is that not what I am doing?" said Eleanor, and she turned once more and began to walk away. The three boys quickly got to their feet and collected their horses, following Eleanor down the dirt pathway once more.

It started to rain from the rainbow cloud and they were astonished to see the droplets of water were also coloured like a rainbow. The three boys began to laugh and held out their hands to capture the coloured rain. Eleanor turned to see what they were laughing at, seeing the look of joy on their faces made Eleanor smile, it was a brief shower of rain that soon passed. "That was amazing," said Henry. They were ready to carry on, and they had reached the edge of the forest, this was their first view of the trees at close range.

"Is everything coloured like a rainbow?" asked Oliver.

"Well, it is the rainbow fairy's kingdom," said Eleanor. All the trees were multi-coloured like a rainbow, but not in lines, but in patches of colour. All up the tree trunk and all the branches, even the leaves were brightly coloured, then they heard a high-pitched voice.

"Well, well, what do we have here then?"

Eleanor said, "Just ignore him."

"Who?" they all asked.

"It's just a tree goblin," said Eleanor.

"A what?" said Henry.

"A tree goblin," said Eleanor. "Take no notice."

"Where are you?" asked Oliver.

"I'm right in front of you," said the goblin.

"Are you invisible?" asked Stephen.

"No. I'm not invisible," said the goblin.

"Then how come I cannot see you?" said Oliver. He was staring at the tree right in front of him. "Something just moved, he said. "I swear I saw something move," said Oliver. Henry stepped closer to the tree, and placed a hand on the brightly coloured tree trunk, it moved beneath his fingers, he jumped back in surprise. A high-pitched laughter rang out from the tree.

Eleanor was growing impatient, and raised her staff above her head and commanded, "Reveal yourself." The tree goblin fell from the tree onto the green grass below. Now they understood why they could not see him before, his skin was scaly and patterned in the same way as the bark of the tree.

"Why did you do that?" he squealed at Eleanor. "I was only having some fun."

"I don't have time for fun," said Eleanor.

This was the first time they had heard Eleanor speak in a severe tone. Oliver bent down to help the goblin to his feet, he stood only about ten inches tall, and had overly large hands and feet, he had round head had large pointed ears, and large disc like eyes, a small flat nose, and a broad mouth. "What are you doing here?" he asked.

"We're on our way to see the rainbow fairy," said Oliver.

"Not if you're going with Eleanor, you're not."

"Be quiet, Samuel," said Eleanor. And even though his lips were moving, there was no voice to be heard.

"What's happened to him?" asked Stephen.

"He talks too much," said Eleanor.

"Why did he say if we went with you we would not be going to the see the rainbow fairy?" asked Oliver.

"He doesn't know what he's talking about," said Eleanor. Samuel had returned to his tree, and with his overly large hands and feet, climbing the tree was very easy. Now back on the tree, he was perfectly camouflaged once more. Oliver was now worried, why would Eleanor stop Samuel from talking, surely, this meant she was hiding something. Then he remembered that Eleanor could read his thoughts. Damn, he had to stop thinking of Samuel, and what he had said, whilst in the presence of Eleanor.

Eleanor was walking on down the pathway. Stephen and Henry followed close behind, Oliver was a little further back. He was going to keep a close eye on Eleanor from now on. As they continued to follow Eleanor through the forest, they were looking all around them at the strange sights, rabbits with small antlers kept appearing and then just as quickly, they would disappear once more. There was a very strange looking animal, its head resembled a lizard, and its body was covered in feathers, but its tail was bare, using its tail for balance it stood on its back legs, raising its body high in the air, it was brown in colour. Henry walked over to get a closer look. As he approached, it scurried away and ran up the nearest multi-coloured tree. Instantly, its colour changed to match the tree, and it became invisible. "A lot of the creatures of the forest use camouflage for protection," said Eleanor.

"Come along," said Eleanor. "We have a long way to go."

"Can we rest for a minute?" asked Oliver, and he sat on the nearest large stone. It was covered in moss and tiny coloured flowers. Oliver had only sat down for a couple of seconds before the stone he was sitting on started to move. He jumped off quickly and stepped away. As he looked on in astonishment, he realised it looked like a picture of a tortoise that he had seen in a book, minus the moss and flowers, but he never imagined they could grow this big. They all watched as it lumbered off into the forest.

"Are you coming?" said Eleanor.

"Yes, I'm coming," said Oliver. He caught up with Henry and Stephen, and said, "I've had quite enough surprises for one day."

After a few more hours of walking, Eleanor stopped. They had reached a river. "This is a good place to have a rest," she said.

"Is anyone hungry?" asked Henry.

"I know I am," said Oliver.

"Me too," said Stephen.

"And what would you like to eat?" asked Eleanor.

"I would love some roast chicken with potatoes and vegetables," said Oliver. Instantly, a plate appeared with exactly what Oliver had said. They could not believe their eyes.

"Is it real?" said Stephen.

Oliver picked up the plate. "It smells real," he said.

"Taste it, taste it," said Stephen.

There was a knife and fork on the side of the plate, Oliver picked up a piece of chicken on his fork. "Oh wow," said Oliver. "That tastes great."

"Can I have the same?" asked Stephen. And a second plate appeared.

"I don't suppose I could have pork instead of chicken," said Henry. But once again a plate appeared with exactly what he asked for. As they sat eating, they realised that Eleanor was not.

"Are you not hungry? Oliver asked.

"Not yet," said Eleanor.

"I could get used to this," said Henry.

They had been sitting by the river for quite some time when they heard a loud splashing noise. They all looked towards the river, there was barely a ripple, but streaks of yellow, blue and pink danced their way across the surface of the water. Then a second splash much louder and this time, they could see multi-coloured ripples on the surface of the water heading towards them at great speed, not knowing what to expect, they sat motionless. Something large turned a few feet from the bank and a large fish tail suddenly appeared above the surface of the water, sending a wave of water onto the bank. Eleanor had moved away from the bank, but all three boys got soaked. Eleanor was laughing.

"You are so foolish," she said. "You could see what was coming but you just sat there anyway."

"Well, we didn't know what was going to happen, did we. But you obviously did. What was that?" asked Oliver.

"A mermaid," said Eleanor.

"But they are not real, are they?" asked Stephen.

"Why don't you ask them yourself?" said Eleanor. The three boys looked back towards the river and there were a dozen or so mermaids, all basking in the sunshine floating on the surface of the water. The water shimmered as they playfully splashed each other, using their tails. There were both male and female, the lower half of the body was scaled like a fish with multi-coloured scales, the top half looked almost human, only more muscular, and without scales. Instead, they had smooth hairless skin that was a golden brown.

"Good afternoon, Eleanor," said one of the mermen.

"Good afternoon, Janus," said Eleanor. Janus was the biggest of the mermen.

"So what do you have there then?" he asked.

"They are humans," said Eleanor.

Suddenly, the mermaids and mermen began whispering amongst themselves. "What are they doing here?" asked Janus.

"They entered our kingdom by crossing the snow river but now cannot get back. I am taking them to the rainbow fairy to help them get home."

"She won't thank you for it," said Janus. "The last time humans came, they tried to steal her treasure."

"But these are mere children," said Eleanor. "They pose no threat."

"Well, on your head be it," said Janus. And with that, all the mermen and mermaids turned, and dived beneath the surface. A succession of tail fins splashed the water's surface, causing ripples that sparkled in the sunlight as they spread out across the river.

"What did he mean, on your head be it?" asked Oliver.

"You don't have to worry," said Eleanor. "Everything will be all right, the rainbow fairy will see that you get home." They gathered their things and started following Eleanor as the path wound its way through the forest, each leading their own horse. It felt like they had been walking for hours.

"Can we have another rest?" asked Henry.

"But we still have a long way to go," said Eleanor. But as she turned around, all three were lying on the ground having fallen asleep. "Sleep well, young humans," said Eleanor.

Chapter 10
Catching Up with Percival

Percival and the guards had been travelling for a couple of days without incident. They were deep in the forest and as it was getting late, they had stopped to set up camp for the night. All traces of snow had now melted away, but it was still cold at night, so they collected wood and started a fire. All the horses had been tied to some bushes and were standing together. Berwyn had gone to find something to eat. After they had eaten, the guards settled down for the night. Slowly, one by one they fell asleep, this was a big mistake. A group of outlaws used this forest as their hideout, they had been watching Percival and the guards from some distance away, hidden amongst the branches of the evergreen trees that grew there. Now they descended to the forest floor. Silently, they moved around the camp from one guard to another, removing all their weapons. Two of the outlaws were holding lit torches that flickered in the cool night breeze. They provided just enough light along with the fire for the guards' weapons to be gathered. Only when they were sure they had all the weapons did they wake the guards from their slumber.

"My name is Cedric, and you have entered my forest. Now, who are you and where are you going?"

"My name is Percival and I am a travelling story teller. These are my friends who seek an adventure."

Cedric was looking at all the guards one by one. "So its adventure you seek, is it?" Nobody answered. As he gazed at Percival, he stopped. "I've seen you before," said Cedric. "I can't remember where, but I'm sure we have met before."

"I don't believe so," said Percival.

Cedric shook a finger at Percival. "Yes, I know I've seen you before." He then turned to look at the guards once more. "So you're hoping to find adventure, are you?" Still nobody answered. "We out number you three to one, so I wouldn't bother trying to resist, as we already have all your weapons." Only now did the guards realise this was true. "Tie them up," said Cedric to his men. Percival was beginning to wonder what had happened to Berwyn, when an almighty roar echoed through the forest. It sent a chill down the spine of every one of the outlaws. Cedric walked up to Percival carrying a lit torch, he bent down and held it close to Percival's face. "It's you," he said. "I knew, I knew you from somewhere," said Cedric. "Where is he?" asked Cedric.

"I don't know what you are talking about," said Percival.

"The bear," said Cedric. "The giant white bear." He had taken a knife from his belt and held it against Percival's throat. "Call the beast," said Cedric. Percival still denied knowing any giant white bear. Cedric pressed the very tip of the knife against Percival's throat and drew blood, it trickled down Percival's neck.

"Stop that," shouted one of the guards. "Leave him alone."

Cedric turned from Percival and called to Ben, "Take my whip and teach that man he should only speak when spoken to." Ben, the largest of the outlaws, a mountain of a man, stepped forward and picked up the whip from the ground. He then walked over to the guard who had spoken. Ben then pulled the guard to his feet, and raised him off the ground with one hand. He tried to resist but his hands were tied behind his back. He wildly kicked at the outlaw, but it made no difference. Ben made him stand in front of all the other guards. He ripped at the guard's shirt to reveal a bare chest, he then took five paces back. The guard looked terrified. "Begin," ordered Cedric. Ben drew his arm back dragging the whip across the ground, with his arm fully extended behind his back, he bought it forward with such speed, the whip cut through the air like a sharp knife. The air crackled and the whip cut open the bare chest of the guard. He screamed in pain. Cedric looked at Percival who was trying not to show any emotion. "Again," ordered Cedric. The ritual was repeated six times. Now all the guards were shouting at Cedric to stop. The guard being whipped was screaming in agony, his bare chest had multiple cuts and was covered in blood, still Percival would not answer. "Enough," said Cedric, "for now." Cedric sat on the ground next to Percival, still pressing the knife against his neck.

"Take him away," he shouted. Ben walked around behind the guard who had now collapsed onto the ground, grabbed him by his right arm and dragged him to one side, and dropped him onto the ground, unceremoniously. He was unconscious.

The two guards who had been sent by King Richard to find Percival were in another part of the forest. They had heard Berwyn roar, although they didn't know what this meant. They were on horseback, each carrying a lit torch which barely showed the pathway through the forest. Some rustling of leaves to their left caught their attention, but it turned out to be nothing more than a couple of badgers searching for food. They were hoping Berwyn would roar again, but nothing for at least half an hour. Then a blood-curdling roar once again echoed throughout the forest, it sounded close, and so they rode quickly in the direction from which they thought the sound had come. Having only two lit torches, the light didn't penetrate very far into the blackness of the forest. They moved forward cautiously, as the path they were following had disappeared. Now avoiding thorny bushes and low hanging tree branches, they came to a clearing in the forest where the moon shone brightly. This helped to reveal a single huge tree, something large seemed to be suspended from one of the branches. As they approached, they could see it was a large net, and caught up in the net was the giant white bear, Berwyn. It was suspended about six feet off the ground. There was no way they could lower the weight of the giant white bear, they would just have to cut through the rope and let the net fall to the ground. With a sharp blade each, it didn't take long to cut through the rope, the net containing Berwyn crashed onto the ground, but he was still entangled. He began to roar once more, and he was struggling to break free. The two guards approached the net. Berwyn was so agitated at being caught up in the net. As the two guards approached, he lashed out with a giant paw, and baring his teeth, he was truly terrifying. The guards stopped moving forward. Suddenly, they were fearful of releasing Berwyn in case he attacked them. One guard slowly stepped forward as Berwyn continued to roar, and struggle against the net. The guard spoke softly as he approached closer. Berwyn seemed to recognise him and so they were able to calm him down. Once he was calm, they could cut through the net and make an opening for him to escape. Once free, Berwyn bounded off through the dark forest, the two guards following on horseback. His white fur seemed to glow in the moonlight, which made it easier for the guards to follow. After about half an hour, Berwyn stopped, as did the guards. Through the bushes, they could see a camp fire glowing in the dark, shadowy figures were barely visible in the half-light that surrounded the fire, but they sensed something was wrong because of Berwyn's reactions. The two guards dismounted their horses and crept closer for a better look. The first person they came across was the guard with his hands tied behind his back who was unconscious after having been whipped. At first, they thought he was dead, he was lying face down and so they rolled him over, the sight made them feel sick. His bare chest was like one big open wound, covered in dried blood, but no, he was still breathing.

The two guards untied his hands, he remained unconscious. They silently moved closer. Now they could see all their friends, they were gathered together, but they were surprised at just how many outlaws were present, dotted here and there around the fire. Then they spotted Percival, he seemed to be sleeping. They moved around the fire, behind the outlaws to reach their friends, trying not to wake anyone. They started to untie the rope that held their hands. However, not waking someone when trying to untie their hands proved difficult. Having been woken by someone messing with his hands, the first guard started to struggle. They had to throw him to the ground and pin him down before he realised who they were. Once he recognised them, he no longer resisted. They soon had all the guards freed, but they could not make an escape because of Percival. Percival was the last one to free, but the most difficult, for Cedric the leader of the outlaws was lying right next to Percival and still held the knife to Percival's throat. They were assessing the situation looking at Percival when Berwyn appeared. He was standing right over the top of Percival and Cedric. The guards stood still and watched, without making a sound, wondering what Berwyn was going to do. At first, he did nothing, but Cedric stirred. He had been woken by a hot wind blowing across his face. Then as he became more aware of his surroundings, he realised there was a rhythm to the hot wind on his face, and there was a smell that went with it. Terrified by the realisation that something big was breathing upon him, he forgot about Percival and jumped to his feet. He turned and was face to face with Berwyn, the giant white bear let out a roar that must have woken the whole forest. Cedric was terrified, and as he went to run away, fell over his own feet and Berwyn was on top of him in a flash, pinning Cedric to the ground with his front paws. The outlaws now awake were watching the giant white bear as it stood over Cedric, as he lay on the ground. All the outlaws were interested in was to get away from this giant bear as fast as they could. Not only did they leave the guards' weapons, but in their haste, they left their own as well. Some of the guards went to give chase. "Leave them," said Percival. "You won't find them in the dark, they know their way around this forest far better than we do." The guards returned.

"So what do we do with this one?" they said.

"You will take this one back to King Richard and tell him what happened, then it is up to King Richard to decide on what is justice."

Then the two guards who arrived with Berwyn stepped forward. "Percival, we were sent by King Richard, he requests that you return to the castle immediately."

Surprised by the news, Percival said to the rest of the guards, "It seems you will have to continue without me. Good luck, gentlemen, on finding Prince Oliver." Percival and the two guards were on horseback and headed back to the castle immediately. Cedric had his hands tied behind his back and was made to walk, Berwyn followed on behind.

Chapter 11
Frolicking Fawns

The three young men woke from their slumber only to find that Eleanor was nowhere to be seen. The three suns were merging once more as it was late in the day. They were deciding what to do when they became aware of faint music being played. "Do you hear that," said Oliver.

"Yes I do," said Stephen. "But where is it coming from?" Henry could hear it also, and was heading deeper into the forest, Oliver and Stephen followed. As the music got louder, they could also hear singing and laughter, they followed the sound. Finally, they could see a clearing with a fire burning bright and dancing around the fire, were...

"What are they?" asked Henry.

"Fawns," said a high-pitched voice, which took them all by surprise. Samuel the tree goblin blinked his huge disc like eyes, this was the only thing that made him visible against the rainbow coloured tree.

"What are you doing here?" said Oliver.

"Eleanor asked me to keep an eye on you, so you don't get into any trouble."

"Why would we get into any trouble?" asked Stephen.

"Not everything in this kingdom is friendly," said Samuel. "You must realise that."

"We hadn't given it much thought," said Oliver.

"Eleanor knows that, which is why she asked me to keep an eye on you."

"So what are fawns exactly?"

"Half goat, half human," said Samuel. "Peaceful creatures generally, unless you upset them, of course. Then they can be quite dangerous." The look of horror that had spread across the faces of the three boys was evident. Samuel leapt from the tree onto Oliver's shoulder. "Don't worry, they won't harm you as long as I'm with you," he said.

"Let's go and say hello." Oliver was always the first to try anything. Besides, Samuel was sitting on his shoulder, this gave him the confidence to step forward. Henry and Stephen were reluctant to follow, but decided they had no choice. As Oliver stepped out from the trees into the clearing, they were spotted. The music suddenly stopped, every head was turned in his direction.

"Hello, my name is Oliver." As soon as he began to speak, all the fawns disappeared into the forest. Henry and Stephen joined Oliver in the clearing.

"What happened there?" they asked.

"Timid little things fawns," laughed Samuel.

"You mean to say that whole thing about them being dangerous was a lie?"

"Of course, they wouldn't hurt a fly." As they stood in the clearing by the fire, slowly the fawns gathered, one by one they reappeared from the forest. Samuel called to them, "Come on out, it's all right, they won't hurt you." Tentatively, they approached.

Oliver said, "Hello," and offered his hand to shake. They backed off, not understanding the gesture. They were about the same size as Oliver and Henry.

When suddenly a deep booming voice said, "Hello," and from the forest walked a fawn that was much bigger than any of the others. He stood on two hairy legs, but had the upper body of a man, with milk white skin, and blue, green hair, he had white flowers growing entangled in his hair, there were deep blue eyes, beneath pale blue eyebrows and pale blue lips, but the crowning glory were the rams horns that grew on his head. They added a sense of power to his appearance, they were thick and curved down the back of his head and then forwards alongside his eyes. Where the rest of his appearance was pale and subdued, the horns were brightly coloured in yellow, orange, pink and blue, which added a majesty to the whole appearance.

"Your Majesty," said Samuel, as he bowed. The three boys looked at each other and followed his example.

"Well, well, what have we here," he said in his booming voice.

"Humans, tell me, who are you?" he commanded.

"My name is Oliver, and these are my friends, Henry and Stephen, Your Majesty."

"What are you doing in this kingdom?" he asked.

"We found it by accident, Your Majesty, but now we cannot find our way home. Eleanor said the rainbow fairy will help us."

"Oh, she did, did she? And did Eleanor tell you that you will have to do something for Cressida in return?"

"No, Your Majesty, we were just told that she would help us."

"Oh I'm sure Cressida will do everything in her power to help you, providing you do something for her first." The three young men looked at each other. "Do you have anywhere to sleep?" asked the fawn king.

"We make camp, light a fire and sleep in the open," said Stephen.

"That is not advisable in these parts of the forest," said the fawn king. "Follow me and we can provide you with shelter for the night."

"Thank you, Your Majesty," said Oliver.

The fawn king turned and started walking through the forest, and everyone followed. Henry asked Oliver, "Why didn't you tell him you are a prince?"

"Because I don't think it would have made any difference." They eventually came to a steep cliff and the fawns with their goat's feet were easily able to scale the wall into an entrance in the rock face, but the humans had no way of climbing. Stranded at the bottom, they were beginning to think this had not been a good idea after all, when the fawn king reappeared and dropped a rope.

He called down, "Grab hold one at a time and I will pull you up."

Oliver told Henry to go first, and then Stephen. "Are you sure, Your Majesty?" said Stephen.

"I will be fine," said Oliver.

When Oliver had been pulled up the cliff face and entered the opening, he was pleasantly surprised. It was not just a cave as he had expected when waiting at the bottom, he walked into a sculpted room, with chandeliers suspended from high vaulted ceilings, and beautiful furniture spread throughout the room, it very much reminded him of home. "Welcome to my palace, my name is Langton," said the fawn king.

"Thank you, Your Majesty," said Oliver, looking around in awe. "This is not what I expected," said Oliver.

"Oh, and what did you expect?" asked Langton. "A stable?" Oliver felt embarrassed, but Langton just laughed. "Do not worry about it," he said. "You are not the first to be surprised, let me show you around." There were three rooms for dining, each had a number of tables.

"Why three rooms?" asked Oliver.

"I would have thought that obvious," said Langton. "One room is where single males eat, one for single females, and one room for mated couples. Do you not have this where you come from?" asked Langton.

"Well, no," said Oliver. "We all eat together." But then he added, "The king's family eat together and those that serve the family eat separately."

"But all fawns are my family," said Langton, "and they all serve me. Let me show you where you will be sleeping." Again, Oliver was surprised to see normal looking beds, this obviously showed from the expression on his face. "What did you expect?" said Langton. "Straw?" A deep booming laugh echoed throughout the cave. "I will leave you to get some rest, we can talk again in the morning."

"Thank you again," said Oliver. Stephen and Henry who had been following Oliver, and Langton had already chosen a bed and were lying down, it did not take long to fall asleep.

Oliver was awake. There was no lighting in the room, it was completely black. At first, he wasn't sure why he had woken, had he been disturbed or just woken up. There was no way of telling the time deep inside the mountain. For all he knew, it could be daylight outside, then he heard it, a faint groaning noise that seemed distant. *That could not have woke me up,* he thought, and so he rolled over onto his side, determined to get back to sleep, and there it was. Only this time, a groaning so loud, it resonated throughout the fawn's cave palace.

He lay silently listening, then out of the darkness he heard a voice, "Oliver, are you awake?" It was Henry.

"Yes, I am," replied Oliver.

"Did you hear that noise?" asked Henry.

"Who didn't?" said Oliver.

"Apparently, Stephen didn't," said Henry.

"How can he possibly sleep through that?" said Oliver, in disbelief. Again and again, the groaning was heard. They didn't know whether to wake Stephen or not, they were half expecting someone to come bursting into the room and tell them to get up, but it never happened and gradually the groaning faded away. It seemed Henry had drifted off to sleep once more because he was no longer talking, but Oliver found himself deprived of any further sleep, as hard as he tried he kept tossing and turning, with so many thoughts running through his head, like, where is Dante, is his father looking for him, do they realise he was missing. All these questions and no answers, and so he lay awake. It felt like hours, and when the others did finally wake. Langton came to let them know it was time to get up. Henry having gone back to sleep seemed ready to get up, and Stephen who had slept all night seemed refreshed and was positively raring to go, but Oliver had spent most of the night lying awake. Firstly because of the loud groaning, and then because of his own thoughts. He was so tired. As he tried to get up off the bed, he found he was too weak to even stand, and so collapsed onto the floor. Stephen who had witnessed this ran over to Oliver, and helped him back onto the bed.

"Are you alright?" he asked.

"I don't know," said Oliver. "I have never felt like this before."

Langton had also witnessed what happened. "Are you feeling all right?" he asked Oliver.

"I have never felt this tired before in my whole life," said Oliver.

"You must rest here, I will try and find Eleanor, and let her know what has happened, she may have the answer," said Langton.

As Oliver lay down once more, too tired to sleep, yet too tired to stand, he told Stephen of the groaning he had heard all night. Henry said that he had heard it also, but it hadn't kept him awake. Stephen went to have a word with Langton but was informed by a couple of fawns standing guard at the entrance to the cave that Langton had already left.

As he looked out across the land below, Stephen could see Langton moving at great speed, running and jumping over large obstacles as if they didn't exist. It was truly impressive, for Stephen knew that no human could run that fast, or jump with the power and agility that Langton possessed. And then, he was gone, in search of Eleanor. Stephen returned to Oliver, Henry was sitting at the foot of his bed. Oliver was facing the wall, but still not sleeping. Stephen told Henry he was going to see if he could find out what made the groaning noise that kept Oliver awake all night. Henry agreed to stay with Oliver. Stephen left Oliver and Henry, and started to explore. Most of the fawns seemed to be having breakfast, and no one was paying any attention to Stephen. He discovered many tunnels branching off the main room, he chose one to enter. He removed from the wall a lit torch, as he carried it in front of his body, it illuminated the tunnel. There were carved steps leading down, the tunnel was easily wide enough for two people to pass by each other. The descent seemed to go on forever. He was thinking of giving up, as he looked back the way he had come the climb looked daunting. He had no idea just how far he had descended into the mountain. The air had become damp, he could hear trickling water, and then he heard it, a deep groaning noise that sent a chill running down his spine. He had reached the bottom of the tunnel, the floor had levelled off, holding the torch high above his head, he could see a door. In the middle of the door was a section of metal bars. Stephen cautiously approached, the groaning had stopped, but movement could be heard. As Stephen stepped up to the bars, he raised the torch to see inside. A hand was suddenly thrust between the bars, grabbing hold of Stephen by the arm. A wild deranged screaming was heard from within. Stephen struggled to break free, but the grip was strong. Stephen had dropped the torch, and it had rolled away from him across the floor. He was trying to release the grip on his arm but it was futile, the grip tightened, causing Stephen to cry out in pain. This seemed to excite his assailant, and the screaming got louder. Suddenly, footsteps could be heard making their way down the carved steps. Langton appeared, with rage upon his face. Stephen was pinned against the door from within, Langton bent down and picked up the torch. He approached the door, thrusting the torch through the bars at the attacker from within. Stephen was released, he collapsed onto the floor in a heap, the screaming had ceased. Langton was talking softly to whoever was locked inside. Eventually, he turned his gaze to Stephen. The rage was still evident across his face. Without a word, he grabbed Stephen by the arm and threw him over his shoulder. He made easy work of climbing the stairs, and threw Stephen to the ground in front of Oliver and Henry. "What is the meaning of this?" demanded Langton.

"I meant no disrespect," said Stephen.

"I took you in and gave you shelter," shouted Langton.

"And we truly appreciate it," said Oliver, now fully awake. Having been given an elixir from Eleanor.

"What were you doing down there?" asked Langton.

"Oliver said that he had heard groaning all night that had kept him awake, I just went to investigate, I didn't mean any harm."

Langton had calmed down, and was sitting on his throne. The throne next to his was covered in cobwebs and dust. Stephen dared to ask, "Who is in that room?"

"It is my Queen," said Langton.

"Your Queen?" said Stephen. "What happened?"

"Ten years ago, we had two fawns born together. We named them Darius and Ferdinand. For seven years, they were our greatest joy. Then three years ago, they were captured by ogres. We have not seen or heard from them since. My Queen has been driven mad, as you have witnessed."

"Is there any hope of them being alive?"

"I hold no hope." It was heart breaking to see Langton look so defeated, he sat slumped on his throne. "We will speak of this no more," said Langton. "Eleanor is waiting for you."

They walked to the entrance of the cave and looked down. There was Eleanor, in her blue patterned robe that caressed the floor and with matching hat. She carried her staff. "Come to me," she said as she lifted her staff into the air, and all three boys were lifted into the air and they gently floated to the ground below. Young fawns raced down the cliff face as easy as walking on flat ground, they playfully raced around jumping over the heads of the three young boys. Langton watched from above. Oliver, Henry and Stephen were trying to catch the fawns, but they were way too fast and agile, with boundless energy, the boys got tired quickly. Eleanor grew impatient. "We must leave," she said. The young fawns didn't want the boys to leave, but they said goodbye, and watched as the three young boys were led away by Eleanor. From above, Langton watched in silence, and to himself, wished them, good luck.

Chapter 12
Searching for Dante

Percival had returned to King Richard's castle. Cedric had been placed into the dungeon upon their arrival. Richard and Percival were alone, Richard handed the note left by Dante to Percival. "In a land you have never seen, in a kingdom like no other, in a valley of tall green trees, I will be waiting."

"Have you ever seen such a place?" asked Richard.

"Your Majesty, I have travelled all my life and seen many things," said Percival.

"But a kingdom like no other?" asked Richard.

"Your Majesty, each kingdom is different from the last. Let me think, in a land you have never seen, in a kingdom like no other, in a valley of tall green trees, I will be waiting," Percival repeated this line over and over as he paced up and down. Richard watched quietly, finally Percival stopped pacing. He turned to face King Richard, Richard's face lit up in anticipation.

"I have heard stories of a magical fairy kingdom that is hidden from view," said Percival. "This could be the land never seen that Dante is referring to."

"So, how can we find it?" asked Richard.

Percival was still pacing up and down. "If my memory serves me right, the story suggests a magical waterfall hidden within misty clouds."

"Can you find this place?" asked Richard.

"I believe we can," said Percival. "It will be quite a journey travelling across many lands."

"Then we will need provisions," said Richard. They decided on a dozen guards with two wagons of provisions, this took a couple of days to organise, plus the ten thousand gold coins, they were placed into ten leather pouches, a thousand gold coins in each, and they were handed out to ten guards. The remaining two guards would drive the wagons, the other ten guards rode horseback. Each carrying a sword and shield, plus bow and arrows, for they had no idea of what they might encounter on this journey. On the day they were to leave, the three princesses pleaded with their father not to go, but he felt he had no choice, he had made a promise to his late wife, he could not abandon his son again.

While Richard had been getting ready for his journey, Dante had been on the move. The slight frame of Nicholas did not slow Dante at all, he moved from tree to tree in order not to leave any tracks, and when he moved between one forest and the next, he simply flew short distances at a time, only touching down briefly, leaving the odd footprint here and there, but no visible trail to follow. Dante was able to keep Nicholas asleep using the black sleeping dust. Unlike King Richard, Dante knew exactly where he was going and how long it would take, three weeks of travelling through forest and open countryside, then up into the mountains. Nicholas was now awake, and had tried to escape, but as Dante pointed out, "Where would you go?"

As they looked out from the side of the mountain, all that lay below them was a vast grassy plain with boulders dotted here and there, with not a sign of life anywhere, apart from the occasional huge bird soaring high in the sky above. "You are free to leave if that is what you wish," laughed Dante. Nicholas decided to stay, for now.

King Richard, Percival and the guards had nothing to go by except for an old story of Percival's. It told of a waterfall in the sky, that was hidden by misty clouds that hid the entrance to an enchanted kingdom. Percival knew of a mountain range that climbed so high into the sky that the top was shrouded in cloud, he could only hope this was the right one. They passed through many a forest on their journey. In one forest, they came upon a wooden cabin. At first, it seemed abandoned. As they dismounted their horses, five young men appeared with pitchforks. They had been watching, hidden in the bushes. They had seen Richard give the command to dismount. Richard now found himself surrounded with three pitchforks held at his throat, the other two stood either side of Percival. Richard ordered his guards to lower their swords, which they had drawn as the young men appeared, Berwyn was nowhere to be seen. An elderly looking woman appeared from within the cabin, she crossed the muddy yard, her eyesight was not the best, yet as she approached, she recognised King Richard instantly. "Fools," she shouted at the young men. "Do you not recognise your king?" Immediately, they lowered their pitchforks and sank to their knees. She attempted to curtsey, but stumbled in the mud. Richard caught her by the arm and prevented her from falling into the muddy ground. "Your Majesty, I can only apologise for my sons' behaviour. We have been robbed so many times, we need to take drastic measures."

"I fully understand," said Richard. Just then, Berwyn came from amongst the bushes, the five young men raised their pitchforks, and stood between Richard and the giant white bear. Impressed by their bravery as they stood unflinching as the giant bear approached.

"It's all right," said Richard. "He is with us." The five young men seemed uncertain of what to do. Percival stepped forward and walked up to Berwyn, who then lowered his head. Percival began to stroke the top of his head, only then did the young men lower their pitchforks, once more.

"What can I do for you, Your Majesty?" said the old woman.

"We are searching for a winged fairy," said Richard, "who may be accompanied by a young boy. Have you seen anyone recently that fits the description?"

"Your Majesty, we have seen no one for over a month," said the old woman. "Come inside and I will prepare something to eat," said the old woman. "You must stay the night."

"I will come inside on one condition."

"What is that, Your Majesty?" said the old woman.

"That you allow us to provide the food in return for your hospitality." The old woman agreed, and so food was unloaded from one of the wagons and in an hour, they were eating heartily, and after, were settling down for the night, with not enough beds for everyone. Richard and his men were happy to sleep on the floor, the old woman wanted Richard to have a bed, but as he pointed out, if they were sleeping in the open, they would be sleeping on the ground, and this was far warmer than sleeping outside.

On the mountainside, Dante had found an opening in the rock face large enough for himself and Nicholas to shelter from the strong winds that scoured the surface. He had lit a fire using low growing shrubs that colonised the area, the fire provided enough warmth for it to be cosy, and Dante slept well in the knowledge that Nicholas had nowhere to run too if he wanted to escape. In the morning, Dante woke first. He left Nicholas asleep as he stepped outside. It was early morning, the sun was just beginning to show itself on the horizon, and the air was cool. As Dante stood looking at the empty sky, he was aware Nicholas had joined him. "Good morning, young Prince," said Dante.

"Good morning," replied Nicholas. "So where are you taking me?" asked Nicholas.

"Oh, it is a place of magic and great beauty," said Dante. "A kingdom like no other."

"And why have you taken me from my father?" asked Nicholas.

It was only now that Dante realised that he hadn't told Nicholas why he had taken him from the castle. "My apologies, young Prince," said Dante. "Many years ago, I was cheated by your father and brother out of a share of gold, and I vowed that one day they would pay for their betrayal. It has taken seven years to find your father's kingdom, and now I intend to collect a payment of gold for your safe return, and if your father doesn't pay, then I will keep you for as long as it takes. I am confident he will come for you." Stones came tumbling from above, this startled both Nicholas and Dante, but, it turned out to be nothing more than a couple of mountain goats dashing across the mountain above.

In the wooden cabin, King Richard and his men were waking. The old woman and her five sons were already outside, working. Percival opened the door and stepped outside, Berwyn followed. "Good morning," said Percival.

The old woman returned the greeting, "Good morning. I hope you are rested," she said.

"I slept well last night," said Percival. Just then, Richard appeared in the doorway, stretched and stepped outside.

"Good morning, Your Majesty," said the old woman. "I trust you slept well."

"Thank you, I slept very well," said Richard. "Once all my men are awake, we will be leaving, is there anything I can do for you?" he asked.

"Take my sons with you," she asked. "I am not long for this world, I need to know they are safe."

"But we are on a journey that will be fraught with dangers, I cannot guarantee their safety," said Richard.

"Your Majesty," the old woman pleaded. "You have seen for yourself how brave they are, they will be no burden." Richard was about to refuse again, as the old woman collapsed to the ground, her breathing was shallow and she clutched at her chest in pain. Percival got to the old woman first and knelt on the ground, he rested her head on his knees, as he did this two of the old woman's sons appeared. Seeing their mother on the ground, they dropped their tools and raced across the yard. They got to her side as she took her last breath.

"I love you, be good," she said and she was gone. They started to cry as anyone would, having witnessed the passing of a loved parent. Sobbing uncontrollably and unashamedly, the two brothers lay their heads on their mother's body. As the guards awoke in the cabin, they had no idea what had happened, but the sobbing brought them outside. They stood beside Richard, who then instructed them to find the other three sons. They asked the two sons where their brothers were. Between the sobbing, they were able to discover, they were on the other side of the river gathering up their cattle. The guards set off at once to bring the brothers home. While they were gone, Richard had managed to talk the two brothers into moving their mother inside, and she was placed onto her bed, where she lay as if she was sleeping. Before long, horses' hooves could be heard travelling at great speed. Percival looked out of the window, and turned to Richard and nodded. The door was flung open as the three sons entered the cabin. The two brothers were kneeling besides their mother's bed, the three sons crossed the room and joined their brothers in their grief.

Richard, Percival and all the guards stepped outside, leaving the five brothers to grieve for their mother alone. As they stood outside, Richard pondered the old woman's request to take her sons with them. He spoke with the guards, "Do you think we can take them with us?"

"They may slow us down, Your Majesty, but they proved their loyalty to you and their bravery in front of Berwyn."

And so it was decided, if they wanted to join Richard and his men, they were welcome to do so, but they had to be ready to leave immediately. Richard went inside and explained to them their mother's request. He pointed out that they were more than welcome to join his party, but would have to leave straight away. The brothers looked at each other through reddened eyes, and the decision was made. Richard left the cabin so the brothers could say goodbye. They followed shortly each carrying a lit torch. Once all five brothers were outside, each one threw their torch back into the cabin, it caught fire quickly. They mounted their horses, and joined Richard and his party. As they rode away, the roar of the fire could be heard, but no one looked back.

They travelled far and wide. Every so often, they would come across a lone farmhouse, but on each occasion, the answer was the same, no one fitting the description of a winged fairy had been seen. It dawned on Percival one day, that maybe Dante had disguised his appearance and covered his wings so as to appear human. "Is that possible?" asked Richard.

"Yes, Your Majesty, if you remember from our first encounter with Dante, we thought he was a small child sitting in the tree above us. It was only when he unfolded his wings and floated to the ground that we did realise he was a winged fairy."

"Yes, that's true," said Richard. "And once he had landed, he folded his wings once more so they lay close to his body. All this time, we have been looking for a winged fairy, with a small child. From here on, we are looking for anyone with a small child." And so they continued to search the countryside for anyone with a small child. It was only two days into the search when they had a break through. A young couple with two small children living on a farm had been visited by a man with a small child. Berwyn's appearance caused the young couple some concern, never had they seen anything like Berwyn. With Percival's reassurance, the young couple let their children approach. Berwyn lay on the ground so the two young children could climb onto his back. He lay still as they stroked his soft white fur. Having observed how gentle he was, did the young couple tell Richard what they knew.

"Do you know the child's name?" asked Richard anxiously. The young couple looked at each other.

"Actually, no. He only ever referred to the child as boy. It was always, 'come here, boy', and 'don't do that, boy'."

Richard didn't know what to think, but then the young woman said something that caught Richard's interest. "The child didn't seem very happy. I felt as though he was trying to tell me something, but the old man kept a watchful eye and we were never allowed to be alone."

"How long ago did they leave here?" asked Percival.

"It was five days ago."

"Are you certain?" asked Richard.

"Yes, I know it was five days ago because it was my wife's birthday. We invited them to stay and celebrate with us but the old man declined, saying he had no time to waste. The young boy pleaded with the old man to stay, and got a clip around the ear for his trouble. My wife stepped in between the old man and the child. The old man apologised for his impatience, but said, "I am sorry we cannot stay a minute longer, come, boy," he said, and he held out his hand and the child walked past my wife and without a glance back, they left."

"Were they on horseback?" asked Richard.

"No, they were walking," said the young man.

"And which direction did they head when they left?" asked Richard.

"They were heading towards the distant mountains," said the young man, as he pointed to the left. Barely visible in the distance was a grey shadow that rose into the sky. Richard thanked the young couple for their help, called his men to mount their horses and they left for the distant mountains.

Chapter 13
Meeting Cressida

They had left the fawns behind, and were following a footpath that followed the flow of the river as it twisted and turned its way through the forest. Every now and then, they could hear the high-pitched voices of tree goblins, but they could not make out what was being said, and no one was visible, until Samuel dropped out of a tree and landed on Oliver's shoulder. At first, frightened by the impact of something hitting his shoulder, Oliver regained his composure upon realising it was Samuel. "You frightened the life out of me."

"Sorry," said Samuel.

Eleanor was leading the way, clearing the path as she went. "Has she told you anything about Cressida?" asked Samuel.

"No nothing," said Oliver. "Why?"

"All I can tell you is that you will need to be on your best behaviour, and expect the unexpected."

Before Oliver could ask what this meant, Samuel had leapt from his shoulder back onto one of the trees and vanished. Eleanor had stopped. The pathway that had been narrow and twisting had widened and was straight, lined on either side by giant trees. The branches overhanging the pathway formed an arch of many colours, the branches away from the path reached down to the ground. Once again rabbits, with tiny antlers were dashing between the lower branches, being ridden by pixies.

"This is the pathway that will lead you to the crystal palace, good luck," said Eleanor, and she turned to walk away.

"Are you not coming with us?" asked Oliver.

"I am not permitted to enter the crystal palace," said Eleanor. "But I have shown you the way as I promised, just follow the path and it will lead you, the centaurs will meet you."

"Wait. What are centaurs?" asked Oliver.

"You will see," said Eleanor. She turned away once more and as they watched her walk away, she vanished into thin air. Suddenly, they felt uncertain about visiting the crystal palace. When they heard horses' hooves, they turned to walk down the pathway towards the crystal palace, and were shocked to see not horses but something else, entirely different.

"Come with us. Cressida is waiting for you." This was more of a command than a request.

"So these must be centaurs," said Stephen.

"It would seem so," said Oliver. The three young men felt compelled to obey. They had the body and four legs of a horse, but instead of a horse's neck and head, they had the upper body of a man. There were six of them, all carrying a long bow and arrows. They led the way down the path beneath the rainbow coloured archway. It was a long pathway, and they travelled along it in silence. When they finally stopped, the six centaurs parted, three on each side. The pathway ahead was now clear and standing before them was the crystal palace. As they stepped out from beneath the arch, a hundred or more trumpets played a fanfare announcing their arrival. Now with three centaurs on either side, they were escorted forward. As they neared the crystal palace, the giant crystal doors slowly opened. The centaurs on either side stopped.

"Enter," called a voice. It had a musical quality, not unlike Eleanor's. They felt at ease once more and entered. The entire palace was made of crystal and shone in multi-coloured light. It took a little getting used to, but their eyes soon adjusted, the palace was huge.

The voice called once more, "Please come and join me." They found themselves drawn to the voice, and even though they couldn't see where the voice was coming from, they were confident they were heading in the right direction. They turned a corner and walked through a doorway. The room was full of fairies, some male and some female, but all brightly coloured. Some were hovering overhead to get a better view of the three humans. "Come, do not be afraid," said the musical voice. Once more, they felt compelled to step forward. The fairies parted as the three young men walked further into the room, revealing the most beautiful fairy of them all. She sat upon a crystal throne, with white skin and gold and silver hair, her wings fully extended revealing the most vibrant of colours. It was obvious why she was called the rainbow fairy, even the gown she wore resembled the colours of a rainbow, and yet, somehow with all the colours on display, she looked delicate and elegant.

From her throne, she introduced herself, "My name is Cressida. I hope the centaurs did not startle you," she said.

Oliver answered, "They were a bit of a surprise." The fairies all laughed.

"They are the guardians of the crystal palace," said Cressida. "No one can enter without their permission. Come walk with me," said Cressida. She floated down from her throne to the floor below, the fairies parted as the three young humans joined Cressida on a walk through the palace. All the floors, walls and ceiling were made from crystal, which meant that it was incredibly bright within the palace, but surprisingly cool. There were fountains, and waterfalls and crystal bridges that crossed a giant indoor lake. The fish that swam within the waters were almost as large as Oliver and Henry. They were coloured with red and white scales, some even had shiny scales that sparkled in the light. Oliver and Henry bent down on the bridge to get a closer look. A shoal of fish gathered in front of them, with a wave of her hand, Cressida launched onto the surface of the water what looked like caterpillars. There was a frenzy of splashing, as the surface of the water bubbled with activity, with so many large fish hungry for food, bodies were momentarily on top of the water as fish from below surfaced for the floating feast, and within seconds, the surface of the water was clear once more, and the fish slowly dispersed to the far reaches of the lake.

"What was that?" asked Oliver.

"A delicacy that they go mad for," said Cressida. "Now tell me, why are you here?" asked Cressida.

Oliver explained what had happened, "Eleanor said that you would be able to help us."

"I can help you," said Cressida. "But first you must prove yourselves worthy of my help."

"And how can we do that?" asked Oliver.

"There is a section of my kingdom where even I cannot enter. You will need to travel to the black mountains, there you will find a lord of darkness. Retrieve the crystal egg that has been stolen and I will send you home."

Oliver, Henry and Stephen looked at each other. "I don't like the sound of this," said Henry. Stephen agreed.

"But what choice do we have?" said Oliver. Oliver turned to face Cressida. "We accept the challenge," he said.

"Excellent," said Cressida.

"There is one thing I would like to ask," said Oliver.

"And what may that be?" asked Cressida.

"Can you provide us an escort so that we may find the black mountains?"

"Of course," said Cressida. "I will provide an escort of centaurs to guide you." She floated back across the lake, skimming the surface with her feet, the fish followed like a magnet. Oliver started back across the crystal bridge, followed by Stephen and Henry.

When Oliver, Stephen and Henry finally made it back across the crystal bridge, a male blue, green fairy was waiting for them. "Follow me," he said. The palace seemed empty.

Oliver asked the fairy, "Where has everyone gone?" but got no answer. Still they followed, through one empty room after another. Then they entered into a room with glass doors that were open wide, leading into the most spectacular garden. The fairy crossed the room and entered the garden, and promptly disappeared. The three young boys followed. As they stepped through the open doors, a fanfare played by trumpeters announced their arrival. There were roses everywhere, some were small shrub bushes, others were growing over archways, some had long stems with leaves and flowers only growing at the very top of the stem, some grew in hanging baskets where the roses cascaded to the ground, but all were brightly coloured and fragrant, so heavy was the air with the scent of the roses that Oliver, Stephen and Henry felt overpowered and quite tired.,

Cressida walked up to the three young boys. "Come join us for something to eat, and then you must rest tonight, for you have a long journey ahead of you tomorrow."

The three young boys woke early the next morning. They were each sleeping on a crystal bed, but far from feeling hard, the beds felt soft and warm. Henry asked the other two, "Do you remember going to bed?"

Stephen answered, "I don't even remember having anything to eat."

"No, nor do I," said Oliver. "And yet I feel satisfied, and fully refreshed."

"Yes, I feel the same," said Stephen.

Before another word was spoken, a centaur entered their room. "Cressida is waiting." He then turned and left. They got off their beds and followed the centaur. Once more, they were led to the gardens. This time, however, there was no fanfare. They were greeted by Cressida and a dozen centaurs.

With no pleasantries exchanged, all Cressida said was, "These are your guides to show you the way to the black mountains." She then turned and entered into the crystal palace, fairies from all corners of the garden streamed above their heads and into the crystal palace just before the glass doors closed.

The largest of the centaurs stepped forward. "My name is Drew, and I have been instructed to take you to the black mountains. Once there, you will be on your own," he said.

"Do you have any idea where the crystal egg is being kept?" asked Oliver. Drew did not reply, he simply walked to the front of the line and the rest of the centaurs fell into single file and followed. "I guess we're off," said Oliver, to Stephen and Henry.

They walked for four days through the rainbow forest without incident, until on the fifth day, they came across a shabby looking stone bridge. It spanned about eighty feet across what looked like an old dried up riverbed. The centaurs stopped, they removed their bows from their backs and each placed an arrow ready to fire. The three young boys had stopped also, they watched as the centaurs inched forward slowly. Then without warning, a giant hand appeared above the bridge and came crashing down. The ground around them shook, the centaurs backed away. "Show yourself," shouted Drew. And with that, the ground shook beneath their feet once more. They watched in horror as the biggest thing they had ever seen stood before them.

"What is it?" whispered Henry.

"It's a troll," said one of the centaurs, standing at least twenty feet tall, it had long shaggy hair that was multi-coloured, and it looked like it had a spider living inside its nose, as long black hairs protruded from inside its nostrils, that quivered with every breath, with sad looking eyes of emerald green. It had a large bulbous nose that was covered in warts of various bright colours, with powerful looking arms and giant hands. He looked as though he could crush any of the centaurs at will.

"Stand aside, troll," shouted Drew. "We are on a mission for Cressida the rainbow fairy."

"What do I care of the rainbow fairy?" shouted the troll. Even his voice made the ground tremble.

"You know what she can do," said Drew. The troll roared defiance, but the centaurs stood firm, with arrows ready for firing. The troll eventually ceased roaring, and with that, lowered his arms, bowed his head and stepped away from the bridge. "Quickly," said Drew. "Across the bridge, before he regains his courage." As they fled over the bridge, Oliver was the last to cross. He stopped to look at the troll who had sat on a large boulder. His head was level with the bridge, on which Oliver was standing. He looked directly into the troll's eyes, and all he could see was sadness.

"Beware the rainbow fairy," said the troll, in a whispered voice. "I was once human, and I displeased her. This is what she did to me." Oliver could hardly believe his ears.

Could this be true, he thought.

Drew had spotted Oliver. "What are you doing there? Get away from him, he's dangerous." Oliver looked at the troll one last time before moving on. The troll sat below a giant rainbow coloured tree that reminded Oliver of a weeping willow back home. With the troll's long shaggy hair that was also multi-coloured, he blended in perfectly, even the warts on his nose were brightly coloured, as were the stones that lay scattered on the ground beneath the tree. As Oliver made his way across the bridge, he could feel the heat from the suns rising. Finally, he caught up with the others.

Drew came over as Oliver left the bridge. In a rage, he asked, "What on earth were you doing?"

"Nothing," said Oliver.

"You're lucky he didn't snap you like a twig," said Drew. As they left the bridge behind, they became aware of a sudden change in the landscape. Although the three suns still shone in the sky above, gone were the multi-coloured trees of the rainbow forest, as if the intense heat had drained all the colour out of them, and in their place was a forest that looked as old and ancient as time itself, trees as tall as mountains, with trunks so thick even the troll they had just encountered could easily have hidden behind. As they continued to follow, Drew and the centaurs, the three young humans were in awe of the size of the trees. They came across one giant tree that was lying at such an angle half its roots were exposed, even its roots were as thick as a normal tree trunk, and its thick branches sprawled out over the ground like fingers, supporting it, preventing it from falling any further.

Drew suddenly stopped, held up a hand to signal to the other centaurs. They all withdrew an arrow held ready in their bow, as a large cat like creature, with foot long conical shaped horns appeared from out of nowhere. Sandy coloured with short fur and a thick tail covered in spikes, this was a formidable foe, covered in battle scars from previous fights. Drew knew from experience that if there was one cat that showed itself, there was normally at least one more hidden from view. The centaurs quickly formed a circle. Oliver, Stephen and Henry were placed into the centre, where they were easier to protect. The large cat was cautious, motionless, watching, only its tail twitched. "What is it doing?" asked Henry.

"Looking for a weak spot," said Oliver. Then without warning, a pack of smaller animals appeared. The cat was now surrounded, his attention now focused on his attackers. Snapping at his heels, the cat turned one way and then the other. Although much bigger than his assailants, he was outnumbered, and out manoeuvred. He thrashed his tail sending one of his attackers flying through the air. Still, the pack attacked undeterred. It seemed this cat was on its own, his only chance of survival was escape. Drew and the centaurs had moved away silently, keeping a careful watch on what was happening. Oliver tried to watch what was happening, but the centaurs kept blocking his view. Henry was terrified. With every yelp of pain, from either foe, he flinched as though he had been stabbed. The pack of smaller wolf like creatures showed no interest in the centaurs. They were only interested in their mortal enemy, the cat, with its powerful jaws and claws, bared its fangs and made a swipe with its large, clawed paws, but missed. Time and time again, it also tried to use its horns to impale its enemy, each time they danced out of reach, it missed time and time again. They knew how to stay out of range, but continually they attacked the cat's weakest point, the rear, even with its thick spike covered tail. Although the cat roared calling for help, none came. The last they saw of the cat like creature was when it collapsed onto the ground and was completely overpowered.

Drew had successfully led them away from the fight. They had walked for a couple of hours, stopping regularly to drink water. It was getting dark, when they made camp for the night and settled. Oliver finally had his chance to be alone with Stephen and Henry. He repeated what the troll had told him on the bridge. "Do you believe him?" said Stephen.

"He had no reason to lie," said Oliver.

"So, what happens if we don't manage to recover the crystal egg?" asked Henry.

"We don't know the answer to that," said Oliver. "We don't even know if we can trust Cressida to keep her word, even if we do manage to retrieve the crystal egg." These thoughts played on Oliver's mind until he finally fell into a restless sleep. He tossed and turned all night, at one point while dreaming, he called out, and woke himself up. Startled by the unfamiliar surroundings, he felt terrified, as there were strange unfamiliar noises calling to each other in the dark. After the extreme heat of the day, the night was cool. Then he remembered where they were and that they had put in place a circle of fire for safety while they slept. Slowly, the realisation of where he was, allowed him to calm his breathing, and eventually, drift off to sleep once more.

When the three young boys woke in the morning, the centaurs were nowhere to be seen. "I can't believe they just left us," said Henry.

"Nothing surprises me anymore," said Stephen. Just then, horses' hooves were heard approaching. Not knowing what to expect, the three boys ducked out of sight behind some boulders. Only when they recognised Drew's voice calling them, did they show themselves. "Why are you hiding?" he asked.

"We thought you had abandoned us," said Henry.

"Why would I do that?" said Drew. "Come, we have found the way, as we approach the black mountains it will become more difficult," said Drew. "There will be swamps to bypass, and there will be monstrous creatures to avoid."

"What sort of creatures?" asked Oliver.

"The likes of which you have never seen before, I can guarantee," said Drew. Oliver was excited by the prospect of meeting some strange creature, but as he looked over at Henry, he could see the fear on his face, which looked as though every last drop of blood had been drained from his body. He looked ghostly white, and then Oliver looked across at Stephen, having heard what Drew had said, Stephen didn't seem to show any emotion. Oliver put this down to the fact that Stephen was older, and he had been on the first journey into the unknown and had already seen some pretty strange sights.

As Drew and the centaurs led the way, Oliver bought up the rear, with Henry and Stephen in front of him. A large shadow appeared and crossed the ground in front of Oliver from left to right, then a second and a third, Oliver looked up into the sky, but with the sun so bright, he could not make out anything, for his eyes had started to water, and then he was sneezing. Upon hearing the sneezing, Drew, who was at the front of the line, turned around, just in time to see a winged harpy swoop down and lift Oliver from the ground, and before he could react, the other two harpies swooped down from above and grabbed Henry and Stephen. They lifted them off the ground with ease, the centaurs had their bow and arrows in hand, but dare not fire for fear of hitting the young humans. All they could do was watch as they were carried away towards the distant black mountain. "There is nothing we can do for them now," said Drew. "We must return to Cressida and let her know what has happened."

Chapter 14
Dante Comes Home

Dante and Nicholas were climbing higher into the mountain. They had to stop often, as the higher they went, the thinner the air, and the more tired they became. They were approaching a mist that lay on the mountain, and there was a sound that resembled rushing water. Dante tied a rope around his waist and then tied it around Nicholas. "What is this for?" asked Nicholas.

"In a minute, we will enter the mist, I don't want to lose you," said Dante. Once more, they climbed. They had reached the mist, the air was wet, but not because of rain. The noise was so loud they could no longer talk to each other. Dante climbed higher and encouraged Nicholas to keep climbing by pulling on the rope around his waist. It was slippery because of the water. Dante climbed without much difficulty, but Nicholas lost his footing and was clinging on by his fingertips. The sudden jolt of Nicholas's weight falling, nearly pulled Dante from the mountain, but, he managed to hang on, and slowly, he pulled on the rope, but it was wet, and slipped from Dante's grasp. Nicholas was now hanging by the rope around his waist. Again, Dante pulled on the rope, inch by inch, Dante managed to pull Nicholas back to where he could get a footing and hold on. Dante took a couple of minutes to get his breath back, and then started to climb higher and Nicholas followed, cautiously. Finally, they had made it through the mist, now there was nothing but blue sky overhead. The tops of the mountains stretched as far as the eye could see, and the source of the water was revealed. On a higher peak, the water was falling from rain clouds, and racing across the surface of the mountain. Still tied together, Dante led Nicholas towards the water. The water disappeared into a hole in the mountain Nicholas had no idea what Dante was up to. Dante approached the water, the noise was deafening once more, and they could no longer speak to each other again. Dante walked towards where the water disappeared. Nicholas didn't understand what was happening, he tried to stop Dante getting any closer by holding onto some rocks, but Dante pulled hard on the rope and Nicholas lost his grip and so continued to follow. Suddenly, Dante disappeared from view. Nicholas was still being pulled towards the water. Terrified of what was going to happen, he suddenly found himself being pulled along a pathway, hidden from view, behind a curtain of water. Dante led the way and Nicholas followed, they had left the water behind, the deafening noise of the falling water was now just a distant memory. Dante untied the rope from his waist and Nicholas did the same. They were able to talk to each other once more. "Where are we?" asked Nicholas.

"When we finally leave this mountain, I will be home, and you will be in a kingdom like no other," said Dante. "We must keep moving," said Dante. "We need to dry these clothes." Nicholas had been so scared of what was happening he hadn't even realise how wet he was. Only now did he realise how much his clothes were clinging to his body, he felt cold. The path they followed led down inside the mountain, but they needed no torch to light the way, for something that covered the walls of the mountain was glowing, a soft pale light. They descended quickly, it was far quicker coming down than it had been climbing up. Even so, they still needed to rest from time to time, but as they got lower into the mountain, breathing got easier and they tired less. Nicholas hadn't noticed at first, but it suddenly dawned on him that his clothes had dried, and he became aware of a warm breeze that was blowing through the mountain. Then the path levelled off, and in the distance, light could be seen from an opening. They made their way towards the light, the opening was too small to walk through. So they laid on their stomachs and crawled into the daylight.

"What a relief to be back in the open, in the warm sunshine." said Dante, he stood looking out at the view that sprawled beneath them, "Welcome to my home," he said. Nicholas stood with his mouth open in awe, his eyes were wide with wonder.

"Where are we?" he asked Dante.

"This is the kingdom of the rainbow fairy," he said.

They had found a way out of the mountain, but were still above the treetops. The first view Nicholas had of this knew kingdom was the rainbow coloured trees, and when he looked into the sky, there were the three suns; yellow, blue and pink. Nicholas was totally mesmerised. Dante stood for a while just glad to be home once more, but the screeching of something in the sky above reminded him of just how dangerous a place it could be. As three harpies flew overhead, each carrying something held in their talons, Dante pushed Nicholas to the ground behind some rocks. He put his hand over Nicholas's mouth and pointed to the sky, they watched as the harpies flew off in the direction of the black mountains. When Dante removed his hand, Nicholas asked, "What on earth were they?"

"They are called harpies," said Dante. "They are servants of Arec, the ogre lord, who lives in the black mountains."

"What's an ogre?" asked Nicholas.

"Something you don't want to meet," said Dante.

"Why?" asked Nicholas.

"Because they would eat you as soon as they look at you." Nicholas gulped, but it had the desired effect, he stopped asking questions. They had sat hidden behind the rocks for a while when Dante decided it was safe to move. "Follow me," he said. "Give me your hand." Dante took hold of Nicholas's small hand. They had almost reached the bottom of the mountain, but the last few feet were quite steep. Dante pulled Nicholas closer into his grasp, he then unfolded his wings and jumped off the side of the mountain, they gently floated to the ground below. Nicholas thought this was great fun and wanted to do it again, but Dante said, "No, we must keep moving. I want to be home before it gets dark."

Dante still had hold of Nicholas by the hand, so that he could not run off, but his eyes were everywhere. He wanted to know everything. "Why are there three suns?"

"It has always been that way," said Dante.

"Why are the trees so brightly coloured?"

"Because the rainbow fairy likes them that way," replied Dante.

"What are they?" asked Nicholas.

Dante looked in the direction Nicholas was pointing. "They are fawns," said Dante.

"What are fawns?" asked Nicholas.

"They are vile, dangerous creatures that eat small children, you had better be quiet, for if they hear us, I fear that will be the end, for both of us." Nicholas stopped talking, but he looked back over his shoulder. The fawns seemed to be playing, they were chasing around jumping over rocks and bushes. To Nicholas, they didn't look as though they would eat him, but he decided to keep quiet, just in case, and so he allowed Dante to lead him through the rainbow forest. As they moved through the trees, they were both unaware of being watched, but Samuel the tree goblin was sitting in one of the coloured trees, invisible. He recognised Dante, he knew Dante before he had left the rainbow kingdom many years ago, and was surprised to see him back. Even more surprising to Samuel, was the fact he had with him a young human boy, but why? As they went on by, blissfully unaware of his presence, he waited and watched. Then he began to follow, he was interested in where Dante was going with the young human, for Samuel knew from experience, he must be up to no good. Day turned to night as the three suns merged to create the purple moon. Dante and Nicholas settled for the night in the branches of one of the rainbow coloured trees. Dante explained to Nicholas, "It is safer than being on the ground." Samuel couldn't agree more.

Chapter 15
Oliver Meets Arec

The three harpies had carried the young human boys all the way to the black mountains. They landed on the ground, released their captives and with heads bowed, they backed away. Henry and Stephen were on their knees, but Oliver had found the strength to stand up. A large black shadow approached on the ground before him, he raised his head to look at what had made the shadow. To his surprise, it was a fawn carrying a tray of drinks. "Welcome, my master lord Arec is excited to meet you. Won't you have a drink of water?" Henry and Stephen got to their feet and stood either side of Oliver.

"What is going on?" whispered Henry.

"I have no idea," answered Oliver. He stepped forward and accepted a drink of water from the tray. "My name is Oliver," he said.

"My name is Darius," said the fawn.

Just then, a second fawn approached. "My name is Ferdinand, please follow me. Lord Arec is waiting."

"Did you hear that?" said Stephen to Oliver. "Their names are Darius and Ferdinand, those were the names of Langton's twin sons."

"I know," said Oliver. "Let's follow and find out what is going on." There was a large entrance at the bottom of the black mountain, it was obvious why it got its name, for all the surrounding mountains were different shades of grey and brown, with their tops covered with snow, but this one was totally black. Darius and Ferdinand led the way, there were fires lit on the ground, they provided light and heat. "Why are we here?" asked Oliver.

"Because our master wishes to speak with you, please come." And so, they continued to follow the two fawns deeper into the black mountain. Their nostrils were assaulted with an odour like nothing they had experienced before.

The two fawns stopped, stepped to one side and said, "Please enter. Lord Arec is waiting for you."

"Are you not coming with us?" asked Oliver.

"We are not permitted to enter the inner sanctum," said Darius. And so, Oliver, Henry and Stephen stepped past the two fawns and entered the inner sanctum. There were metal cages hanging from the ceiling, where all manner of different creatures were being held captive.

Lord Arec called to them from across a vast room. "Come join me," he said. As they walked between the cages suspended overhead, the stench of urine burnt their nostrils and made their eyes water. They could hardly breathe, it was so strong. Lord Arec called again as they approached, "Welcome, gentlemen. Welcome to my home." Lord Arec was an ogre, he sat upon a stone seat, he was easily twice the size of a normal man, with a large domed head that had only a few wispy hairs on top, a broad nose and deep sunken eyes, his mouth was broad and in the corners of his mouth, large four-inch fangs grew up from the lower jaw, down one side of his face were open sores that were weeping a clear fluid that trickled into the corner of his mouth. He wore a suit of armour that covered his upper body, covered in large spikes, his giant hands were completely covered in sores like the ones on his face. His legs were bare, again with sores that were constantly weeping. Two fairies were tending to the sores on his legs, he flinched in pain every now and then. "Come sit with me," he said. "How is it that you are here in this kingdom?" asked Arec.

It was Oliver who spoke, "My lord Arec, it is an honour to meet you. Arec laughed. Oliver continued, "We came to this kingdom by accident and now cannot find our way home."

Arec laughed again. "Why would you want to leave such a beautiful kingdom?" He gazed around the room with great delight.

Oliver was finding it difficult to pick the right words without insulting lord Arec. "You have a wonderful home," said Oliver. Arec was out of his seat in a flash. Oliver knew instantly he had said the wrong thing.

"Look around, you young human, does this look like a home to you?" snarled Arec. "This is as much a prison for me as it is for those that I keep in these cages." He picked up a stone and threw it at one of the cages, the beast inside roared in defiance, this caused all the creatures in all the cages to react, the noise was deafening. Even Arec himself found the noise intolerable. "Follow me," he shouted. He led them back to the opening of the mountain, and stopped. "You may leave if you wish, for I cannot stop you once you have left the sanctuary of the mountain."

"I don't understand," said Oliver.

"I cannot step into the light," said Arec. "Not even the moonlight, so, if you wish to leave, I cannot stop you. But be warned, if you do choose to leave, then I cannot protect you, the choice is yours," said Arec. He then turned and walked back into the darker section of the cave, leaving the three young humans at the entrance to decide on what they wanted to do.

"Cressida wanted us to come here to retrieve the crystal egg," said Oliver.

"And she promised to send us back home if we found it," said Henry.

"Well, there's no point in leaving as we are already here," said Stephen.

"Now we need to find the crystal egg," Oliver called after Arec. "We have decided to stay," said Oliver.

"A wise choice, said Arec. "Come, we will eat."

Oliver; Stephen, and Henry looked at each other. "I wonder what will be served for dinner," said Henry. "I hope it's not something from one of those cages," he said. Instead of going back to the room they had come from, Arec took a tunnel that led them in the opposite direction. They finally entered into a large cave that had a large table in the centre of the room. Arec walked to one end of the table where a large armed chair was waiting. He sat in his chair at the head of the table, there were a dozen more chairs.

As Oliver, Stephen and Henry approached the table, Arec called them, "Come, sit this end, so we can talk." Once seated at the table, Arec lifted a large bell that had been sitting on the ground besides his chair. He shook it once, the sound echoed around the room. Darius and Ferdinand appeared. To the delight of Oliver, Stephen and Henry, they were each carrying a silver platter loaded with fruit. Two fairies followed with trays of vegetables.

"I hope you like fruit and vegetables," said Arec.

"Yes we do," said Oliver.

"You seem surprised," asked Arec.

"It was not what we expected," said Oliver.

"And what had you expected?" said Arec. "That I was going to eat you?"

"It had crossed our minds," said Oliver.

Arec laughed. "Don't worry, young humans, I don't like meat."

"So why all the creatures in the cages?" asked Oliver.

"Ah," said Arec. "You thought I had captured them to eat them."

"Well, yes," said Oliver.

"All those creatures that you see in those cages were not caught for me to eat, they were all sent to kill me," said Arec.

"But who would want to kill you?" asked Oliver.

"Can you not think of anyone?" asked Arec.

"Surely, you don't mean Cressida," said Oliver.

"I know she covets the crystal egg I have in my possession." Henry's eyes lit up at the mention of the crystal egg. "So you know of the crystal egg," said Arec. Oliver looked round at Henry and Stephen, he knew instantly from the guilty expression on Henry's face that he had been the one to give it away. "What did she promise you," asked Arec. "What did she offer you, if you stole the crystal egg?"

Oliver hesitated to answer, "Not sure whether to tell the truth or not."

"Come, come," said Arec. "You can tell me, I will show you exactly where the egg is after we have finished eating."

After giving it much thought, Oliver finally decided to tell Arec the truth. "Cressida promised us that if we retrieved the crystal egg, that she would help us to return home."

"I knew it," said Arec. "Rather than come visit me herself, she is still using others to do her bidding for her, she will never change."

"What does that mean?" asked Oliver.

Before Arec could answer and without any warning, a giant golden bull appeared. It charged straight at Arec. Arec was surprisingly light on his feet considering his size. He jumped to one side just as the golden bull lowered his horns to strike, they became embedded in the chair where Arec had been seated. As the bull shook his head from side to side, smashing the chair against the table and then the wall, it splintered and fell apart. Now the bull was pacing the room, searching for Arec. He took no notice of the young humans who had moved to the opposite side of the table. The two fawns stood still, paralysed with fear. The bull approached, towering over them. He sniffed each of them in turn, they were not what he was seeking, he moved on in his search. The two fairies had flown to the top of the cave, out of the way, the golden bull looked up, again not what he was seeking, and so kept searching. Suddenly, a terrifying roar came from the darkest corner of the large cave. Arec wielding a giant club, covered in six-inch spikes, struck the golden bull on the side of its head, it crumpled to the ground, momentarily stunned, but, within seconds, it was back on its feet, seemingly uninjured. It charged at Arec again, this time, Arec misjudged the speed of the golden bull. Before he could move out of the way, a glancing blow was delivered to Arec's right leg. It was now his turn to crumple onto the floor, it seemed he was at the mercy of the giant golden bull. The bull lowered its head in preparation to charge, pawing at the ground with its front feet, and snorting loudly. It gathered speed as it raced across the cave. It seemed finally Cressida had found someone to do her bidding that would be successful. As Arec struggled to get to his feet, a second ogre appeared unexpectedly, even bigger than Arec. He carried a metal spear that he thrust into the side of the giant golden bull. This intervention had caught the bull by surprise. Once more, he crumpled to the floor. Arec had finally pulled himself to his feet and struck down on the bull's head with his giant club. This time, the six inch spikes became embedded, and the bull took its last breath. The effort needed to deliver the final blow had caused Arec to fall to the floor again. The second ogre crossed the cave and helped Arec to his feet, the two fairies had returned from the ceiling to the floor and began to tend Arec's wounded leg. The second ogre turned and spoke to Oliver, Stephen and Henry, "My name is Reif, Arec is my brother. Are you unharmed?" he asked.

"Yes," said Oliver. "The bull only seemed interested in Arec."

"Another one of Cressida's, no doubt," said Reif.

"Are you sure?" asked Oliver.

"There is no one else who would constantly send one creature after another to kill Arec and myself," said Reif.

"But all this for one crystal egg?" said Oliver.

"So you have heard of the crystal egg," said Reif. "But do you know what it is capable of?" asked Reif.

"Well no," said Oliver.

"My brother, Arec and I were made guardians of the crystal egg," said Reif. "If Cressida ever got her hands on it, she would have untold power over the whole kingdom. We cannot let that happen," said Reif.

Oliver, Henry and Stephen struggled with this news. "Why, would that be so bad?" said Oliver.

"Did Arec not tell you?" said Reif.

"Tell us what?" asked Oliver.

"We were once human," said Reif.

The three young humans were stunned into disbelief with this declaration. "No," said Oliver. "It cannot be true."

"And why is that?" asked Reif. "I have no reason to lie to you."

Arec, who was being tended by the two fairies, called out, "It is true, we were once human."

"But why?" asked Oliver.

"Cressida knew we had been made guardians of the crystal egg, and she asked us to give it to her, but, it was her parents who had entrusted its safety to us. Neither Cressida nor her brother Dante, were allowed to have the crystal egg. We were told to bring it here and hide it for all eternity. Cressida and Dante followed but what she didn't know is that a spell had been placed on the black mountain preventing her and her brother from entering. That is when she cursed us to look this way, and he trapped us inside with a spell that prevents us from stepping into the light."

Arec said, "That's enough questions for tonight, I need to rest." With the help from his brother, Reif, Arec got to his feet, where Reif lifted him off the ground and into his arms, he carried his brother with ease from the cave and down a tunnel. The three boys followed silently. Reif carried Arec to a bed where he gently lay him down, making sure his brother was comfortable, he turned to leave the room. Oliver, Stephen and Henry were standing in the doorway, as Reif walked past, he said, "Follow me." They did what he asked. He took them to a room where the fawns, Darius and Ferdinand slept. "I am afraid I have no beds to offer you but at least it will be warm and safe."

"Thank you," said Oliver.

"You're welcome," replied Reif. He then left them to get comfortable for the night. Darius and Ferdinand had returned, they did not seem surprised to see the young humans. Oliver wondered whether to mention Langton, but decided it could wait until morning.

Chapter 16
Richard Enters the Kingdom

Richard and Percival had reached the mountain, Berwyn would have to stay behind. It was too steep, which also meant the horses and wagons would be left, and so, they reluctantly left Berwyn at the bottom of the mountain, unloaded what provisions they might need, and started the climb. As they got higher, it became harder to breath, especially for the guards who were each carrying a pouch of heavy gold coins. They needed to rest often, as the higher they climbed, the air grew thinner. They were approaching the mist that shrouded the mountaintop, there was a thundering loud noise. "What is that?" asked Richard.

"It is water," said Percival. "That is what causes the mist, from here on, it will get very wet and slippery." Percival had suggested a rope be bought along, now was the time to use it. Everyone was joined together by the rope, just in case someone fell. Richard checked to make sure everyone was ready, the answer came back yes, and so they pressed on. As those leading the way disappeared into the mist and out of sight, panic spread through those at the rear. The youngest of the five brothers did not want to go any further, he was frightened of what was ahead. His brothers rallied around him with encouragement, and up they went. At the front, the head guard Robert and King Richard had made it through the mist. They were soaked, but, what a glorious sight, blue skies and mountain tops. They were followed closely by the rest of the guards. When suddenly one guard lost his footing and slipped on the wet rocks, this pulled everyone else off balance, a bag of gold got ripped and was lost into the hole, gone forever. Slowly, everyone managed to get back to their feet, Percival, and the five brothers followed at the rear, as they came up through the mist the second of the five brothers lost his footing on the slippery wet mountain. The first of the brothers was pulled from the mountain, and was hanging between Percival and the second brother. Percival was unable to grab hold of anything that wasn't slippery and was being pulled down towards the cascading water. As the first of the brothers dangled dangerously close to the waterfall, his siblings were doing their best to pull him back up. With fear etched on his face, his screams were silent, drowned out by the thunderous sound of the water. Meanwhile, the guards were struggling to stop Percival from disappearing into the hole where the water flowed, with the rope being so wet it was hard to grip, for either group. Percival had slipped perilously close to the edge but had managed to wedge himself between two rocks. The weight of the brother dangling in the hole was causing Percival incredible pain, as they were joined together by the rope tied around their waist. Slowly, the four brothers pulled on the rope. The guards and Richard could do nothing to help, all they could do was stand and watch with bated breath. Percival cried out in pain as the rope slipped through the fingers of the four brothers and the weight of the first brother again tightened the rope around Percival's waist. Richard was considering cutting the rope to save Percival, but that would have meant sacrificing the brothers to fend for themselves, something he didn't want to do. Once more, the four brothers pulled on the rope. Finding strength from somewhere, they slowly managed to pull their brother clear of the hole, totally soaked and exhausted they collapsed onto the side of the mountain. Richard let them rest for a couple of minutes, but eventually, he said, "We cannot stay here, as it gets dark the temperature will drop, unless we can find some sort of shelter we will be in trouble." Nobody could hear what Richard had said above the noise of the waterfall, but the hand gesture to move was unmistakeable, and so they all struggled to get to their feet and very cautiously climbed higher. Clear of the mist, they could see where the water was coming from, and see where it disappeared.

"That is where we have to go," pointed Percival.

"What do you mean?" asked Richard.

"If I am correct," said Percival. "There is a pathway that takes us behind the waterfall and into the mountain." Richard trusted Percival, and so that was where they headed, it wasn't far but it was still slippery from the spray of the water. Carefully, they found their way onto the path, it headed straight to the waterfall. As if by magic, the guards at the front disappeared, everyone followed cautiously for the pathway was still very wet. Still tethered together, they followed the path, which did indeed lead behind the cascading waterfall. It was so loud, there was no way of communicating, a hand gesture to keep moving forward was all they could use. As they moved deeper inside the mountain, the deafening noise of the water faded away, like a distant memory. At the same time, they had become aware of just how warm it had got, the further they travelled into the mountain. The next thing to dawn on them was how bright it was inside the tunnel they were following. Something that covered the walls of the tunnel was producing light bright enough for them to see where they were going. The pathway led them down through the mountain. Suddenly it opened into a large cave, where they decided to rest a while. Richard noticed as Percival struggled to sit down, this was the first opportunity Richard had to ask Percival if he was all right. Watching as Percival lowered himself onto a rock, Richard knew the answer before asking the question.

"Are you all right, Percival?" asked Richard.

"Yes, I am fine," came the reply.

"I think we can remove the rope now," said Richard. And so, everyone started to untie themselves from the rope. Richard helped Percival remove the rope and then lifted his shirt to look at his stomach, there was a burn around Percival's waist caused by the rope as the brother had fallen from the mountain.

"That needs to be looked at," said Richard.

"It will be fine," said Percival.

But Richard was having none of it, he called to one of the guards, "Can you have a look at this for me?" The guard walked past the five brothers to where Percival was sitting. As everyone looked on, with Richard standing by his side, Richard lifted Percival's shirt so the guard could see the mark around Percival's waist.

"Oh wow, that's nasty," said the guard.

"Can you treat it?" asked Richard.

"Back home, it wouldn't be a problem. I mean, with the right plants I could wrap some leaves over the burn to ease the pain, but here, I don't have anything."

"It will be all right," said Percival. "If you reach inside my pocket, there is a small container." The guard reached down into the pocket indicated by Percival, there he found a small round bottle. "If you just pull the stopper for me." The guard did as instructed and passed the tiny bottle to Percival. He placed it to his lips. As he tilted the bottle, a pale blue liquid dripped from the bottle onto his tongue, which he drew into his mouth. He pulled a face of disgust. "My mother always told me, the worse the medicine tastes, the better it is for you," said Percival. As Richard and the guard stood watching, the burn around Percival's waist glowed blue, as the blue slowly faded away so did the burn. "Ah, that's better," said Percival. Richard and the guard looked on amazed, stunned into silence.

"What is that stuff?" asked Richard.

"Just a little concoction of my mother's," said Percival. "Always handy to have around, only works on burns though." Percival then got up and walked over to the five brothers, "Now then, let's have a look at you, Jacob," Jacob was the brother who had been hanging in the air, having been pulled from the mountain when his brother Joseph had slipped. Again, he had a burn that went all around his middle. Percival removed the stopper and lifted the bottle to Jacob's mouth. "Just one drop on your tongue is all it takes." As one drop of the blue liquid hit Jacob's tongue, he recoiled in disgust. "I know," said Percival. "But it works." And as with Percival, Jacob's burn glowed blue and then faded, along with the pain. Percival then went from one to another checking the hands of everyone. Each time they tasted the blue liquid, they either choked or recoiled, but they had seen it work, and so the disgusting taste was a small price to pay. They were all feeling tired after the exhausting day they had been through. With no idea of the time of day, and no food to eat, they settled down to sleep. It was warm in the cave, and their clothes having been soaking wet, were now dry, and so they slept.

It was the youngest of the five brothers, Joshua, who woke first. Not wanting to disturb anyone else, he slowly crept away from where everyone was sleeping. He followed the only pathway available from the cave, it led him down deeper into the mountain. He had no way of knowing how long he had been walking, and there had been no sign of life. That was until he heard some heavy breathing, he stopped instantly and found a large rock to hide behind. The breathing seemed to be coming from behind him, but he could not be certain because of the sound echoing off the walls. He sat quietly, trying to determine where the sound was coming from. Then he felt it, on the back of his neck, the warm breath of a monster. He began to tremble with fear, he dare not turn around. Suddenly, he felt a large hand placed on both his shoulders. As more hands grasped at his body, he found himself being hauled from behind the large rock where he had taken refuge. He screamed for help as he was raised into the air, screaming for his life, only to hear laughter. For it was his brothers who had found him and decided to have some fun. They released him and continued to laugh.

"That was not funny," he cried. Richard and his guards had heard the screaming and raced through the tunnel with swords drawn.

Richard was not amused by what he found. "What the hell is going on?" he raged. "Where do you think you are going?" he asked.

"We just wanted to explore," they said.

"You're making all this noise, and you have no idea whether or not this mountain could be inhabited," said Richard.

"We're sorry," they said. "From now on, we stick together, and try to make as little noise as possible."

"Agreed?" asked Richard.

"Agreed," said the brothers.

They still had no idea what time of day it was, and so they pressed on, descending deeper into the mountain, the only audible sound was their footsteps and breathing, apart from that, silence. Percival noticed that the ground beneath their feet felt different, whereas before it felt like solid rock, now it seemed softer to walk on. He bent down to touch the ground with his hand, it was dirt, he pointed this out to Richard, who stopped walking and tested the ground for himself. "You're right," said Richard. "But what does this mean?"

"I believe it means we have reached the base of the mountain," said Percival. "Now we just need to find an opening that leads us to the outside." They told the others what they suspected, excitement spread quickly.

"Remember," said Richard. "If anyone finds an opening, let someone know. Don't step outside alone, we don't know what might be waiting for us." They all agreed. Richard had his doubts about the five brothers doing as they were told, but knew he could rely on his guards. They were standing in a cave with many exits. Richard suggested two men try a tunnel together. "Be wary of any sounds you hear, and be careful of the floor, we have experience of tunnels that suddenly produce giant holes." They all nodded in agreement. The guards all paired off, as did the four eldest brothers, leaving the youngest. "You shall join Percival and myself," said Richard. The youngest brother was not very happy about being with the King and Percival, he had wanted to explore by himself, but now felt his every move was being watched. Fortunately for him, it was, as he walked down the tunnel in front of Richard and Percival, he was not paying enough attention to the floor as suggested, he was about to take one more step, when Richard grabbed him from behind and pulled him backwards with such force, he flew beyond where Richard was standing, and landed at the feet of Percival.

"What did you do that for?" he shouted as he stumbled to his feet. His face red with rage.

"Look," said Richard. He was pointing to the ground, directly in front of where he stood, there was a large hole. Feeling embarrassed, the young boy turned away without saying another word. They walked back to where the tunnel began, marked the entrance with an X. "This would let everyone know that this tunnel had already been checked."

It was only the second tunnel they had checked, when they got their big surprise. Richard, Percival and Joshua, youngest of the five brothers, were making their way along the tunnel when a faint light appeared in the distance. After what had happened down the first tunnel, it was Richard who led the way. As they approached the source of the light, the tunnel turned to the right, and there it was, a massive opening to the world outside. They stepped towards the entrance without actually stepping outside. "A kingdom like no other," said Percival. They could hardly believe their eyes, the young boy had pointed out the three suns of yellow, pink and blue, and Richard was captivated by the forest of rainbow-coloured trees sprawled before them.

"We had better go back and let the others know we have found the entrance to the kingdom," said Percival.

"You go and I will wait here," said Joshua.

But Richard was having none of it. "We will all go back," he said. The young boy reluctantly walked away from the opening, and followed Richard and Percival back down the tunnel in search of the others. By the time they made it back to the cave, all the others had returned having exhausted their search, only the two eldest of the five brothers had not returned. Richard was about to send two guards down the tunnel in search of the brothers when they did finally reappear.

"We found a source of light coming from outside, but the gap in the rocks was too small to get through," they said. The youngest brother in his excitement told them of the opening they had found. "Is this true?" asked the brothers.

Richard nodded. "It is."

"Then let's go," said the brothers.

"Just remember," said Richard. "When we get there, not to go dashing off. This is a kingdom we know nothing about." Richard was still troubled by the brothers' eagerness, he knew the guards would do as he requested, but the five brothers, he was not so sure. They had reached the opening, the view was as impressive the second time around as it had been the first. The youngest of the five brothers pointed out to his siblings the three suns and Richard stood with his arms folded next to Percival. Everyone was stunned into silence by the beauty of the rainbow-coloured forest that sprawled before them. Richard turned to Percival. "So what now?" he asked.

"I honestly don't know," said Percival.

Chapter 17
Dante Arrives Home

Morning had arrived and Dante was already awake. He watched Nicholas as he slept. A loud squealing from the ground below startled them both. Nicholas woke up in a fright, Dante put a hand over his mouth, to silence him. As he peered over the side of the branch they were sat upon, there below was a hunting party of centaurs. They had slain a wild boar, one of the centaurs threw the boar with ease so it lay across his back, and they walked off, satisfied with their kill. As Dante removed his hand from Nicholas's mouth, Nicholas asked, "What were they?" Dante kept forgetting Nicholas had never seen this place before.

"They are centaurs," said Dante. "They are servants to Cressida, the rainbow fairy. We must stay out of their way, at, all times." Nicholas was fascinated by the centaurs, and watched as they walked away.

A high-pitched voice interrupted the silence. "Good morning," said Samuel, which caught them both by surprise.

"Who is there?" asked Dante, a little annoyed. Nicholas turned away from watching the centaurs.

"Do you not recognise your old friend?" the voice asked.

A grin appeared on Dante's face. "Samuel, is that really you?" he asked.

"Of course it is," said Samuel. He stepped away from the trunk of the tree, and as he did so, he became visible to them both.

"Wow," said Nicholas. "What is that?"

"Excuse me, young human, but I am a tree goblin," said Samuel. Nicholas was so happy to see such a strange creature, and it talked.

"Can I touch you?" asked Nicholas. Samuel was surprised by the request, but agreed to it. "Wow," said Nicholas. "It feels just like the tree."

Not sure what to make of Nicholas, Samuel turned to Dante. "So what brings you back home?" he asked.

"I just felt it was about time," said Dante.

"And what about the young human?" asked Samuel.

Dante seemed a little flustered, he had wanted to reach his old home without anyone knowing he was back, he certainly didn't want Cressida to know. As if Samuel was reading his thoughts, he asked, "Will you be visiting your sister, Cressida?"

"I would like to get home first and get settled," said Dante.

"I quite understand," said Samuel. He felt uneasy as Nicholas continued to stare in awe. "But what of the young human?" Samuel asked again.

"I rescued him," said Dante. "He was lost and alone, and needed someone's help."

As the three suns rose higher into the morning sky, a mist came down. Nicholas marvelled at the multi-coloured mist, and Dante was pleased to see the mist for it provided cover from prying eyes. Samuel realised it was time to leave, and as quickly as possible. Dante was confident his old friend, Samuel, would not say anything. As he watched him disappear into the mist, after bidding them farewell, and wishing them good luck, Nicholas asked, "Will we get to see him again?"

"Oh, I am sure of it," said Dante. He took Nicholas in his arms, opened his wings and floated to the ground. The air was damp, as was the grass beneath their feet, the multi-coloured mist afforded them sight of only a couple of feet.

Nicholas asked, "How come we didn't stay in the trees? I thought it was safer than being on the ground."

"Normally, it is safer in the trees," said Dante. "But not when the mist descends."

"Why?" asked Nicholas. But, before Dante could answer, a chorus of squeals and groans rang out over their heads. "What was that?" asked Nicholas.

"That is the sound of death," said Dante. He then explained. Each multi-coloured tree in the forest had come alive, feelers from the trunk of each tree extended along the branches at great speed. Anything sitting on a branch was quickly overpowered by the feelers and drawn back to the trunk, an opening appeared and everything that had been caught was consumed.

Dante knew of the danger of the trees, but on the ground with visibility of no more than a few feet, he was aware anything could appear through the mist. On his own, Dante would have made himself invisible, but because he had Nicholas with him this was not an option. Dante led Nicholas by the hand, listening intently for any sound of movement. Nicholas went to speak, but Dante placed a hand over his mouth. Dante stopped walking, which forced Nicholas to stop also. Out of the mist came a family of rabbits with tiny antlers, they scurried across their path, and vanished into the mist once more, closely followed by a red fox, with five multi-coloured bushy tails, coming out of the mist and running into Dante and Nicholas. It was startled, it faltered briefly in its chase of the rabbits, standing perfectly still, staring at Dante and Nicholas, and then it was gone, disappearing into the mist once more, with five bushy tails stirring the coloured mist as it passed on through and vanished. Dante and Nicholas continued walking through the mist without speaking, still listening intently, strange noises could be heard, which seemed dulled because of the mist. Nicholas physically jumped on more than one occasion, but tried his best not to make a sound. Then as quick as it came down, the mist began to thin. The path ahead revealed, they were leaving the rainbow forest, in the distance was a valley covered in tall green trees. A smile spread across Dante's face, he was nearly home. Nicholas, now able to speak, asked, "Why did that fox have five tails?"

Dante explained, "The more tails he grows and the more colourful they are, increase his chance of finding a mate, it proves he is a successful hunter and can provide for a family of cubs."

"I see," said Nicholas.

Full of joy, Dante was skipping his way down the path, still holding Nicholas by the hand, who had to run to keep up with Dante. Suddenly, Nicholas tried to stop, he had heard laughter, he was sure of it. Dante wanted to keep going, but Nicholas wanted to investigate, he struggled and struggled to break free of Dante's grip. Finally, he wriggled free, as he broke away, Dante lost his footing and fell to the ground. This gave Nicholas the head start he needed. Dante dare not call out for he wanted to remain hidden. As Nicholas raced away from the path towards the tall trees, the laughter grew louder. He was right, but, he was in for a shock, so excited by what he could hear, Nicholas raced between two large trees into a clearing, and ended up face to face with a group of ogres. They were sitting around a fire. At first, Nicholas didn't realise what they were doing, but, as he watched silently, frozen to the spot, he realised they were plucking fairy wings like you would pluck a chicken, as they tore the wings off, the bodies were discarded onto a pile, and the wings devoured. Nicholas felt sick to his stomach, as he took a step backwards, he stepped onto a twig which snapped, the ogres turned in his direction, he was spotted. They roared in anger at the sight of Nicholas and they stood up, only now they were on their feet did Nicholas realise just how big they were, twelve to fifteen feet tall, wide shouldered and barrel chested, with huge arms, and powerful looking legs. Nicholas's own knees trembled, he wanted to run but was paralysed with fear. The three ogres, each holding a large club, approached, one threw his club at Nicholas who ducked just in time. He started to run as the ogres gave chase, with their long strides they were closing in fast. Nicholas was dodging between the trees, the ogres smashed the small trees out of the way, when one of the ogres hit the tree Nicholas was hiding behind, he was sent flying through the air. And as the ogres watched, out of the sky, a harpy swooped down, grabbing Nicholas by the shoulders in its talons and carried him away. Dante had observed all this happen from the safety of one of the tall trees, out of the ogres' reach. They screamed as they watched the harpy fly away, the ogres roared in defiance, one of the ogres threw his club at the harpy but missed, as it soared high in the sky. Dante was angry, knowing that without Nicholas, he would not get the gold he so desired from King Richard. The ogres returned to their catch of fairies and resumed pulling off and eating their wings. Dante felt sick, watching the ogres plucking the wings off of the fairies, there must be something he could do. Turning himself invisible, he floated down from the tree. As he crept towards the ogres, he stumbled as he kicked a stone, and cursed, he had been heard, they looked in his direction. He bent down and picked up the stone, and threw it against one of the tall trees. As it bounced off the tree trunk, they were enraged by the interruption, all three ogres were now on their feet. Once more,

Dante, again bent down and picked up a larger stone, it crashed against the tree trunk. The three ogres roared as they went in search of the intruder. This enabled Dante to move quickly and release the remaining fairies from the trap in which they had been caught. The ogres returned shortly after having found nothing, only to see the last of the fairies fly away. One of the ogres launched his club into the air, narrowly missing one of the fairies, the escape was complete. Dante, still invisible, left the pile of five fairy bodies, there was nothing he could do for them now, they were already dead. As the harpy flew over the treetops, Nicholas had passed out, the harpy headed towards the black mountain. As she reached the entrance to the cave she landed, released Nicholas onto the ground and backed away, she was rewarded with food brought out by the two fawns, Darius and Ferdinand. Nicholas's limp body was picked up by the fawns and covered in a blanket, they carried the body into the black mountain. Oliver, Stephen and Henry were with Arec, totally unaware of what had happened outside. Still passed out, the two fawns carried the small body to Arec, he was seated talking with the three young humans. The two fairies were tending to the sores on his legs as usual. Darius and Ferdinand placed the small body on the ground at Arec's feet, they were all curious as to what the fawns had carried in, as the blanket was removed, it revealed Nicholas's limp body. Oliver burst into tears, he fell to the ground by his younger brother's side and cradled him in his arms. Arec turned to Stephen and Henry. "Who is this?" he asked.

It was Stephen who answered, "This is Prince Nicholas," he said. "Prince Oliver's younger brother."

Arec then turned his attention to the two fairies, tending his sores. "Check the boy," he asked. They placed the bowl with the soothing liquid for Arec's sores on the table beside his chair. Oliver was reluctant to let go of Nicholas, but knew the fairies were only trying to help. He lay Nicholas's body on the ground and stepped away. One of the fairies lay her head on the chest of Nicholas and without saying a word, started feeling his legs and arms. After checking all his limbs, when finished, they approached Arec.

"He has no broken bones, and his heart is beating strong," said Arec. "He is merely sleeping." Oliver was crying again, only this time with tears of happiness. Stephen and Henry were either side of Oliver also crying. As they watched on, Nicholas began to stir, Oliver was on the ground by his brother's side, tears splashed down onto Nicholas's face. He woke up startled, for he had passed out after being caught whilst flying through the air, by some strange creature, as he was about to be attacked by ogres. He struggled against the arms that held him.

Then he heard a voice he recognised. "Nicholas, Nicholas, it's alright, it's me, Oliver." Oliver released his hold and Nicholas stood up and faced his brother. At first, he could not believe his eyes, they were back together. He flung his arms around Oliver and hugged him tightly.

"But how did I get here?" he asked.

Reif entered the room. "It was a harpy that saved you from the ogres," he said. Nicholas hadn't realised anyone else was in the room, until he heard Reif's deep voice. As he turned away from Oliver, the first one he saw was Arec. Once more, being tended by the two fairies, on seeing the ogre, it sent a chill that ran down his spine, his instinct was to run, but once more he was paralysed with fear. He continued to turn, there was a second ogre, larger than the first. Nicholas couldn't understand what was going on. Continuing to look around the cave, there was Stephen and someone Nicholas didn't know, and finally, he was looking back at Oliver, who was smiling at him.

"What is going on?" he asked.

"It's all right," said Oliver. "You're not in any danger, we are amongst friends." Nicholas was still wary of the two ogres, but was pleased to see two fairies. He began to relax, that was until he saw the two fawns Darius and Ferdinand. He shouted at Oliver, to run, but Oliver just looked at him strangely. Nicholas grabbed Oliver by the hand and tried to pull him away from the two fawns who were approaching.

"What is wrong with you?" asked Oliver. "I told you we are amongst friends."

"But they are vile, evil creatures that will eat you as soon as look at you," Nicholas said.

Oliver started to laugh, Nicholas didn't understand. "Why are you laughing?"

"Who told you they would eat you?" asked Oliver.

"Why, Dante did," said Nicholas.

Only now did it occur to Oliver to ask, "How did you get here, Nicholas?"

"Dante bought me here."

"What?" said Oliver.

"It was Dante, he said something about you and father stopping him from getting some gold, he took me from my bed and brought me here, if father wants me back, he has to pay for me in gold, or something like that."

It was Arec who spoke, "So Dante is back."

"It seems so," said Reif. "But why after all this time has he returned? I wonder if Cressida knows her brother is back," said Reif.

"I doubt that very much," said Arec. "Not after the way he left."

"Why what happened?" asked Oliver.

"We don't know exactly what happened, but they had a falling out, and Dante left, vowing never to return." Nicholas had lots more questions he wanted to ask his brother Oliver. And so, Oliver, Stephen and Henry took Nicholas to one side, and sat in a circle, they talked late into the night, explaining everything, until Nicholas had no more questions, they finally fell asleep on the ground, all huddled together.

Chapter 18
Saved by Eleanor

Richard and Percival had been discussing what to do next. Percival had asked to see the note Dante had left behind when he took Nicholas. Richard had it folded in his pocket, he passed it to Percival, who unfolded it and read it once more. "A land you have never seen, a kingdom like no other, a valley of tall green trees, we have to find a valley of tall green trees," said Percival. "But we have no idea which direction to take, I suggest we all stay together," said Percival. "We have no idea of the dangers."

"Agreed," said Richard. They decided to set forth and head down the first pathway they came across, hopefully, they would meet someone who could help them on their quest. As always, the king's guards led the way. Richard and Percival walked side by side, the five brothers were at the rear. They hadn't gone very far when the youngest of the brothers Joshua stopped.

"What are you doing?" his siblings asked.

"I can hear music," he said. "Listen."

"I can't hear anything," said another.

"No wait, there it is again."

This time, they all heard it, and before any of his brothers could stop him, the youngest Joshua had dashed off in search of the source of music, without letting Richard know what was happening, the four remaining brothers chased after Joshua. When they finally caught up with him, he was standing still, for he was at the edge of a lake. He did not respond to them when they touched his arm and asked, "What are you up to?" He seemed focussed on something in the water. The music continued softly and they followed his gaze, and there she was, whatever she was, floating on her back on the surface of the water, as it sparkled around her, playing a strange looking instrument, it resembled a harp, only much, much smaller, they all became transfixed. She lifted a pearly white hand that appeared ghost like and beckoned them towards her, all five brothers stepped into the water and were drawn towards this strange creature, unable to resist her charm, as they waded out into deeper water she kept playing. Eventually, they were swimming. Once they were close enough, she reached out a webbed hand, grasped one of the hapless brothers and was about to pull him under the surface of the water. Suddenly, from the bank behind them, a beam of blinding coloured light shot across the surface of the water, the temptress dived below the surface unable to withstand the brightness of the light, releasing him as she disappeared below the surface, once the music had stopped the five brothers were released from her spell. Not knowing why they were in the water, or how they even got there, they started to make their way back to the bank. None of them were very good at swimming. By the time they had reached the bank, they were exhausted, the first of the brothers struggled to haul himself clear of the water, then proceeded to help his siblings, the youngest of the brothers Joshua was the worst swimmer, and being fully clothed, the weight of the water was pulling him under as he became more exhausted. Too tired to jump back in, his brothers shouted encouragement from the bank, but he sank below the surface and out of sight. Only now did they become aware of someone standing ten feet away, dressed in a long blue gown that brushed the floor as she walked closer to them, she carried a staff, patterned in red, black and white on the stem, covered at the top in multi-coloured berries and flowers, it was Eleanor. She raised her staff above her head and said, "Come to me, human." She then pointed the staff at the water. A bright light shone from the staff penetrating deep into the water, and the surface of the water bubbled, and as the brothers watched the youngest brother Joshua, reappeared on the surface. Two siblings now jumped into the water to retrieve their youngest brother, they floated his body to the bank. The two brothers on the bank attempted to haul his body out of the water, grabbing a shoulder each, they lifted his head and shoulders onto the bank. The two brothers scrambled out of the water, once more, and between them, they managed to pull his limp body away from the lake. "Place him on his side and stand clear," said Eleanor. She moved closer, standing over his body, with her staff she traced up and down his spine. As she did this, the staff glowed once more. All four brothers watched in desperation, praying their brother would survive.

"What is going on?" they asked. Eleanor stood firm, continuing to trace up and down the spine, then without warning, the young boy coughed and spat out a large amount of water. This happened three times, before he stopped coughing.

He then rolled onto his back, opened his eyes and asked, "What just happened?" They were so relieved that he was alive. For a second, they forgot about Eleanor. Then she turned to leave.

"Wait, who are you?" they asked.

Before she answered, King Richard said, "Yes, I would like to know the name of the lady who saved my companions." Eleanor turned to face Richard, only now did he realise she was not human.

"My name is Eleanor, and I am a gnome," she said. "And you are King Richard."

"How do you know that?" asked Richard.

"I know many things," said Eleanor. "I know you have come to rescue your son, for it is Nicholas you seek. But what of Oliver? Does he not concern you?" she asked.

"What do you mean?" asked Richard.

"Oliver is here also, for I have met Oliver, and I took him to the crystal palace of the rainbow fairy."

"Oliver is here, you say, you've seen him?"

"I would not have said so, if it was not true," said Eleanor.

"And Nicholas, have you seen him?"

"I have not yet come across Nicholas," said Eleanor. Richard's mind was racing. Both his sons were here, he could not believe it.

"Can you take us to see the rainbow fairy?" asked Richard.

"I can," said Eleanor.

"You should rest here a while," said Eleanor. "I have things to do, but I will be back." They watched as she disappeared into the rainbow forest, her long blue robe brushing the ground as she went, leaving no trace of footprints to follow. Percival was checking on Joshua, the youngest of the five brothers, while Richard sat alone. His thoughts were racing through his head, *how is it possible that Oliver is here*. Richard wasn't sure having both his son's here was a good thing or not. Instead of concentrating on finding just one of them, he now had both to worry about, and this was the dilemma that he now faced, which of his sons should he look for first. These thoughts were recurring in Richard's mind. Percival, satisfied the youngest brother would survive his ordeal, approached Richard. "Your Majesty," said Percival. Richard had been staring at the ground and was unaware of Percival's presence, as he lifted his head Percival could see the anxiety written across his face.

"I don't know what to do," said Richard.

"Try not to worry, Your Majesty," said Percival.

"How can I not?" said Richard. "Both my sons are in this magical kingdom, of which I know nothing about."

From out of nowhere, a high-pitched voice interrupted Richard and Percival's conversation. "I have seen them both."

"Who said that?" asked Richard anxiously.

"Why, I did," said Samuel.

"Where are you?" asked Richard.

"I am right in front of you," said Samuel. Richard was beginning to get frustrated, for he could not see anyone.

"Tell me what you know," pleaded Richard.

"All in good time, Your Majesty," said Samuel. He was enjoying his invisibility.

"What do you want from us?" asked Richard.

"You have nothing I need," said Samuel.

"Then why won't you help us," begged Richard.

"I never said I wasn't going to help," said Samuel. Richard was on his knees in desperation, all eyes were now on Richard, as he knelt before a group of trees.

The musical voice of Eleanor commanded, "Reveal yourself." And with that, Samuel fell out of the tree and landed in front of King Richard. Eleanor's return had taken them all by surprise, including Samuel. "Tell them what you know," she commanded.

Samuel got to his feet, bowed and said, "Your Majesty, I first met Oliver and his two friends over a week ago."

"What do you mean two friends?" asked Richard.

"He had two companions," said Samuel. "Eleanor knows this to be true."

"What were their names?" asked Richard.

"Stephen and Henry," said Samuel.

"Stephen," said Richard, surprised. "And what happened to them?" asked Richard.

"Why, Eleanor took them to see the rainbow fairy."

"This is true," said Eleanor. "I have already told you this."

Richard then asked, "What of Nicholas? When did you see him?"

"I saw him two days ago, with Dante," said Samuel. Eleanor's face revealed a surprise at this news, but was instantly replaced with her usual composure. Only Percival had noticed.

"Where did you see him?" asked Richard.

"They were in the rainbow forest heading towards the valley of tall green trees, where Dante used to live."

Richard's eyes lit up with excitement. "Can you take us there?" asked Richard.

"I can only take you so far," said Samuel. "For it is a land that provides me no protection."

"Eleanor can take us the rest of the way," said Richard.

"I'm afraid I cannot," said Eleanor. "For my magic does not work there. I would be at the mercy of the ogres that live there, and they show none. I can do for you what I did for Oliver, I can take you to the crystal palace of the rainbow fairy, if anyone can help you, she can."

Chapter 19
The Crystal Egg

Arec, had promised to show Oliver the crystal egg that had been entrusted to him and his brother Reif to keep safe, from Cressida and her brother Dante, Oliver was expecting some elaborate safety measures, to stop the crystal egg from being stolen, and so, as Arec led the way Oliver followed, no one else was allowed access, Reif blocked the way. Nicholas; Stephen and Henry protested at not being allowed to follow, Reif stood his ground, which meant he completely blocked the entrance to the tunnel that led to the crystal egg. Knowing Reif would not relinquish his position, they went back to the entrance of the mountain, and sat looking out. Oliver was excited to see the crystal egg, for he had imagined it to be truly beautiful, when Arec finally stopped walking he stepped to one side, Oliver didn't understand, there was no crystal egg, they had reached the end of the tunnel, all that stood before them was a solid wall, Oliver looked at Arec, "Cressida does not know this, but only a human hand can retrieve the crystal egg from beyond the wall, you must believe and reach through the wall," said Arec, and so Oliver tried, he placed his right hand on the wall and pushed, nothing happened, he pushed harder, still nothing happened, he turned to look at Arec.

"What is wrong, why can't I push my hand through the wall," he asked.

"It is because you are pushing," said Arec, "you just have to believe and your hand will pass through, try again," and so Oliver tried once more to pass his hand through a solid wall, it did not happen, because Oliver could only see the wall as a solid object, his mind would not allow him to believe, and his hand could not pass through, after several attempts he gave up, all he got for his efforts was an aching shoulder.

"I cannot do it," he said, disappointed with himself he went to find the others. Reif was still blocking the tunnel, Arec tapped his brother on the shoulder and he stepped forward allowing Oliver to exit. They followed him down the tunnel, as Oliver went to find the others, Arec and Reif went to the main cave.

"Did he manage to retrieve it?" asked Reif.

"No," said Arec.

"Then we must get one of the others to try," said Reif. He left Arec and went in search of the young humans. Oliver had found Nicholas and the others sitting at the entrance, looking out. It was raining multi-coloured droplets of water, and the suns were shining, it was like the whole sky was a rainbow, never before had anything looked so stunningly beautiful, Reif approached, but stayed back out of the light, he called to the humans, "I expect Oliver has told you what happened, who else would like to try?"

"I would like to try," said Henry.

"Follow me," said Reif, this time no one followed, as they walked back into the mountain, Reif was explaining to Henry what he needed to do, they had reached the wall. When Henry first volunteered to try, he had been confident, but now stood facing the wall his confidence waned.

"Remember," said Reif, "All you have to do is believe your hand can pass through the wall, and it will," Henry took a deep breath, and placed his hand on the wall just the same as Oliver had done, but once again the wall remained solid, Henry took a step back.

"Try and clear your mind," said Reif, "There is no wall, just reach forward and take the crystal egg." Again Henry stepped up to the wall, and as before he failed, Reif was trying to control his frustration, but not very well, Henry was feeling a little uneasy in Reif's presence, and so gave up and re-joined the others. Reif had gone back to his brother Arec, "Henry has tried to retrieve the crystal egg," he said, "but has failed, just like Oliver. It is getting late, they need to rest. There is another day tomorrow." The humans were summoned to eat, and then to bed.

They were all feeling tired and so after they finished eating, sleep was a welcome comfort, but not for all. Nicholas only pretended to sleep, he had been waiting for a chance to visit the wall. He knew where to go and what had to be done, just pass your hand through a wall that wasn't really there. *Easy*, or so he thought, he had managed to reach the wall without disturbing anyone else, he wanted to try this on his own. He stepped forward, without feeling nervous or scared in any way, he put his hand upon the wall, there was nothing there, as he stretched forward with his arm, more and more of it disappeared, then he felt it, small and egg shaped, *like a chicken's egg*, he thought, he gently grasped it with his fingers and closed his hand around it, then slowly he withdrew his hand from the wall. The small crystal egg gave off a soft glow, now he had it, *what to do with it*, he thought. As everyone was sleeping, he would return to bed and show them in the morning what he had done.

Morning came abruptly, as the young humans were woken from their sleep by loud roaring, before they had a chance to get to their feet, Arec and Reif entered. "Where is it," they raged, no one knew what they were talking about, no one but Nicholas, upon seeing the two ogres in such a rage he was too scared to tell them what he had done. He stayed hidden behind Oliver, with the crystal egg in his jacket pocket. "It had to be one of you," the ogres said, "Give us the crystal egg," said Reif, only now did Oliver understand what was going on.

"I don't have it," said Oliver. Henry, who was terrified couldn't speak, he began to sweat, it was like fear oozing from his pores, he had no control over it. Arec realised what they had done.

"Brother calm yourself," he told Reif, who then took a step backwards and slowed his breathing. "We didn't mean to scare you," said Arec, "But someone has taken the crystal egg, this is important to us, only a human could have retrieved it from beyond the wall. Which of you managed to retrieve it?" Oliver, Stephen and Henry all looked at each other.

"I don't have it," they all said.

Oliver turned to Nicholas, "Do you have it?" he asked, "You won't get into trouble, I promise."

Nicholas who was so pleased with himself the night before when he accomplished what Oliver couldn't, was now too scared to admit what he had done.

"No I don't have it," said Nicholas.

Oliver knew his brother was lying, but turned to the ogres and asked, "How do you know it has been taken?"

"The protecting wall is no longer there, and the crystal egg is missing," said Reif.

"Only a human hand could reach through," said Arec, "Please let us have it, we need it to return to our human form." Oliver turned to Nicholas once more, he didn't say anything this time, he just held out his hand. Nicholas reached into his jacket pocket and passed the crystal egg into Oliver's outstretched hand, Arec and Reif could not believe their eyes, ten years of being trapped in these bodies and trapped inside of this mountain were about to come to an end, Oliver handed the crystal egg to Arec. He held it in his right hand, Reif placed his right hand over the top of the crystal egg, so they both held it between them. At first nothing seemed to be happening, but very slowly their hands were beginning to glow, then as the four boys watched the glow started to travel up their forearms. The two fawns Darius and Ferdinand watched on from the doorway, the fairies who tended to Arec's sores were floating overhead. The glow intensified as it passed beyond their shoulders to their chests, across to their left arm it travelled, then down through their body, and lastly into their legs. As it reached their feet the glow was so bright everyone had to look away, the two ogre brothers screamed in pain and agony, and then silence. Oliver was the first to open his eyes, the glow had ceased, he turned to look where the ogres had been standing and in their place on the ground were two human forms. He quickly raced to their crumpled bodies, as he called their names everyone else opened their eyes. They could not believe what had just happened, the two fairies had fled the room as the glow got too bright, now that the light had gone, they were back.

"Can you help them?" asked Oliver.

Without a word being said they approached, the clothes they had worn as ogres now lay covering their bodies like a giant net. Gently, the fairies removed the clothes, and covered both brothers in a blanket.

"They are sleeping," they said.

Everyone watched on in amazement, waiting for them to awaken, Oliver had picked up the crystal egg and placed it into his pocket for safe keeping. It seemed like hours before Reif finally awoke. Reif opened his eyes, and tried to get up, but found his legs unsteady. He seemed confused, not fully awake, and so he fell to the ground once more. As he sat there quietly, he slowly became more aware of his surroundings and his body. He raised an arm, and saw a human hand, he put his hands to his face, it felt human also, he ran his hands down over his body. Although he had a muscular body, he was nowhere near as big as he was before, and there were his feet, normal, once again. He began to cry, then he realised there was another body on the ground, next to him, and remembered it was his brother Arec. The body was facing away from Reif, he turned it over so as to look upon the face, his brother Arec did not stir.

"Something's wrong," Reif cried, "Help him."

The two fairies bent over Arec, they slowly ran their hands over his body.

"I am sorry," they said, "He has gone."

"You must save him," cried Reif.

"There is nothing to be done," said the fairies.

Reif screamed at everyone to get out, he wanted to be alone with his brother, and so, everyone quietly left. The crying could be heard throughout the mountain, as it echoed off the walls. There was no escape, everyone felt Reif's pain. Sitting alone, cradling his brother's human form, Reif cried. "Why did we do this, why didn't we just stay as we were?" He was angry; frustrated, and inconsolable. When Darius and Ferdinand, the two fawns, asked if he needed anything, all they got was a, "No." They offered to move Arec, but Reif defied them to touch him. They backed away and left Reif sitting on the floor, rocking backwards and forwards, holding his brother, as the tears flowed.

For three days Reif had sat holding his brothers body, for three days he had refused any food or drink, in all that time he had not slept. On the fourth day he passed out, he had slumped to the ground, finally releasing Arec's body. The decision to remove the body had been made, the decaying process was underway and the body had started to smell badly. The fawns, Darius and Ferdinand, removed Arec's body, they carried it to the bed where he slept, now in human form he looked tiny on the giant bed that had been Arec's when an ogre. Once laid out with his arms crossed over his bare chest, Oliver, Stephen, Henry and Nicholas came to see the body, to pay their respect. All four, standing around the body, had tears in their eyes, Darius and Ferdinand stood at Arec's head. They were giving a blessing to the spirit of Arec, a ritual fawns went through upon death of a loved one, as they wished his spirit a safe journey to the promised land. Out of his body rose the spirit of Arec, it appeared as almost transparent, it seemed to be searching the room, with its empty eyes, then they settled on the doorway, a faint smile appeared on its face, then as they all watched in amazement the spirit rose higher towards the ceiling and vanished from view. Only now did everyone turn towards the doorway, Reif was standing there tears streaming down his face. He was looking up at the ceiling where his brother's spirit had disappeared, as he lowered his head he saw that everyone was looking at him, he was not ready for this attention, not yet, he turned and quickly ran away. Oliver called after him, but Reif kept running, wanting to be left alone. Oliver understood, and respected his need for privacy, at this time. They stood in the doorway and watched him go.

Chapter 20
Richard and Cressida Clash

Eleanor had taken Richard, Percival and all his companions as far as she could. They had arrived at the long straight pathway that passed beneath the rainbow-coloured trees. Walking beneath the multi-coloured arch formed by the interlocking branches from trees either side of the path, was like passing beneath a guard of honour, and beyond the trees they could see the crystal palace, bathed in sunlight from the three suns. They were about half way down the pathway when they were surprised, as they were suddenly surrounded by centaurs. Each one had a bow and arrow in hand ready to fire.

"Hand over your weapons," They demanded.

Richard's guards looked towards their king, he nodded. They removed their swords and dropped them to the ground, half a dozen centaurs came forward and removed the swords.

"Why are you here?" asked one of the centaurs.

"We have come in search of Cressida, the rainbow fairy," said Richard.

"And what is your business with Cressida?" asked a different centaur.

Richard turned to face the centaur, "I am hoping Cressida can help me find my son," he said.

"You are not welcome," said a different centaur, "You must turn back."

Again Richard turned to face the centaur who had spoken, "I only seek guidance to find my son, we mean you no harm,"

Two of the centaurs were speaking softly, one then galloped off down the pathway, towards the crystal palace.

"We wait," said the centaur, who had spoken first. All the centaurs still had their bow and arrow aimed, ready to fire. The wait was intense, Percival was getting tired. He slumped to the ground, one of the centaurs ordered him back to his feet. One of Richard's guards moved between the centaur with his bow drawn, and Percival.

"He needs to rest," said the guard.

"He can rest when I tell him to," said the centaur, "Move out of the way."

The guard refused. King Richard tried to intervene, but found himself faced with three arrows pointed at his chest, he backed away. Percival slowly struggled back to his feet, the centaurs also backed away, still with their arrows ready to release. The wait continued, until finally the centaur returned. "Cressida wishes to meet with King Richard alone, the rest of you must return. Eleanor will be waiting for you," the centaur said.

The guards were reluctant to let their king out of their sight, but he agreed to see Cressida alone, for all he could think of was how to save his two sons. Percival and the guards were led back to the start of the path, as told, Eleanor was waiting.

King Richard was escorted towards the crystal palace. Centaurs announced his arrival with a fanfare of music. As he stepped into the crystal palace, all eyes were upon him, fairies of all ages, stood staring as he walked amongst them. With a regal air befitting a king, he walked on by, as he passed from one room to the next, there she was, sat upon a crystal throne, high in the air, her wings spread out like a giant fan, it was easy to see why she was called the rainbow fairy. Her wings were brightly coloured, as was the gown she wore, she called down to King Richard.

"Why have you come to my kingdom," she asked, all talking amongst the fairies had ceased, everyone present was now listening to their conversation.

"I have come in search of my two sons," said Richard.

"Two sons?" said Cressida.

"Yes, Your Majesty," said Richard, the whispering started, soon the whole room was talking.

"I have met Oliver," said Cressida, "but I was unaware of a second prince."

"He arrived after Oliver," said Richard, "He was brought here by Dante."

An audible gasp went around the room. Cressida floated down from her crystal throne above, with all the grace and beauty of a princess.

"Tell me about this second child," asked Cressida.

"His name is Nicholas," said Richard, "And he is just five years old. Dante took him from his bed in my castle, leaving a note which led us here. He is demanding I pay him in gold for the return of my son."

"In this note, did it say where you are to find Dante?" asked Cressida.

Richard had noticed that every time Dante's name was mentioned there was a reaction amongst the fairies, "It said something about a valley of green trees," said Richard.

Cressida, turned away from Richard, beat her wings and soared gracefully through the air, back to her crystal throne. Richard watched on, he didn't understand what was happening, he asked Cressida if she could help him, she did not answer. Then, without warning, both Richard's arms were grasped in a vice like grip, and he was lifted from the floor, he struggled to break free, but the grip tightened.

"Remove him," ordered Cressida.

Richard called out, "Why won't you help me, what are you doing?"

Two large centaurs one either side of Richard carried him out of the crystal palace, he continued to struggle, as all the fairies looked on. Once outside, the centaurs released Richard's arms, he fell to the ground.

"Why won't you help me?" Richard called again.

"You are not welcome here," said the centaurs.

The large doors to the crystal palace closed behind them, six more centaurs appeared, each carrying a bow and arrow pointed at Richard, he had to concede defeat. Richard dragged himself up off the floor, he had hurt his right leg when he was dropped. He stumbled down the pathway beneath the glorious arch, created by the rainbow-coloured trees, followed all the way by the six centaurs. When he finally reached the end of the path, there was Eleanor, in her blue robe, with her red hair, she was gazing up at the coloured arch, her staff was standing alone. She felt his presence before she looked away from the arch.

"You were unsuccessful?" she asked.

"Yes," said Richard.

"And she didn't give an explanation," said Eleanor

"How did you know that?" asked Richard.

"I know many things," said Eleanor.

Finally she lowered her gaze to look at Richard. She watched as he stumbled down the path towards her, she placed her hand on her staff. As she wrapped her fingers around the stem, the roots were withdrawn from the ground. She touched the staff to Richard's leg, it glowed and instantly his leg felt better.

"Ah, that feels so much better," he said.

"I know," replied Eleanor. Without another word being said, she turned away and Richard followed.

It was not a long walk to Eleanor's home, as they passed through a forest of coloured trees, but it was not what Richard had expected. It was a moated castle, with many turrets, made from large grey stonework, with many narrow windows. As Eleanor approached, the staff glowed and the drawbridge lowered. As they passed over the drawbridge, Richard looked down into the water, it was murky and dark, it seemed lifeless. Until a bird landed on the surface of the water, instantly a large mouth appeared, grabbed the bird, and pulled it beneath the surface of the water.

"What was that?" asked Richard.

"Protection for my home," said Eleanor.

They passed on through the gateway, as they left the drawbridge, it rose back into place. Percival was the first to greet Richard.

"Your Majesty," he said, "How did you get on with Cressida?"

"I didn't." replied Richard, "She will not help us," he said. "We will have to find another way."

"That will not be easy," said Eleanor, "If Cressida will not help you it is doubtful anyone will."

"What about you?" asked Richard, "You have helped us so far."

"I only helped you to find Cressida, but if she chooses not to help you, there is little I can do to help." said Eleanor.

Percival asked Eleanor, "What happened to Oliver after you took him to see Cressida?"

Richard hadn't thought to ask Cressida that, all eyes were now on Eleanor, for the first time she looked uncomfortable, but it lasted a mere second.

"I believe he was sent on a quest for Cressida, for something she wants, and in return she would send him home," said Eleanor.

"Have you any idea where she sent him?" asked Percival.

"Alas! I have not," said Eleanor.

Percival was watching her very closely, she could not read his thoughts, and this worried her.

"Tell us about the harpies," asked Percival.

How could he possibly know of the harpies, thought Eleanor. She struggled to remain composed.

"What do you want to know about them?" she asked.

"How long have they been under your control?" he asked.

Eleanor's composure began to unravel.

"I don't know what you mean," she said.

"Oh I think you do," said Percival, "Where did the harpies take Oliver and his friends?"

Eleanor was really getting flustered.

Percival pressed on with the questions, "Where is the black mountain, why does Cressida want the crystal egg, so badly?" Eleanor had never before met anyone like Percival, she could not hear his thoughts, but he knew all of hers. She felt faint, and before she hit the ground she had passed out. Four of Richard's guards raced forward and picked Eleanor off the ground, they carried Eleanor into the castle and gently placed her on one of the large sofas that sat opposite a great fireplace in the vast sitting room. Richard and Percival had each taken a seat opposite where Eleanor lay. She was restless in her unconsciousness, what started out as a minor twitch of the hand, had developed into more extravagant movement. One minute she was shielding her face, the next she was on the attack, thrusting at some invisible foe. And then the screaming started, it started out as aggressive, but before long had turned into a whimper of fear, she was sweating with a fever, and then suddenly, it all stopped. She lay perfectly still, the screaming had stopped and her breathing was back to normal. Percival leant over her body to check she was all right, Eleanor's eyes slowly opened, she recognised Percival, and smiled.

"You wanted to know about the harpies?" she said calmly.

"Yes," said Percival.

"There is a lot to explain," said Eleanor.

"Take your time," said Percival, as Richard leant in close, so he could hear what was being said.

"I have an understanding with the harpies," said Eleanor, "If they do my bidding when asked, I allow them to hunt on my land, without reprisal."

"And what of the black mountain?" asked Percival.

"There are two brothers who reside in the black mountain, for all purposes they are ogres. They were sent there by the old king and queen of the fairies, sent with a crystal egg, it was to be placed in the mountain where no one would ever be able to reach it, unless they were human. They were human once, the two brothers I mean." said Eleanor, "Only once they had reached the black mountain the king and queen transformed them into ogres, and to make matters worse, they trapped them in the mountain with a curse that does not allow them to step into the light, neither sun or moon. They were imprisoned by those they admired above all others, in order to keep the crystal egg from being retrieved, they were made guardians, transforming them into ogres meant they could no longer reach the egg and so, it was safe."

"Why would they feel the need to hide the crystal egg in the first place?" asked Richard.

"Because of their children, they had twins, Cressida is one, and you already know the other." said Eleanor.

"Dante," said Percival.

"Exactly," said Eleanor, "They were always fighting over who should take over from their parents, and so when it was time for the king and queen to depart this world, they decided the power of the crystal egg was too great. They couldn't destroy it, no one can, but to put it out of reach, and there it remains, locked away in the black mountain, guarded by two ogres."

Chapter 21
Cressida Seeks Her Twin

Learning that her brother, Dante, was back in the kingdom, did not sit well with Cressida, for many years she had held a grudge against him. She was first born, she should have inherited the power of the crystal egg. She had summoned the centaurs, and they had answered her call, she sat upon her throne looking down upon the centaurs, "I have heard that my brother Dante is back, and that he is heading home, to the valley of green trees. I wish you to find him and bring him to me," said Cressida. Whispering spread amongst the centaurs, "Silence," screamed Cressida, then calmly, she said, "Maybe I should make myself clear, I was not asking you to do this for me, I was ordering you to do this for me." The older centaurs bowed, but some of the younger centaurs resented the way Cressida had power over them to do her bidding whenever she wished, they remained standing, heads held high with pride. She stared down at them as they looked up at her with defiance in their eyes, she smiled at them, and with a simple gesture, a wave of the hand, and all those looking up at Cressida were bowled over. She laughed at them as she leapt from her thrown and glided out of the room, leaving the older centaurs to help those knocked off their feet to stand once more.

"We should not be doing her bidding," said the younger centaurs.

"We have no choice," said the older centaurs, "You have seen what she can do."

Two hundred centaurs marched from Cressida's crystal palace that morning. This did not go unnoticed. Samuel, the tree goblin, sat amongst the branches that formed the archway over the path that led from Cressida's crystal palace. He didn't know what it meant, but to have so many centaurs together at one time leaving the palace, and all fully armed with bows and arrows, he knew something was wrong. He followed them down the path, racing along the branches, keeping out of sight. He suddenly froze, an arrow had just narrowly missed hitting him, one of the young centaurs was gazing up into the trees.

"What is it?" asked another.

"I thought I saw something moving amongst the branches, probably just a bird," he said. They turned and continued to follow. Samuel blinked and let out a sigh of relief, he would have to be more careful around centaurs, he told himself.

When the centaurs reached the end of the pathway, they turned left. Samuel turned right, and headed straight for Eleanor's castle. Standing at the edge of the moat, the tiny tree goblin wondered how to let Eleanor know of his presence, there were no trees for him to use, and he knew the moat to be deadly. Even as he watched, a large bird landed on the surface of the water, within seconds a large mouth had risen from the depths, and before the bird could attempt to fly away, amid wild splashing of water, it was consumed. The predator that lived within the murky waters of the moat, had struck again. This did not bode well for Samuel. With no trees to hide upon, he was exposed and vulnerable. He decided to wait in the trees that stood a short distance from the moat. As he scurried across the ground, a large black shadow appeared overhead, instinct told him not to move, if he stayed perfectly still he may not be noticed, but from high above his brightly coloured body shone like a beacon on the green grass. Suddenly, clutched in a firm but gentle grip he was airborne. Flying towards Eleanor's castle, they circled once above the castle. Samuel could see Eleanor standing in the open, then they swooped down to the ground, once landed the harpy released her grip.

"Thank you," said Eleanor.

Without a word the harpy flapped her wings and disappeared over the castle turrets.

"Hello Samuel, you are a long way from home," said Eleanor.

Only now did Samuel feel truly exposed, he looked around and saw all the guards, Richard and Percival and the five brothers, never had he seen so many humans in one place. Richard stepped forward and stood beside Eleanor. Samuel cowered before the human king.

"There is no need to be afraid," said Richard, "We mean you no harm, we are only here to find my two sons," he said. Samuel looked nervously at Richard, and then Eleanor.

"We believe we know of Oliver's whereabouts," said Eleanor.

"Have you seen his younger brother, what can you tell us of Nicholas?" asked Richard.

"As a matter of fact, I have seen Nicholas," said Samuel.

"Where did you see him?" asked Richard.

Samuel felt uncomfortable talking to Richard, and so he addressed his answers to Eleanor, "I saw the young human with Dante, they were heading to the valley of tall green trees."

"That's it," said Richard, "Can you take us there?" he asked excitedly.

Samuel ignored Richard and continued to address Eleanor, "They were heading to the valley of green trees, when they had a bit of trouble with some ogres, the young human was whisked away by a harpy right from under their noses," said Samuel.

"Where did they go?" asked Richard.

Samuel was gaining in confidence, and getting rather annoyed at all the questions, especially as they were coming from a human, he continued to ignore Richard. "All I can say," said Samuel, "is that they were heading in the direction of the black mountain."

"Thank you," said Eleanor.

"That is not why I came to visit," said Samuel, "I have other news."

"What might that be?" asked Eleanor.

"Cressida has sent an army of two hundred centaurs to go to the valley of tall green trees, in search of Dante," said Samuel.

"That's good to know," said Eleanor, "For while they are searching for Dante, it will give us a head start towards the black mountain."

With so many centaurs on the move and fully armed, the news spread quickly amongst the forest. Langton, king of the fawns, was curious as to why so many centaurs were armed, he made his way to the path they were taking.

"Was there trouble with the ogres?" he asked.

An old friend of his stopped briefly, "We have been ordered by Cressida to search for Dante in the valley of tall green trees."

"You mean to say Dante is back?" said Langton.

"It seems so," said the centaur.

Langton had his own reasons for his dislike of Dante, for he believed it was because of Dante that his twin sons were missing. Now this might be his chance to find out what happened to them. Langton, raced back to his home, gathered as many fawns as he could.

"We may have to fight," he said, "are you ready for that?"

"Yes," came the reply, and so they set off heading for the valley of tall green trees.

While forces were gathering in the hunt for Dante, he was at home in his tree house pondering his next move, he had lost Nicholas, to a harpy, but where had the harpy taken the human, he knew that without Nicholas, when Richard arrived he would not be able to exchange the boy for the gold he so desired.

For three days the centaurs marched through the forest in order to reach the valley of tall green trees, but, they did not know that Langton and his fawns had taken a more direct route, over the mountain, with their superior climbing ability, and extreme agility they had arrived the day before. Dante had watched them descend from the mountain, he knew they came for him, he also knew that by staying high in the trees they would not be able to detect where he was hiding. Langton called Dante's name, but received no answer.

"Come face me you coward," he called.

Dante was well aware of what Langton was trying to do, but he did not move, and silently watched from above, all the noise the fawns were making had attracted an ogre, drawn like a moth to a flame, he rampaged through the green forest, only to find himself in a clearing, surrounded by a large group of fawns. He started to swing his club wildly, but the fawns were too quick, and so he missed. The ogre realising they were too fast, stopped lashing out with his club, and started watching them, as they circled around, looking for a weak link. Langton gave the order to attack, as half a dozen fawns attacked the ogre from the front, he began to swing his giant club once more, this opened the way for an attack from the rear. Two fawns raced forward each wielding a large knife, they made a cut on the back of each leg. The ogre roared in defiance, continuing to fight, once more the giant club crashed onto the ground, just missing a fawn who leapt to one side at just the right moment. Langton ordered another attack, once again with six fawns attacking from the front, he could not repel those attacking from the rear. Again two fawns made deep cuts into the back of his legs, this time the ogre fell to the ground, unable to stand. The end was swift, by the time the centaurs arrived, Langton and his fawns had already killed off the ogre.

"Why are you here?" asked Aegeus.

"We are here for Dante," said Langton.

"You must know that Cressida has ordered us to catch Dante, and take him to her," said Aegeus.

"I am aware of that," said Langton, "but Cressida does not order fawns about."

Many of the centaurs were riled by Langton's remark, "You will be, once Cressida has her hands on the crystal egg."

"She has to retrieve it first," said Langton.

"We are leaving," he said to Aegeus, "Good luck finding Dante."

Some of the younger centaurs wanted to challenge Langton for the remarks he had made, but Aegeus blocked their way as they tried to pass, "He is no concern of yours, we are here to find Dante, and take him back to Cressida, nothing else."

Langton knew that with so many centaurs in the area all Dante had to do was stay hidden high amongst the trees. Once far enough away from the centaurs, Langton gathered the fawns together.

"We will move onto the mountain and observe," he said, "Stay out of sight, it is not the centaurs we are watching, look into the trees, for it is the green fairy we hunt." They all ascended upon the mountain, and disappeared, into crevices and behind boulders, to watch and wait.

The centaurs under the leadership of Aegeus had spread out into the forest of tall green trees.

"Be careful of ogres," he said, as green squirrels raced from the forest floor into the trees, and small birds feeding on bugs on the ground took flight, all, to get out from under the heavy-footed centaurs.

Aegeus, called to Dante, "We know you are here, Cressida has asked us to escort you to the crystal palace." Dante watched from above, without answering. "It has been a long time," said

Aegeus, "She misses her twin brother, she bears no ill will." Dante pondered what to do, and finally agreed, "All right, I will come with you," he said, and from the tallest green tree he leapt into the air, and gently floated to the ground. Aegeus had not expected it to be this easy, and Langton sitting on the mountain side hidden, was also taken by surprise, he had not expected this either, but with two hundred centaurs to protect him for now, Dante was out of reach.

Chapter 22
Leaving the Black Mountain

Eight days had passed since Arec's spirit had left this world, Reif had been left alone in this time, now on the ninth day Reif sought out everyone in the black mountain, he had called them together. "I am leaving the black mountain," he said.

"Are you sure?" asked Oliver, "The crystal egg is no longer locked away, I fear I cannot protect it by myself," said Oliver. "But, can you leave?" asked Oliver.

"There is one way to find out," said Reif.

Reif made his way to the entrance, the three suns were rising above the mountain, he took a deep breath, as he stepped into the sunlight, behind him they all waited anxiously, they all held their breath. It was good to feel the sun again, warm on his back, he breathed a sigh of relief, as they all raced from within the mountain to congratulate Reif.

"Free at last," he said.

Then a familiar voice was heard. Oliver, Nicholas, they turned away from Reif in disbelief, for it was their father Richard, he raced towards them with open arms, as they raced towards him. He dropped to his knees, as the two boys jumped into his arms, they embraced in sheer joy. Eleanor smiled at the touching scene, but walked on by, she was surprised to see Reif, human, once more.

"And where is Arec?" she asked, but she knew the answer before Reif spoke.

"Arec is no longer of our world," said Reif.

It was like a dagger to Eleanor's heart, for she had found Arec and Reif as small children, and taken them into her home and raised them. Now it was Eleanor and Reif who embraced, but in grief.

"How did this happen?" asked Eleanor, "Who retrieved the crystal egg?"

"Arec had taken Oliver to where the egg was hidden, but Oliver was unsuccessful, it was Nicholas who managed to retrieve the crystal egg," said Reif.

"And who has it now?" asked Eleanor.

"I believe Oliver has it," said Reif.

Eleanor called Oliver over, "Do you have the crystal egg," she asked.

"Yes, I have," said Oliver.

"May I please have it?" asked Eleanor, as she held out her hand. Oliver was glad to pass it over, he reached into his pocket, closed his fingers around the crystal egg and placed it into the palm of Eleanor's outstretched hand, it instantly changed from a clear crystal egg, into a rainbow coloured egg.

"Why has it done that?" asked Oliver.

"Because it senses magic," said Percival.

Oliver and Nicholas had let go of their father and made their way to Percival, who embraced them both.

"Where is Berwyn?" asked Oliver.

"We had to leave him behind," said Percival, "The mountain we had to climb to get here was too steep."

Stephen was speaking with Richard, and introduced Henry, and the two fawns, Darius and Ferdinand, while the two fairies stayed back. It was only when Eleanor called the fawns forward did they move. She asked the name of the two fawns.

"Darius and Ferdinand," they said.

Surprised, Eleanor said, "You are the sons of Langton."

"Yes," they nodded.

"I am pleased to meet you your highness," said Eleanor, as she bowed her head, "And who do we have here?" she held out a hand, the two fairies looked much older in the sunlight than they had inside the mountain.

"They have never spoken to us," said Darius, "We don't know what happened to them, they just appeared one day at the entrance, and lord Arec took them in, kept them safe, gave them a place to stay, and in return they tended his sores."

Eleanor addressed the two fairies, "If you wish you can have a place at my castle, you will be safe and well looked after." They bowed their heads in acceptance of Eleanor's offer. "I think it's time we left," said Eleanor.

As they started to move away from the mountain, a dark shadow appeared on the ground from above, circling in the sky overhead, a single harpy. Eleanor advised them all to stand still, as she stepped away from the others the harpy landed in front of Eleanor, taller than Eleanor, she looked down on the gnome. Facially, she was female in appearance, she had long brown hair, a pale skinned face, with oval eyes, the colour of gold, and pale pink lips, but from the neck down she was covered in feathers, with huge wings that folded close to her body when on the ground. They could hear Eleanor talking to the harpy, and the harpy responded, but they were too far away to make out what was being said, as quickly as she appeared, the harpy took flight. Eleanor turned to the rest of them and said, "The centaurs have Dante, and are taking him to Cressida at the crystal palace, we must move fast." said Eleanor, "We need to get back to my castle before Cressida finds out the crystal egg has been retrieved from the mountain. Undoubtedly, she will send the centaurs, and if we are found with the crystal egg in our possession we will be out numbered, and not able to escape."

With Eleanor leading the way they started on their journey to her castle, while in the skies overhead storm clouds were gathering. Cressida was in a rage, the centaurs had arrived back at the crystal palace.

Dante greeted his sister, "How are you dear sister, it has been a while,"

Cressida was in no mood for playing games, she had reason to believe the crystal egg had been retrieved from the mountain. She sat upon her throne looking down at Dante.

"What do you know of the crystal egg?" she asked.

"It is held within the black mountain," said Dante.

The room was full of fairies, all watching eagerly, waiting to see what Cressida would do with her twin brother.

"Are you sure of that?" said Cressida.

"As sure of your ever growing beauty," answered Dante.

"Did you or did you not bring a young human into our kingdom?" asked Cressida, a gasp was echoed around the room.

"I did," answered Dante.

"And was the purpose of this young human to retrieve the crystal egg for you?" asked Cressida.

"No, no dear sister, I took him in exchange for a king's ransom," answered Dante.

"If that is the case, where is he?" asked Cressida, her voice tingling with menace.

"He had the misfortune to run into an ogre, but was whisked away from under the ogre's nose by a harpy," said Dante.

"And you expect me to believe this?" screamed Cressida. Dante stood unfazed by his sister's aggressive demeanour.

"Why dear sister, you do not trust me?" he said.

Dante knew very well what he was doing, he stood there smiling up at Cressida, as she struggled to control her temper. She called for the guards, four centaurs entered the room.

"Take him and lock him away," she ordered.

Without a struggle, Dante bowed and allowed himself to be escorted from the room, he knew that Cressida could not physically hurt him without hurting herself. Being twin fairies meant pain and suffering was shared.

Eleanor was leading her companions through the rainbow forest. She knew the signs, brightly coloured clouds were merging, becoming darker, blocking out the three suns, and becoming more menacing, turning day into night.

"We must find shelter, immediately," she said. As she looked around she spotted standing together a couple of ancient trees, with their lowest branches as thick as the trunk, they curved down to rest on the ground, this was the best shelter available. "Quickly," said Eleanor, "under here." They gathered under the two giant trees, as the first flash of coloured lightning spread across the black sky, followed by a loud clap of thunder. Then the rain began to fall heavily, only, without three suns to give the rain its colour, the rain was black, making it feel incredibly eerie as they huddled together under the trees, where it was pitch black, and only when lightning flashed across the sky was anything visible, and in the blink of an eye the image was gone. Eleanor had experienced this before, but for the humans, this was their first experience of black rain. Richard and the guards seemed quite unfazed, as did Percival, but for the younger humans, Oliver, Nicholas and Henry, this was quite terrifying. Then, a flash of lightning, and a scream, as the lightning had flashed across the sky, Henry had seen a face, and then it disappeared into the pitch black once more. They were not alone under the trees, under the darkened skies and heavy black rain, shadows appeared with each flash of lightning, and like a ghost vanished into the dark, the shadows seemed to be getting closer with each new flash, heading towards the two giant trees. Eleanor and her companions looked on, not knowing what was heading their way, they watched anxiously. Henry feeling scared had hold of Oliver's arm in a vice like grip, a flash of lightning that lit up the whole sky for a second revealed a group of fawns soaking wet, as they dashed under the branches to escape the worst of the weather. At first the fawns were unaware anyone else was there, as they shook themselves to remove as much rain water as possible.

"Hello, Langton," Caught totally by surprise, he turned to face Eleanor. She held her cane aloft which glowed softly, revealing the soaked fawns as the black rain ran down their faces, leaving dark streaks of water.

"Why Eleanor, what are you doing here, caught out in this storm?" asked Langton.

"I have a surprise for you," she said.

She then stepped to one side, Darius and Ferdinand stepped from the back of the group. Langton almost collapsed in disbelief, Darius and Ferdinand raced forward to be re-joined with their father, as the tears flowed between them, Langton asked, "How is this possible?"

Eleanor explained what the two young fawns had told her, how they had been playing and got lost, then they had been chased by an ogre. He had been easy to escape from, but then they didn't know where they were, and finally they were caught by two harpies, and carried off towards the black mountain. They thought they were going to die, but the harpies landed at the foot of the black mountain, and released them. Still scared the harpies were going to kill them they raced inside the black mountain, only to find themselves face to face with Lord Arec, an ogre.

"It turned out Arec the ogre was your old human friend Arec, who had been transformed, and his brother Reif is here with us now, transformed once more into human form," said Eleanor.

"What happened to Arec?" asked Langton.

Reif stepped forward, ten years younger than Arec, he knew who Langton was, but they had never been friends. "He died," said Reif, "When we were transformed back into human form."

"I am sorry to hear that," said Langton, he stepped forward and put his arms around Reif as he pulled him closer, "Your brother was a good friend, I miss him dearly."

They waited for what seemed like hours for the storm to end, but eventually the rain stopped and the skies cleared, as the three suns reappeared daylight was resumed. With all the rain that had fallen during the storm the ground was soaked and black puddles had formed, as they stepped out from under the ancient trees, Eleanor stopped and put her hand on Langton's arm, he stopped also.

"I have something to tell you, Reif and Arec were transformed back into human form because the crystal egg was retrieved from the black mountain." said Eleanor.

"Who managed to retrieve it?" asked Langton.

"It was the young human, Prince Nicholas," said Eleanor.

"And where is it now?" asked Langton

"I have it," said Eleanor.

"Does Cressida know it has been retrieved?" asked Langton.

"We cannot know for sure," said Eleanor, "but I need to get back home."

"She sent two hundred centaurs and they found Dante," said Langton.

"I have been warned of this," said Eleanor, "Which is why I must get back to the safety of my home."

Cressida had sensed something had changed within the kingdom, she wasn't sure, but was afraid it had something to do with the crystal egg. She had sent centaurs to investigate, Dante was still locked away, Cressida decided to pay her brother a visit. As the door was unlocked and opened, Dante stood. As Cressida entered Dante bowed.

"Good morning, dear sister," he said.

Cressida did not answer, she slowly paced the room thinking of what to say. Dante's gaze followed his sister around the room, she looked resplendent in her rainbow coloured gown that shimmied with every movement she made, and sparkled in the light. She stopped suddenly with her back towards Dante, and without turning to face him she asked, "Why do you need a king's ransom?"

Dante told his sister of what had happened in the past, with Oliver and the green-striped zebra, "But I don't understand why you need this gold, when you can have whatever you desire right here," she said.

"Dear sister, if only that was true," said Dante. She knew what he meant and chose to ignore the comment.

"If we joined forces we could rule this kingdom without anyone to stop us," said Cressida.

"True dear sister true, but if I remember rightly the last time we tried this I had to flee for my life," said Dante.

"Why dearest brother, that was just a misunderstanding, you know I can never harm you," said Cressida.

Cressida had sent a dozen centaurs to visit the black mountain, Aegeus led the way. They were to try and gain access to the mountain, normally they would be repelled by the ogres that lived there, but if she was right and the crystal egg had been retrieved, the mountain would be empty. Eleanor had expected Cressida to do something and had asked the harpies to keep watch over the black mountain and let her know if anyone arrived and searched inside. It would take the centaurs five days to reach the black mountain, the harpies could be there within hours, and so they waited.

Eleanor had made all the introductions between human king Richard and fawn king Langton. Langton had agreed to join with Eleanor and Richard and escort them safely back to Eleanor's castle. Darius and Ferdinand were happy to be back amongst the fawns. Friends they hadn't seen in years and thought they would never see again, were amongst the group that had accompanied their father in the search for Dante. After being introduced by Darius and Ferdinand, Oliver, Nicholas and Henry tried to keep up with the fawns as they played, but they were no match for the speed and agility of the fawns, and the humans got exhausted very quickly. This made the young fawns laugh at how quickly the humans tired, after sitting for a short while Oliver got to his feet.

"I bet I could catch you," he said to Darius.

"Come on then," Darius called, "Catch me if you can,"

Oliver watched closely as Darius raced around the bushes, jumping high into the air to clear the large boulders that were dotted around, once, twice, three times he raced around, taunting Oliver with his agility and speed. Oliver had a piece of string, he set a trap. As Darius was showing off to the other fawns, Oliver raced at Darius who leapt out of the way easily avoiding Oliver's outstretched arms, and as Oliver had intended, Darius set off on his race around the bushes, he leapt into the air to clear the same boulder he had already cleared three times. As he landed, he tripped over the piece of string Oliver had set up, he fell to the floor face first, all the fawns started to laugh, along with the young humans. Oliver walked over to Darius, offered him his hand and pulled the young fawn to his feet, Darius was also laughing, "That was fun." he said.

Langton called over to his sons, "We don't have time for games."

"Sorry, Father," they replied.

Richard called to Oliver, "Come here."

"Yes, Father," he said.

They walked over to their parents, still full of energy and wanting to continue playing, but they knew they had to do as they were told. Richard explained, "We need to help Eleanor get back to her home without drawing attention to ourselves."

"Yes, Father," said Oliver.

Percival was watching Eleanor, something about her made him feel uncomfortable, the moat around her castle, the creature that lived there and devoured anything that touched the surface of the water, the fact that she could talk to the harpies, something didn't feel right, he just couldn't be sure. They had been travelling for almost three days, and Eleanor's castle was in sight, as they approached the moat she held her cane aloft, the drawbridge lowered, and they crossed over the murky black waters below, once inside the castle the drawbridge was raised.

"I can't believe we made it back without any trouble," said Eleanor.

For Reif it was like being back home, the castle held fond memories of his brother Arec, from when they were younger. Langton, having helped escort Eleanor home, made his apologies for leaving straight away.

"I have someone who is desperately, in need of seeing these two," he said.

And so with Darius and Ferdinand by his side, Langton left Eleanor's castle and headed home, with the rest of the fawns following on behind.

After Langton had left, Eleanor went into her home, King Richard and his guards followed, along with the five brothers. Percival watched as she led them indoors, Oliver, Nicholas and Henry were outside with Reif and Stephen. Reif was telling them all the things that he and his brother Arec used to get up to in the castle. Down in the depths of the castle was a dungeon and torture room, Henry asked if it had ever been used.

"Of course," said Reif, "but not since Eleanor has lived here."

"Can we see it?" asked Oliver.

"I don't see why not," said Reif, "Arec and I used to play down there."

In the far corner of the courtyard stood a heavy wooden door, they excitedly crossed the courtyard. Reif tried to open the heavy wooden door, it was locked.

"I've never known that door to be locked before," said Reif.

"Maybe there's a reason it's locked," said Percival.

"I know of a passageway that leads to the dungeon from the castle chapel, this way," said Reif.

They all followed, the youngsters were excited by the thought of a dungeon and torture room, Percival went along because something about this place felt wrong, he sensed fear and danger. Reif's memory served him well, he found the trap door easily, even though it had been covered over with a large rug, he pulled it to one side. Reif grasped the large round handle and pulled, this way was not locked, and the trap door lifted easily, fully opening the door so it stayed open. Reif took a lit candle from the chapel wall, and started down the stone steps. They went down quite a way before they reached the bottom, the ground levelled off, it was dark, and the passageway narrow, they had to follow in single file, with only one candle between them. Percival at the rear could see nothing but the faint glow from the candle, and the shadows it cast on the ceiling and walls. A scream, and they were suddenly plunged into complete blackness.

Percival called out to the young princes, "Are you all right?" They both answered, "Yes."

It seemed everyone was all right.

"So who screamed?" asked Percival.

No one knew. A chill in the air passed over them as they stood in the dark, Percival wanted them to go back, but Reif wanted to keep going, as did everyone else. Percival had no choice being at the back, slowly Reif placed one foot in front of the other, with both hands on the wall. Nicholas was excited and tried to move too fast, he bumped into the back of Reif, his strong muscular body was like walking into a brick wall.

"Ouch!" said Nicholas.

Reif laughed, "Slow down," said Reif.

"Is everything all right?" asked Percival.

"Yes, we're fine," shouted Reif.

Then another scream, a chill ran through their bodies. It was louder than before, they must be getting closer to where it came from. Percival was worried by what they might find. According to Reif, since Eleanor had lived in the castle she had never used the dungeon or torture room. Percival felt his suspicions about Eleanor were right, there was something about her that made him uneasy. His thoughts were interrupted by yet another scream, but this time it sounded different, childlike.

"What's happened?" shouted Percival.

A blinding bright light appeared in front of Reif, he raised his right arm to shield his eyes, it was Eleanor.

"What are you doing down here?" she asked.

"I just wanted to show them the dungeon and torture room," said Reif.

"This is no place for young children," said Eleanor, "Follow me."

With her staff shining brightly, she led them up a flight of stairs and when they stepped out of the passageway they were back in the courtyard.

As each child stepped into the open she smiled and said, "Please don't go down there again, it isn't safe,"

She was shocked to see Percival appear last from the dark passage, "I didn't know you were accompanying them," said Eleanor. Percival smiled at Eleanor.

"Quite interesting," he said as he walked on by, "I must speak with King Richard," said Percival.

Percival found Richard and the guards in one of the sitting rooms, as he entered Richard called, "Where have you been?" Percival moved between the chairs as the guards sat watching, when he reached King Richard.

"Your Majesty," said Percival.

Richard indicated for Percival to take the seat next to his so they could talk. Percival spoke softly so that only Richard could hear what was being said. Percival told Richard of his concern regarding Eleanor, Richard looked surprised at Percival.

"After everything she has done to help us," he said.

Percival pointed out to Richard, the moat with the sinister creature that consumed everything that touched the surface, the fact that Eleanor could speak to the harpies, and just now as they were making their way to the dungeon and torture room, they heard screaming.

Richard interrupted, "You were going down to the dungeon and torture room?"

"It was Reif who wanted to show them to the young princes. I tried to stop them but they wouldn't listen, so I went along to try and keep them safe. Eleanor found us and brought us back to the courtyard," said Percival.

Richard was more concerned with his two young sons being shown a dungeon and torture room, than he was with some mysterious screaming.

"Where are they now?" he asked Percival.

"They were still in the courtyard, when I came to find you, Your Majesty."

Richard was not happy, he found his two young sons still in the courtyard talking to Reif, he walked straight up to Oliver and Nicholas, grabbed each by the hand, and told Reif,

"I do not want you anywhere near my sons again, is that understood?" said King Richard.

"Yes, Your Majesty, I am sorry if I have offended you," said Reif.

Richard did not say another word, but marched back into the castle leaving Reif standing alone. Eleanor watched on, hidden in the shadows.

Chapter 23
Cressida's Fears Realised

Cressida watched from her palace as the centaurs returned from the black mountain. She knew before she spoke with Aegeus the answer to her question.

"What did you find at the black mountain?" asked Cressida. "Nothing your majesty, we searched the whole mountain, there were a few wild animals in cages, that had been abandoned, but they were the only sign of life we came across," said Aegeus.

"Then it is true," said Cressida, "The crystal egg has been retrieved from the black mountain, but where is it, and more importantly, who has it?"

Percival and Richard were alone in the flower room at Eleanor's castle. Totally made from glass, with a tall ceiling, it was extremely hot inside, and it housed a variety of strange plants, unlike any plants found anywhere else. Like a plant with small multi-coloured leaves and a large purple flower on a single stem that was heavily perfumed, or a small smooth round plant, but when touched exhibited from beneath its outer skin two inch spikes. Percival had discovered that the hard way, as he had placed his hand upon the ball shaped plant. Then, there was a plant that could move on its own to maintain its position in the sunlight. Percival had wanted to speak with Richard in private, and once more he told Richard of his concerns about Eleanor. Richard listened without interruption for he held Percival's opinion with the highest regard. The heavily scented air from all the flowers, and the heat generated from the sun shining through the glass made them feel quite drowsy. Richard was the first to feel the effect, as he stumbled forward and fell against Percival. Under the weight of King Richard, Percival too found himself unable to stand. He struggled to lower King Richard to the floor, and as he lay there, Percival began to feel light headed. He slumped forward and lay on top of Richard. Eleanor appeared from behind the largest plant in the flower room, with leaves so big she was easily concealed, Eleanor had heard everything.

Four of Eleanor's servants also appeared from behind the giant plants, with bald heads, no mouth to speak and no ears to listen they looked very odd, with large round eyes but no visible nose apart from four small holes, two beneath each eye, only added to their strange appearance. They were dressed in long grey robes that gave no indication as to whether they were male or female. Two took hold of Percival and easily lifted his body from where it lay on top of King Richard, the other two servants lifted the unconscious body of King Richard from the floor. As the servants made their way through the flower room carrying Percival and Richard, some of the plants became animated, with long feelers extended towards Richard and Percival. Eleanor lightly touched the feelers with her staff, the plants quickly withdrew their feelers as if they had been stung. Without her knowledge it was now Eleanor's turn to be spied upon, for Oliver had been about to enter the flower room when he saw Eleanor's servants pick Percival and Richard up off the floor, he watched from outside as they headed towards the rear of the flower room, and quietly entered, watching them silently. A concealed door at the back of the room opened as Eleanor approached. As she stepped through the doorway, torches mounted on the walls burst into flames. A set of steps made of stone led down beneath the castle. As they passed by the flames, each one in turn expired, only darkness followed as they ventured deeper into the depths beneath the castle, heading towards the dungeon. The door had closed before Oliver could reach it, unable to open the door he went in search of the guards and Nicholas. Eleanor arrived at the torture room, torches on all the walls burst into red flames, it gave a warm but terrifyingly eerie glow. Three long benches lay side by side through the centre of the room, with chains and leather straps attached to each bench, for holding a prisoner in place while being questioned, and ultimately tortured.

Eleanor passed between these benches, followed by the servants, carrying the still unconscious, King Richard and Percival. There were seven cells that made up the dungeon, two were already occupied. The servants placed King Richard in one, and Percival in the one furthest from King Richard. This meant that if they wanted to talk, they would not be able to whisper, but would be forced into speaking loudly.

Eleanor walked away from the cells once she had checked they were properly locked, as she did so, the torch flames expired, and they were plunged into darkness once more, tinged with a feeling of guilt, for she liked King Richard, but Percival was a problem, with his suspicions, he could ruin everything.

Eleanor was back in her flower room when she came across Nicholas.

"Good morning, Nicholas," she said.

"Good morning, Eleanor," he replied.

She bowed her head, keeping her eyes firmly fixed on his, "You really shouldn't be in here you know, not on your own, some of these plants can be quite dangerous." She blew breath onto the small ball shaped plant, it immediately thrust out two inch spikes.

"Wow!" said Nicholas.

As a further demonstration, she then stroked a long thin leaf with her hand, the leaf coiled around her wrist and tried to pull her towards the plants head. Other leaves twitched excitedly, trying to get a hold on her arms and legs, she used her staff, once more, gently touching the leaves made them recoil as if being stung.

"Have you seen my father?" asked Nicholas.

"Your father and Percival left early this morning to visit Cressida at the crystal palace, now that he has found both you and Oliver. he is eager to leave and return home," she said.

Nicholas excitedly left Eleanor in the flower room, and raced off to find Oliver, he eventually found Oliver talking with the guards.

"I asked Eleanor had she seen father, and she said he had gone to see Cressida at the crystal palace about helping us go home," blurted out Nicholas.

Oliver knew this was not true, but didn't want to upset Nicholas.

"That's great," said Oliver.

He had already told the guards what he had seen, but they all followed Oliver's lead.

"That's great news," they said.

Nicholas was in a very good mood, and went off to find Reif, to tell him the good news.

"Why would Eleanor lie?" said Oliver, after Nicholas had left, "It doesn't make sense, there's more going on here than we are aware of."

Eleanor entered the room, her sudden appearance surprised them all. Trying to remain calm, Oliver said, "I understand father and Percival have gone to see Cressida."

"Yes, they left first thing this morning," said Eleanor.

"It seems rather odd they didn't take any guards with them," said Oliver.

"I suggested he visit Cressida without any guards," said Eleanor, "It would seem less threatening, especially as he was going to ask for help in returning home."

Oliver pretended to be happy with Eleanor's explanation, just then Nicholas returned having found Reif, asking Oliver to come outside and play.

As Oliver approached the doorway, Nicholas ran off, calling, "Catch me, if you can."

Eleanor placed a hand on Oliver's shoulder and reassured him everything would be all right. Oliver struggled to keep his emotions in check, for he did not want Eleanor reading his thoughts, for he knew his father had not gone to see Cressida, as he had witnessed the bodies of Richard and Percival being carried away. What Oliver didn't know was why the bodies had been taken, that was something he was determined to find out.

After being told they were not allowed to go down to visit the dungeon, Nicholas, while trying to hide from Oliver decided to go up instead. He had gone into the castle and was heading towards the narrow staircase that led to the highest tower. He couldn't help think it was nothing like their castle back home, with no paintings hanging on the walls: no tapestries, and no suits of armour, just plain bare walls. Then he spotted two of Eleanor's servants cleaning the dining room. Fascinated by their appearance, he forgot about Oliver and decided to go and say hello. As he walked up to them, they backed away, with no mouth they could not speak, but the look in their eyes expressed sheer terror. Nicholas kept on walking towards them, he wanted to show them they had no reason to be scared of him.

"What are you doing here?" asked a commanding voice, it was Eleanor.

"I only wanted to say hello," said Nicholas as he turned to face Eleanor.

The two servants raced past Nicholas as they left the room, Eleanor turned her head to watch them leave, without saying a word. While she was distracted by the servants, she didn't notice Nicholas leave by a different door. He found himself in a part of the castle that somehow felt older, the brickwork was rough to touch, and there was no stone flooring, just bare dirt. With no torches on the wall, he fumbled his way along with his hands on the wall, the passageway turned twice each time to the right, it was completely dark, the only light came from a distant source. Nicholas felt beckoned, he had to go and look. So quietly, he crept down the hallway. The walls were completely bare as was the floor, he was able to move without making a sound. The light at the end of the hallway intensified as he got closer, he held his breath, he could hear voices, his imagination of what might be in the room ahead momentarily paralysed Nicholas with fear. He had two choices, to either turn around and go back or to carry on. His hands were all sweaty, and his heart was racing, still he was determined to find out what was at the end of the dark hallway. Just as he approached the door, Nicholas stumbled and fell to the floor, he hurt his wrist and cried out in pain. Suddenly, the door was opened, and bright light flooded the dark hallway as he lay face down on the ground. Two strong hands reached down and lifted Nicholas off the floor. Kicking and screaming, he was carried into the light, as he struggled to break free from the monstrous grip, he became aware of laughter, his eyes were slowly getting used to the light after having been in the dark hallway. The laughter continued, then a familiar voice,

"What are you doing?" asked Oliver.

His eyesight fully restored, Nicholas looked at his brother and then at Reif, whose strong arms had lifted him off the ground, and now gently placed him onto one of the beds Eleanor had provided for her guests. The guards were all present in the room also, it was they who had been laughing.

"What are you all doing here?" asked Nicholas.

Oliver told Nicholas to sit down and keep quiet.

"I know our father didn't go to see Cressida, because I saw four of Eleanor's servants carry our father and Percival from the flower room," said Oliver.

"Where did they take them?" asked one of the guards.

"I don't know," said Oliver, "The doorway they used closed before I could reach it, and then I could not open it to follow."

The head guard stood up and said, "I thought it was odd when Eleanor told me your father went to meet with this rainbow fairy, Cressida, without telling us first."

"I know," said Oliver, "but we have to be smart, we need to try and find out what Eleanor is up too, without her finding out."

All eyes turned towards Reif.

"She raised you, we know, so where do your loyalties lie?" asked Oliver.

"Eleanor cared for my brother Arec and I," he said, "But my loyalty lies with King Richard."

Eleanor had followed Nicholas down the dark passageway, staying back just out of the light. She had heard everything and was disappointed that Reif chose to be loyal to King Richard, but she also knew that the rest of them were suspicious, she would have to be more careful.

Cressida visited Dante in the dungeon cell where he was being held. As the door opened, Dante got to his feet, and bowed,

"Why hello dear sister and what have I done to deserve such an honour?" said Dante.

"Shut up, Dante," said Cressida.

She turned around to leave.

"Why Cressida whatever is the matter?" asked Dante, with mock compassion in his voice, she stopped at the door and turned to face him once more.

"I am worried about the crystal egg and who has it," she said, "If it falls into the wrong hands and they know of its full power, our way of life could be over."

Dante remembered the stories told by their parents when he and Cressida were younger.

"But surely you have the crystal crown," said Dante, "All the time you have that, the crystal palace cannot be damaged or entered by armed forces."

"But, dear brother, even a crystal palace can become a prison, if one cannot leave," said Cressida.

Dante now understood what Cressida was getting at.

"So, what can we do?" he asked.

"We need to find out who has the crystal egg," said Cressida, "We must find out who visited the black mountain, the centaurs found nothing but an empty cave, and some wild animals in cages," she said.

"We, must visit the black mountain," said Dante.

"But you know I cannot leave," said Cressida, "I have to stay and keep safe the crystal crown."

"Then I will go," said Dante, "I will be quicker by myself, anyway."

"Surely you do not intend to go by yourself," said Cressida.

"Why sister, it sounds like you care," said Dante.

"Oh shut up, Dante," she said, with a smile on her face.

"I will leave immediately," said Dante, "I can be back in three days."

"And while you are gone, I will try to find out as much as I can," she said.

Cressida had sent for Samuel the tree goblin, with his abilities to appear invisible on the multi-coloured trees, he would make a good spy, for he sees many things, Aegeus the centaur had been given the task to find Samuel.

"How am I supposed to find him if he chooses to stay hidden?" said Aegeus.

"Because I have something he cannot resist," said Cressida. She gave Aegeus a crystal bottle containing a green liquid, "Show this to Samuel, let him smell it, let him taste it, and he will tell you anything you ask."

Aegeus set off first thing in the morning, the three suns were in the process of separating, sat in a cloudless sky. He went alone, into the forest.

"Too many centaurs may scare Samuel off." said Cressida, but alone, Cressida knew Samuel's curiosity would prevent him from running. And so, Aegeus entered the rainbow forest. It was early morning, the three suns shone brightly, as the forest was coming to life, birds were awake in the trees, and their dawn chorus filled the air. As Aegeus moved deeper into the forest small animals were scurrying about on the ground only to disappear as he approached. He started to call Samuels' name, and then he listened, no response. He could not help but feel this was hopeless, the rainbow forest spread out as far as the eye could see, how was he supposed to find a tree goblin amongst all these trees? He called again, still nothing, ducking below low hanging branches, and having to turn around and go back, for the thickets were too dense in places to walk through. Aegeus kept searching, scratching a mark on the bark of the trees to show which direction he had travelled, only for the colours on the bark of the trees to run down the trunk and cover over his scratch marks once more, all the while Aegeus was unaware of this happening. Aegeus spent two days looking for Samuel, at times he felt as though he was going round in circles, but that wasn't possible for he had marked the trees as he went. He decided to rest beneath the tree he had just marked, he lay on the ground and closed his eyes, the noises of the forest slowly faded as he drifted off to sleep. When he awoke a short time later, he got to his feet and to his horror the mark on the tree had disappeared. He felt sure he had marked the tree, or had he? He couldn't be sure, for he had been so tired. He decided he could not have marked the tree because there was no mark, and so he marked the tree once more, but this time he scratched a mark on the ground also. The noise from the dawn chorus had ceased, the birds had flown off to feed elsewhere, only a few remained to feed on the bugs on the trees. Ground dwelling animals could be heard running amongst the forest litter that carpeted the ground, suddenly a loud thud, and a squeal. Aegeus stopped, listening intently, he could hear voices, he slowly crept through the forest without making a sound, instinct taking over, for he knew there was danger. As he got closer to the voices, he recognised them as ogres, they had caught a large wild boar. The squeal Aegeus had heard was the animal being crushed by a large club covered with six inch spikes. *I wonder what they are doing here*, thought Aegeus. Just at that moment something hit Aegeus on the back. Startled, he spun around to see what was behind him, only to find Samuel sitting on his back with a big grin.

"Hello, Aegeus," said Samuel, "you were calling for me?"

"Yes," said Aegeus in a whisper, "I have something for you from Cressida."

Samuel tilted his head to one side and looked at Aegeus suspiciously, and then he asked, "What is it that Cressida has sent for me?"

Aegeus had a pouch around his neck, he reached inside to reveal the crystal bottle with the green liquid, Samuel's eyes lit up when he saw the bottle.

"Give it to me," said Samuel.

Aegeus passed the crystal bottle to Samuel who eagerly opened it and drank down the green liquid, as Aegeus watched Samuel's eyes glazed over, remembering what Cressida had told him, Aegeus started to ask questions.

"Do you know who took the crystal egg?" asked Aegeus.

"Yes," said Samuel.

"Do you know who has the crystal egg now?" asked Aegeus.

"Yes," said Samuel.

I need to be more specific, thought Aegeus.

"Who took the crystal egg?" asked Aegeus.

"It was the young prince Nicholas who managed to retrieve the crystal egg from the black mountain," said Samuel.

"Who has the crystal egg now?" asked Aegeus.

"Eleanor now has the crystal egg in her possession," said Samuel.

"And where is Eleanor right now?" asked Aegeus.

"She is at home in her castle," said Samuel.

"Thank you," said Aegeus. He lifted Samuel from his back and placed him on a branch where he instantly blended in, becoming invisible, for Aegeus knew this was the safest place for Samuel. Even more so when he was in this state of unconsciousness.

Aegeus knew he had to get back to the crystal palace as soon as possible, with the information he had learnt from Samuel, but he was aware of the danger of the ogres who he could sense were still nearby. Ogres were loud and noisy, and if you listened properly they could be easily avoided, but what happened next caught Aegeus by complete surprise. He lowered his head to duck below a low branch, and when he stood up he was face to face with a young troll. The troll reached out a giant hand to grasp Aegeus, but the centaur was far too quick. Unlike the ogres who were loud and noisy, who would charge at you swinging their clubs wildly, trolls were the master of ambush. They could wait without moving in one position for days if necessary, just waiting for something to walk by, but this was only a young troll, for it was about half the size of a full grown adult. This worried

Aegeus, for a young troll would never be left on its own. There must be an adult nearby, and he was proved right, for suddenly he found himself in a vice like grip holding onto his back legs, then another appeared at the front, he knew his life was over, for there was no way to escape from two trolls on his own. Aegeus closed his eyes, prepared to die, when suddenly loud screams approached, and his legs were released. He quickly opened his eyes as three ogres stood face to face with the two adult and one juvenile troll. Under normal circumstances the two mortal enemies would avoid each other, but on occasion they would fight, and when they did it was brutally fierce. Adult trolls were bigger than ogres but the fact they had a youngster to look after made them more dangerous but also more vulnerable. The ogres with their giant clubs with six inch spikes attacked, the trolls fought back by throwing large rocks plucked from the forest floor. There was a loud cracking noise as one of the ogres was crushed by a direct hit from one of the rocks, this enraged the other two ogres to a higher level. With clubs swinging wildly the roar they emitted travelled throughout the forest. One of the trolls was hit on the shoulder with a giant club, the six inch spikes embedded into his shoulder. Screaming in pain, he grabbed the club from the grasp of the ogre and kicked him to the floor. Slowly and painfully, he withdrew the spikes from his shoulder, now he was the one wielding the club. The ogre still on the floor backed up against a tree and stood up, as the troll swung the club the ogre ducked out of the way just in time, the club became embedded in the tree, now the two were fighting hand to hand. Normally the troll would have the advantage, but, with his injured shoulder it was impossible to say who would win. Meanwhile, the other troll was doing his best to protect the juvenile from the ogre, the troll had uprooted a small tree, with its branches he used them as a shield to keep the ogre at bay. The ogre was trying to smash the branches with his giant club, the third ogre lay motionless on the ground, seemingly dead. And so, the fight raged on, blow after blow was being struck by both opponents, with bloodied faces and broken noses there seemed to be no end in sight. That was until four more ogres appeared, then totally overwhelmed by sheer numbers it was all over. The screams from the ogres had alerted more to come to their rescue, once they arrived the inevitable ending was swift. As the final blow was landed, Aegeus crept away unnoticed. The six ogres roared in triumph as they stood over the bodies of the three defeated trolls.

With knowledge of Eleanor being in possession of the crystal egg, Aegeus knew he had to get back to Cressida as quickly as he could. He also knew that Cressida would be interested to know that ogres and trolls were in the rainbow forest, for this was not their normal habitat. For two days he raced through the rainbow forest heading back to the crystal palace. Finally he arrived, it was late evening the suns were in the process of merging to form the purple moon, as night time approached. Aegeus arrived at the doors to the crystal palace and they slowly opened, the room was empty, which surprised Aegeus. Then he heard Cressida's voice calling, as he passed from one room to the next he was aware of just how quiet it was, only his footsteps on the glass floor echoed onto the glass walls. He had never been here before when it was empty. He eventually found Cressida, not sitting on her throne as he expected, but standing looking out over the gardens, with her back to him. As he approached, she spun around.

"Good evening, Aegeus," she said, "have you news for me?"

"Good evening, Cressida," said Aegeus, "I do have news, the crystal egg was retrieved by a young prince Nicholas," said Aegeus.

"And it is now in the possession of Eleanor," said Cressida.

"Yes, how did you know?" asked Aegeus.

"Apart from Dante, Eleanor is the only one I know who covets the throne," said Cressida.

"Oh, and I almost forgot, there are ogres and trolls in the rainbow forest," said Aegeus.

"Are you sure of this?" asked Cressida, with a hint of panic in her voice.

"Yes," said Aegeus, "I witnessed a fight myself, six ogres overcame three trolls," said Aegeus.

"It has begun," said Cressida.

"What has begun?" asked Aegeus.

"Eleanor is gathering her forces to launch an attack on the crystal palace. Sound the alarm," said Cressida, "Gather all your warriors, we need a war council."

"Right away," said Aegeus.

"Oh, and Aegeus, I need you to find Langton, tell him it has started, he will understand," said Cressida

Chapter 24
Eleanor on the War Path

Eleanor was hidden away in the tallest tower of her castle. With her, she had the most powerful of all the harpies. "After all these years I finally have the crystal egg," said Eleanor. "It is now my turn to rule." The harpy bowed her head. "You know what to do," said Eleanor. The harpy turned and walked to the window, without saying a word, she leapt from the window and the warm air lifted her into the sky. Eleanor watched as she disappeared into the distance. Eleanor placed the crystal egg on a blue velvet cushion, held her staff aloft, and said, "Deceive." It slowly vanished from sight. Believing it safe, for the door was locked and bolted. Eleanor then left the tower and made her way through a secret passageway down into the depths of the castle, down into the dungeon. As Eleanor entered the dungeon, the torches on the wall's burst into red flame. Richard and Percival watched from their separate cells as Eleanor approached, the glow of red flame gave the impression of warmth. In reality, it was menacing and eerie.

"Why are you doing this?" asked Richard.

"I am sorry you got caught up in this," said Eleanor.

"Caught up in what?" asked Richard.

"A battle for power," said Percival.

"When this is all over, I promise I will set you free, and you will be able to return to your own land," said Eleanor.

Then she turned and walked away. Richard called out to Eleanor, he had more questions he wanted to ask, she ignored him, and approached the tables used for questioning and torture. Laid out on two of the tables were the two fairies, from the black mountain. Their wings had already been removed, and they were held in place by leather straps around the wrists and ankles. They had been advisers to the late king and queen of the fairies. "Are you ready yet to tell me how to use the crystal egg?" asked Eleanor.

"We will never tell you," said the fairies.

"Don't be so sure about that," said Eleanor. "I have ways of getting people to tell me what I want to know." She put her hand into her pocket and removed a small box, she released the catch which held the lid firmly in place and lifted the lid. Inside were two small slugs, luminous green in colour. Eleanor put on a pair of gloves before handling the slugs, then she placed one slug on each of the fairies. Placed on the sole of the foot, they sat there seemingly without doing anything. Then the fairies started screaming as the slugs began to burrow into the soles of their feet, luminous green in colour. They were visible through the skin as they slowly made their way up the leg of both fairies. The screaming intensified and their whole bodies began to shake violently. "I can make this stop," said Eleanor. "Just tell me how to use the crystal egg."

"We will never tell you." The slugs moved higher up the body. Eleanor had never known anyone to endure such pain, she lifted her staff and touched the leg of each fairy. As the staff touched the skin above the slug, it was drawn through the skin and Eleanor with her gloved hand picked them up and placed them back into their box. Eleanor needed the fairies alive to find out how to use the crystal egg, they would be no use to her dead. It seemed they would rather die than tell Eleanor how to use the egg, so, if they didn't value their own lives, who did they care about, above all others. Then a smile appeared upon Eleanor's face. *Why, Cressida, of course,* thought Eleanor. In the shadows, four of Eleanor's servants had been waiting. As Eleanor walked away, the servants approached the tables, unstrapped the fairies and walked them back to their cells and locked them in once more. As they left, the torches ceased to burn and once more the dungeon was plunged into darkness.

Richard asked, "You are the two fairies we found at the black mountain when we found my two sons, are you not?"

"We are indeed the fairies from the black mountain, Your Majesty."

"Why did Eleanor had your wings removed?"

"To prevent us from flying away, of course."

"But you can survive without your wings?" asked Richard.

"We suffer a little pain at first, but they heal quickly, they are of no real consequence, we can survive perfectly happy without them, as does Eleanor."

"Wait a minute, Eleanor used to have wings?"

"No," said the fairies. "Eleanor was born of a human mother and a fairy prince, who went on to become king, but she has never had wings."

It was beginning to make sense to Percival. "Let me see if I understand this correct. Eleanor was the first born child of the fairy king."

"Yes," said the fairies.

"But being born to a human mother, she was rejected by the fairy king, and lived with her mother in isolation, and now being first born, she wants to claim what she sees as being rightfully hers, the fairy kingdom."

"Yes," said the fairies. "But there is more. Unbeknown to the fairy king, the human mother was a witch. That is no ordinary staff that Eleanor carries with her at all times, each time she places it into the ground the roots penetrate and withdraw magic from the soil."

"So what if we can take away Eleanor's staff?"

"Then she will have no more magic than you," said the fairies.

Nicholas was bored, he wanted to find the torture room and dungeon. He knew there had to be secret passageways in the castle, it was just a matter of finding them. Room after room, he searched, all the usual places, the surrounds of a fireplace, a bookshelf, a wall candle holder, nothing, he sat on a brown leather chair trying to think, he was sitting opposite a full size painting of Eleanor. Then it dawned on him, there was not a single painting on any wall in any other room of the castle. He crossed the room, and placed a chair next to the painting. He then climbed onto the chair and ran his hand down the side of the picture frame. First one side and then the other, nothing. He had been sure this would be it. He put the chair back where he got it from, and sat looking at the painting once more. One last try, he approached the painting and ran his hand along the bottom of the frame. Click, there it was, he took hold of the frame and pulled, it opened easily, and there, was Eleanor. Stunned by her sudden appearance, Nicholas slammed the painting shut, and meant to race out of the room. As he looked back, Eleanor didn't need to open the painting, for she just stepped right through. First a foot appeared, then a hand, and as Nicholas watched in amazement, she completely passed through. "Hello, Nicholas," said Eleanor, with her musical voice. "Where were you going?" Nicholas was rooted to the spot with fear, Eleanor approached. Terrified of what was going to happen next, Nicholas shut his eyes. Eleanor bent down and kissed Nicholas on the forehead. This was not what Nicholas had expected.

When Nicholas awoke, he opened his eyes and he was in bed, but, he had no memory of going to bed. Oliver entered and said, "Oh you're awake at last." Nicholas told Oliver he didn't remember going to bed. Oliver explained, "That is because Eleanor found you asleep on the sofa, and she carried you and put you to bed." Nicholas had no memory of any of this.

Meanwhile, Eleanor had sent a message to the harpies, to be spread amongst the ogres and the trolls, "Help me over throw the rainbow fairy and you will have freedom to roam wherever you wish." The ogres agreed readily, for they wanted nothing more than to have freedom to hunt anywhere. The trolls were not so easy to win over, they understood that by helping Eleanor defeat the rainbow fairy, and allowing the ogres to roam and hunt wherever they wanted, that they would be in more danger than they are now. The trolls refused to help Eleanor win her battle against the rainbow fairy.

Three days had passed since Eleanor last spoke with the harpy. For three days, she had anxiously been waiting for the response from the ogres and the trolls. Eleanor had been confident the ogres would help, but she had been concerned the trolls might say no. Eleanor was in the tallest tower waiting, as the harpy appeared on the horizon. Eleanor waited in anticipation, she sat calmly, as she watched the harpy approach. The harpy landed on the balcony and entered the room via the window. "What news have you?" asked Eleanor, impatiently.

The harpy bowed her head, "As you guessed, the ogres have agreed to fight, but the trolls have said no."

"Damn those trolls," screamed Eleanor, revealing the anger that was hidden behind the calm exterior she portrayed. "Without their support, this will prove more difficult than I had hoped." Taking a deep breath to calm herself, Eleanor said, "Very well, this may be more difficult than I had hoped, but not impossible, once I learn how to enhance the power of the crystal egg."

Chapter 25
Oliver Visits Cressida

It was morning and everyone inside Eleanor's castle was getting restless, the five brothers, the guards, Oliver and especially Nicholas. They asked Eleanor if she could lower the drawbridge and allow them to go and explore outside. Wanting to keep up the pretence of friendship, she agreed. They were beginning to get on her nerves. "Don't go too far," she called, as the drawbridge raised shut behind them. They could not believe it was that easy, the plan was they would head towards the forest but remain in sight, only Oliver would enter. This way, hopefully, Eleanor would not miss one person, and therefore, not become suspicious, it was up to Oliver to find his way back to Cressida's palace as fast as he could.

When Eleanor had led them from the crystal palace to her castle, it hadn't seemed very far. Oliver had believed he knew the way, but as he made his way through the rainbow forest, he began to realise he must have gone the wrong way. This was taking far too long, he was tired and exhausted and so sat down to rest, with his back leaning against a large rock. He had not noticed at first but slowly became aware that what he thought was a rock was in fact moving, in a slow rhythm, up and down. He then realised that what he had thought was a gentle breeze was actually breathing, something very big was sleeping, and he was leaning up against it. His first instinct was to get away as fast as he could, but, any sudden movement could awaken what he was leaning against, and so he tried to move as slowly as possible. Firstly to stand, with his arms held out wide for balance, his legs were shaking because of fear. Slowly, slowly, he managed to get to his feet, he now started to creep away. He stepped on a twig which snapped loudly in the silence, he froze on the spot. The breathing continued in its unbroken rhythm. He now dared to look over his shoulder to see the troll from the stone bridge, they had come across before. As he was looking back, he started to walk away once more, not looking where he was going, he tripped and fell, right into the palm of the troll's giant hand. The fingers immediately closed, he was trapped. It had been a reflex reaction, for the troll was still fast asleep. Oliver tried to prize open the trolls fingers, using all his body weight to lean against a single finger proved futile. He was hot and sweating because of his efforts. There was a small gap between finger and thumb, he tried to crawl through, but was too big.

He sat down trapped, with his legs pulled into his chest and his arms wrapped around them. He rested his forehead on his knees. Suddenly, without warning, he felt himself being elevated. He fell to one side and looked out through the opening between the finger and thumb. The troll was awake and standing up. Slowly, the giant fingers unfurled, he was surprised to see Oliver, so small in the palm of his hand. Oliver was looking for a way to escape, it was too high up for him to jump down to the ground. Unless it was like jumping from the hill, when they first met Eleanor. He decided to take the chance, for the troll would surely kill him anyway, and so he raced along the middle finger and leapt from the tip. As he hurtled towards the ground, he suddenly stopped. Not because he had reached the ground, but because he had been caught by the troll once more. "Why on earth did you do that?" he said in a softly spoken voice. "Why try to kill yourself?" asked the troll.

"Well, you are going to kill me anyway," said Oliver.

"Why would I do that?" said the troll.

Oliver looked at him with a puzzled expression on his face. "You're not going to kill me?" he asked.

"I only kill to eat," said the troll, "and quite frankly, you wouldn't even touch the sides on the way down." And then he laughed, Oliver laughed nervously, still uncertain about the troll.

"You're the troll from the bridge are you not?"

"I am indeed," said the troll.

"What are you doing here?" asked Oliver.

"I am on my way to the crystal palace to see Cressida," said the troll.

"Why would you do that?" asked Oliver. "Is that not dangerous for you? Surely, the centaurs will attack."

"I have a warning to give Cressida that she must hear."

"What's happened, what have you heard?" asked Oliver.

"Eleanor has asked the ogres and trolls to help her over throw the rainbow fairy, she already has the harpies on her side and now the ogres have agreed to fight."

"And what of the trolls," asked Oliver.

"We will not join forces with Eleanor." said the troll.

"I was on my way to the crystal palace also," said Oliver, "to let Cressida know that Eleanor has the crystal egg."

"So it is true," said the troll. "She has it."

"Yes," said Oliver. "I was the one who handed it to her."

"Why on earth would you do that?" said the troll angrily.

Oliver, terrified once more, said, "Because she had promised to help us get home."

"Damn fool," said the troll, as he sat down once more. "Never trust a witch."

"You mean to say that Eleanor is a witch?"

"Of course she is, with that magic staff of hers."

"Do you know the way to the crystal palace?" asked Oliver.

"Only I seem to have got lost, it's been a long time since I last saw the crystal palace, I was human back then." Whilst they were deciding on which way to go, a dark shadow appeared on the ground.

"A harpy," said Oliver. "I hope it hasn't spotted me."

"Well, I'm damn sure it spotted me," said the troll. They watched as it flew off, but, it didn't appear to be flying towards Eleanor's castle, which was a relief. A high-pitched voice broke the silence.

"Well, well, what have we here, a human and a troll, an unlikely couple to be travelling companions."

"Hello, Samuel," said Oliver, recognising his voice. "You can help us, can't you?"

"Depends on what you need help with," said Samuel.

"We need you to show us the way to the crystal palace."

"Oh that's easy," said Samuel. "Follow me." He skipped from one branch to the neighbouring tree and pointed. "There it is." Lo and behold, in front of them was the long straight pathway with the archway of rainbow coloured trees that led to the crystal palace.

"I think maybe I should go alone," said Oliver.

"I cannot let you do that," said the troll. "I will accompany you."

"But the centaurs will shoot on sight."

"That is a risk I am prepared to take," said the troll. They started down the pathway. The troll being so tall had to duck beneath the lower branches. Samuel raced along overhead, every little noise Oliver heard as they made their way down the path made him nervous. He was expecting centaurs to appear at any moment, but surprisingly, they didn't.

As they stepped out from beneath the archway, the troll stood upright once more. He towered over Oliver as they approached the crystal palace. Dante greeted them, for he had just arrived back from the black mountain. "Why, hello, Oliver," he said. "How nice to meet you again." He then sneered at the troll, "And what do you want?"

"We wish to speak with Cressida," said Oliver.

"That will not be possible," said Dante. Without warning, the crystal doors opened and out of the surrounding forest, charged an army of centaurs, while Cressida floated in the air so she was face to face with the troll.

"It's been a long time," she said. The centaurs all held arrows in their bows ready to fire on Cressida's command, she lowered her hand and they lowered their bows. As she looked into the troll's eyes, she remembered happier times when they were together, when he had been human. "Why did you betray me?" she asked.

"I never did," said the troll. "Why did you transform me into this?" he asked.

"I didn't," she said. He pleaded with her to be honest with him.

"Oh this is very touching," said Dante. "It was I who told our parents about you two. They transformed Frederick into the troll to stop you from running off with him, and they let it be known that it was you who transformed him into this hideous creature."

"Why you," said Frederick. "I ought to crush every bone in your body," as he turned to face Dante. Cressida raised her hand once more, the centaurs raised their bows.

"Hold," she commanded. "Frederick, why did you come here, today."

"I came to warn you that Eleanor has the crystal egg, and she has asked the ogres and trolls to fight with her against you."

"And what was your answer?" asked Cressida.

"The ogres have agreed to fight alongside Eleanor, but the trolls have said no."

"That pleases me very much," said Cressida. "Follow me," said Cressida. The troll, Oliver and Dante entered the crystal palace, the army of centaurs remained outside. Cressida led the way down to the lower chambers of the crystal palace. With its high ceilings, Frederick the troll was able to walk upright. How he remembered this place, when they used to escape from prying eyes and meet down here. Cressida entered a room that Frederick had never seen before, and there on a plinth in the centre of the room was the crystal crown. Cressida made everyone wait outside, they watched as she stepped onto the multi-coloured floor. She stepped carefully from one square to another, sometimes taking a step backwards, sometimes diagonally, moving forward and sideways. She eventually reached the crystal crown, she gently lifted it from its plinth and placed it upon her head.

"You may now enter," she said.

"What was that all about?" asked Oliver.

"Only the rightful heir to the crown can enter the room and see safe passage across the floor," she said. She ascended into the air once more to face Frederick. "Give me your hands," she asked. He raised his hands, they were shaking in anticipation, she placed her tiny hands onto the palms of the troll. "I promise this won't hurt." He smiled, for he trusted her. "By the power of the crystal crown, transform this troll into the human form he once was." Cressida's tiny hands began to glow, then the troll's hands lit up, the light passed along the forearms and up the biceps, then the shoulders were alight, it spread across his chest and down his body to his legs and feet, his face was all aglow, the light radiating from his body intensified, too bright to look at. Everyone present closed their eyes. A moment later, the light faded, and when they opened their eyes once more, there standing before Cressida was Frederick, the human she had dared to love. They looked into each other's eyes, as Cressida caressed Frederick's face. "We really don't have time for this," snapped Dante. "We need to find a way of stopping Eleanor." The mention of her name bought Cressida back to reality. Frederick's clothes were now dragging on the floor. Cressida asked Dante to fetch some clothes into which Frederick changed. Oliver tried to ask for Cressida's help, explaining that his father King Richard was being held prisoner in Eleanor's dungeon. One of the palace centaurs descended the stairs.

"Langton is here, your majesty." She ignored Oliver's plea for help. Quickly, Cressida took to the air and flew over their heads. Langton was waiting in the room that overlooked the gardens.

"I know Eleanor has the crystal egg," she said. "And I know she has asked for help from the ogres and trolls in taking over the kingdom."

"I have heard this, Your Majesty. The ogres have agreed to join with Eleanor, but the trolls will not."

"Will you fight alongside us?" asked Cressida.

"I am happy with the arrangement we have at this time," said Langton.

"Does that mean you will fight with us against Eleanor?"

"I do not want to see trolls in the rainbow forest," said Langton. "Yes, you can count on us."

Chapter 26
Eleanor's Torture Chamber

Eleanor was in her castle tower, she was seated, looking upon the crystal egg, pondering, how to unleash the magic within. She knew the two fairies in the dungeon knew the answer to her question, but how to get them to reveal the crystal egg's secrets, that was the problem. If only she could capture Cressida, but how, she would have to come up with a plan to lure her away from the safety of the crystal palace, but that would have to wait, for she had a splitting headache and needed to lie down in a dark room in complete silence.

Reif having returned to the castle had gone in search of Eleanor, he knocked on the tower door. "Please, go away," said Eleanor. "I have a splitting headache." Reif knew, from previous experience, when Eleanor had a splitting headache, they could last for days. King Richard's guards and everyone that Eleanor had let leave the castle had returned, everyone, except Oliver, but because she was incapacitated, Oliver's absence had gone unnoticed. The guards had told everyone to behave as normal, as they went back to their room to think about their next move, the five brothers had gone with the guards, that left, Stephen, Henry and Nicholas, in the courtyard.

"So what do we do now?" asked Henry.

"We have to behave as normal so Eleanor doesn't suspect anything," said Stephen.

"I want to find my father," said Nicholas.

"I think we need to check out the dungeon again," said Reif, who had returned to the courtyard unnoticed. "Our best chance will be tonight," said Reif. He explained about Eleanor's headache, so they went and found the guards and five brothers. The decision was made, after dark the guards and five brothers would keep watch, the fewer of them that went the better, if caught, Reif could just say that he wanted to show off the dungeon. So while Reif would lead Stephen and Henry down into the dungeon, it was decided Nicholas should stay with the guards. The scene in the dungeon may be too gruesome for a five year old to witness, this didn't sit well with Nicholas but he had no choice. As night descended on the castle, everything was silent. Now was the time to act. Reif carried a small candle which gave off just enough light to see where they were going. They made their way to the chapel and the trap door. Reif's only worry was that this entrance may now be locked. To his surprise, it wasn't, the rug was rolled up and laid to one side, and the trap door lifted. Each of them took a candle from the chapel and followed as Reif led the way. Stephen being the eldest was bringing up the rear, with Henry in between the two. Henry was feeling rather sick and wished he could have stayed behind with Nicholas. The only sound was their footsteps on the stone stairs that descended below the castle, and the sound of their breathing. The only thing visible was each other carrying a candle, and the shadows which they cast onto the dark walls. Reif stumbled forward as he reached the bottom of the stairs unexpectedly, he warned the others, to be careful. They were grateful for the warning and all negotiated the transition from stairs to level ground without any mishaps. As they left the passageway and stepped into the dungeon, the torches on the wall burst into red flames. This had not been expected and made Henry jump with fright, he screamed. "Who's there?" called a familiar voice, standing peering through the bars of his cell he watched as three dark figures silently approached.

Nicholas had been lying on his bed, wondering what was happening when he remembered the secret passageway that led from the bedroom to the room where he had tried to speak with Eleanor's servants. He quickly made his way to the door and opened it silently, taking a candle for he knew there was no light in the passageway. Quickly, he ran along the dirt floor which muffled the sound of his footsteps. He entered the room at the end of the passageway, and froze. The room was full of Eleanor's servants, no one seemed to have noticed him enter. Then he realised they were all sleeping standing up, he crept between them, brushing up against one he felt sure they would awaken, he held his breath, but his heart was racing. Yet, no one stirred.

Eventually, he made it out of the room, he couldn't believe his luck. From there, he kept to the shadows and made his way to the chapel, the trap door was open so he knew that Reif and the others had made it this far. Trying not to make a sound on the stone steps that led to the dungeon, he moved quickly. He had caught up with the others just as they entered the dungeon. As Richard had called, "Who's there," Nicholas dropped his candle, raced past the other three who were unaware of his presence, and reached through the bars to embrace his father. In the cell furthest away, Percival also stirred. "How did you know we were here?" asked Richard.

"Oliver saw Eleanor and her servants removing you and Percival from the flower room," said Stephen. "Eleanor told the guards that you had gone to see Cressida alone, but, they knew you would never leave without telling them first."

Richard said, "Listen carefully, we must remain here so Eleanor does not suspect anything, but, you must get word to Cressida. Eleanor has the crystal egg but at this present time does not know how to unleash its magic, she has the two fairies that were advisors to the late fairy king and queen. She has already started to torture them into telling her how to release the power of the crystal egg, so far they have resisted, but who knows how long they can hold out."

Percival called Reif over, "Eleanor knows the two fairies would rather die than reveal their secret. Tell Cressida to beware any meeting Eleanor sets up, it will be a trap, for the two fairies would reveal the crystal eggs secrets for the safety of their fairy princess."

It was decided Reif would be the one to go and warn Cressida. First they had to find a way out of the castle. "I will swim across the moat," said Reif.

"Are you mad?" said Stephen.

"Have you not noticed?" said Reif. "There are fish that swim in the moat and the monster that waits beneath the surface ignores them, if I can swim beneath the surface, I think I have a good chance of making it. It only takes whatever lands on the surface."

"And what about when you need to get out of the water?" asked Stephen, Percival suggested that if they watched Reif swim just below the surface, they throw something into the water just before he needs to get out, that way they can distract the monster of the moat. Stephen didn't like the idea, but could not think of anything better, and Reif was raring to go. They had to practically tear Nicholas away from his father, who assured him everything would be all right in the end. The dungeon was plunged into darkness once more as the four youngsters left. The fairies who had been silent throughout, now spoke.

"We do not hold out much hope for their success, crossing the moat is one thing, but travelling through the rainbow forest at night is something else." As Reif led the way, all four had retrieved their candles and quickly climbed the stairs that led them back to the chapel, the trap door was closed, and the rug placed back into place, no one could know they had been to the dungeon. Reif started to undress, he explained he could swim faster without his shirt and shoes, they would only slow him down, these were the items to be thrown into the water as he approached the other side.

"Here I go," he said.

There was a loud splash and a lot of displaced water, as Reif disappeared feet first beneath the water's surface. As he dropped to the bottom of the moat, a large yellow eye passed by, followed by a massive body, the fins brushed against Reif's body, and then the tail. Reif pushed up from the bottom of the moat towards the moonlight, just below the surface he began to swim towards the bank. Looking down from above, Stephen and Henry thought the monster of the moat must have got Reif, but as the water settled once more, the pale skin of Reif's body shone in the moonlight just beneath the surface, making it easy to follow his progress. They cheered silently. There was a large swirl on the surface of the water just behind Reif, but they could not see what had caused it, but surely, it was the monster fish, the mood had suddenly changed. They were fearful for their friend. As he approached the bank, a huge dark shadow followed. He was almost there.

"Now," said Stephen. Henry had tied Reif's shirt around his shoes, and when he dropped Reif's shirt, they smashed onto the surface of the murky black waters. The shadowy figure spun round, up out of the water. The large mouth gaped wide and cleared the surface in one mouthful. Meanwhile, Reif had scrambled out of the water, and they could see his pale-skinned

193

body illuminated by the moon, dashing across the ground heading for the rainbow forest. They could hardly believe he had made it, neither could Reif, who felt as though his heart was going to explode in his chest. Having reached the trees, he sat on the grass to catch his breath. He knew the forest could be dangerous at night and so climbed up the nearest tree to wait for daylight. It was a good few hours before daylight arrived, so Reif settled for the night, he was glad of his position in the tree, for on the ground he could hear animals moving around, occasionally catching a glimpse of something large. Grunts and squeals continued all through the night, the sounds of death, the rainbow forest beautiful and yet dangerous by day, deadly at night.

Reif was on the move at the first sign of daylight, out of the tree and sprinting through the forest as fast as he could. He stumbled upon a wild boar that had just woken up, bad-tempered as usual, the boar gave chase. Reif had to climb onto the trees once more. The boar snorted loudly as he looked up into the tree. For now, Reif was safe, and the boar didn't wait around for long and soon lost interest. He was preoccupied with one thought, food, and his favourite mushrooms were only above ground in the dawn light. Once the suns got too bright, they receded beneath the surface of the ground until the next day. Reif continued on his way, when he finally made it to the long pathway that led to the crystal palace, he ceased running. For blocking his way were three centaurs fully armed with bow and arrow. "I must speak with Cressida," he said.

"There is no chance of you seeing Cressida," said the centaur standing to the right. "Go back."

"But I must speak with Cressida," Reif pleaded. The centaur to the left fired an arrow which landed right between Reif's feet, a warning shot.

He said, "Next time I will aim higher."

"Ok, I'm going," said Reif. He turned and began to walk away. The centaurs watched closely, not believing he would give up that easily. Then a strange whistling sound came from above the centaurs, they all looked away from Reif briefly. He took his chance, the outer branches of the trees that formed the archway over the path were low enough for Reif to climb upon. As the centaurs looked back, he was nowhere to be seen.

"Where is he?" asked one of the centaurs.

"I don't know, I was distracted," said another.

"Why didn't you keep an eye on him?" said the third. And they started to argue amongst themselves. Reif had climbed on top of the tree branches where he saw Samuel, whistling away to himself.

"Thank you," said Reif. The branches that formed the multi-coloured arch, were so intertwined, they gave a stable platform for Reif to run along. The centaurs having stopped arguing realised their mistake. As Reif raced above, the centaurs raced along the pathway beneath, gathering speed they could see him through the branches, a mere shadowy figure. Arrows were fired, but the branches were so intertwined, no arrow could penetrate. Again and again they fired, hitting the branches right below Reif's feet. He could feel the vibration through the branch as the arrows hit, but still he kept running. Then he had reached the end. With no more trees to race along, he had nowhere to go, he was so close, the crystal palace stood like a beacon before him. Once again, he found himself face to face with the three centaurs, they opened fire immediately as he appeared. He dropped down onto his stomach as the first three arrows narrowly missed, the arrows kept coming, two of the centaurs went underneath the canopy of branches, they fired continuously. As Reif lay on his stomach, every arrow fired, vibrated through the branches on which Reif's body lay. He was not confident the branches would last much longer, panic began to set in. As he thought, *how the hell am I going to get out of this mess?* To his relief, the doors to the crystal palace opened, but, only to reveal more centaurs, his heart sank, his brief moment of hope extinguished, he lowered his gaze, as the centaurs stepped forward.

"Halt," shouted Aegeus. "Lower your bows," was the order. Reif could hardly believe his ears, the branches upon which he lay had stopped vibrating, he slowly raised his head so he could see over the edge of the canopy. As he looked down upon those on the ground, he was caught by surprise as Cressida suddenly appeared right in front of his gaze.

"Hello, Reif," she said. "Why did you risk your life to see me?" she asked.

"Your Majesty," said Reif, "I have important news to tell."

Two male fairies appeared either side of Reif and each took hold of an arm. They lifted him from the canopy and floated to the ground. Once on the ground, he was released. Oliver raced forward to greet Reif. "Follow me," said Cressida. They walked back to the crystal palace. Once inside the safety of the palace, Cressida asked, "What news do you have for me?"

Reif explained, "Eleanor has the two fairies who were advisors to the late king and queen, she is asking them how to unleash the magic within the crystal egg."

"So she has the crystal egg, but does not know how to use it," said Cressida.

"Exactly," said Reif. "Eleanor has started to torture the two fairies and we do not know how long they can resist. It is imperative that you strike now."

"We need to be careful," said Cressida. "We cannot just rush in."

"But, Your Majesty, when I left, Eleanor was unwell. When Arec and I were younger, growing up in Eleanor's castle, she used to get these headaches, they could last for a week. She had to retreat to her bed in total darkness, unable to move."

"And this is important," said Cressida.

"Your Majesty, when I left, Eleanor had taken to her bed with one of these headaches, she cannot function until it clears."

Four centaurs were present in the room with Cressida, along with Dante, they asked Reif to wait outside while they now considered what Reif had told them. "If it is true that she is incapacitated this could be our chance," said Dante. The centaurs were more cautious.

"But what if this is a trap?" They argued back and forth over what Reif had told them. As Reif waited in a smaller room, he paced up and down. He could not understand what was taking so long, he had Oliver for company, they waited in silence.

When suddenly, Oliver asked, "How did you escape from the castle?" Oliver then listened in awe as Reif explained how he managed to swim across the moat beneath the surface, how he had seen the bright yellow eye, and the giant body, then as he was about to leave the water he heard the loud splash as his clothes hit the surface, that was his signal to climb out of the water. He had looked back as the large mouth had opened and cleared the surface of the moat. "That was brilliant," said Oliver.

Just then the door opened and Reif was beckoned to enter, Oliver followed.

"We have considered your information and have decided that this is not the right time for action."

"You are mad," cried Reif.

"Be silent," yelled Cressida. "We need more time to gather our defences," she said. Dante disagreed, and let it be known. "Be silent, brother," she said, "Or you will find yourself locked away again." He bowed and excused himself from the room, she was glad to see him leave, they could never agree on anything. She spoke to Reif, "I am grateful for the information you have supplied us with, but under counsel with my centaurs, we cannot act straight away, you are most welcome to stay with us at the crystal palace."

"I thank you for listening, Your Majesty," said Reif. "And I respect your decision, but I must say that I think you are missing a great opportunity." He bowed and backed out of the room, Oliver followed. Cressida was sat upon her throne, drumming her fingers against her leg, she could not help wondering if she had made the wrong decision.

Dante had entered the palace garden, where he was joined by Reif and Oliver. The heavily scented rose garden reminded Oliver of Eleanor's flower garden room, this evoked memories, of his father and Percival being carried off to the dungeon. He was disappointed that Cressida was not going to act, and felt rather strange to think that he and Dante were on the same side. Oliver watched as Dante and Reif were in conversation on the other side of the garden, Reif was still shirtless and Oliver could not help but notice how white Reif's skin was. Then he thought to himself, *I suppose that's what happens when you are locked away from any sunlight for ten years*. He was trying to imagine how that must have felt when Reif approached and he was brought back from his daydream.

"Dante believes he can persuade some of the centaurs to help us attack Eleanor's castle," said Reif, "but we have no time to waste."

"How will we get across the moat?" asked Oliver.

"With Eleanor being unwell, she will not be aware of anyone approaching. Dante will be able to fly over the moat and once inside the castle can lower the drawbridge."

"Excellent," said Oliver. "When do we leave?"

"That's just it, we both think it is better if you stay behind."

"That's rubbish," said Oliver. "There is no way I am going to stay behind. If you try and leave me I will tell Cressida."

They had not expected that. Reif went back and spoke with Dante once more. There was a lot of arm waving and hand gestures in what looked a very heated discussion, eventually Reif came back and agreed

"All right, you get your way." said Reif.

Oliver was pleased, for he didn't want to be left behind but his joy was short lived. Reif and Oliver had been left in the garden as Dante went to drum up support for an attack on Cressida's castle. He had to be careful how he approached the centaurs for the last thing he wanted was Cressida to know of his plans, he was disappointed with the response, not one centaur showed any interest in his plan. He would have to think again, he returned to the garden where he found Reif and Oliver still waiting. When he told them the response, they were dumbfounded.

"Why can they not see it is in their best interest to stop Eleanor before she gets too powerful, what about asking Langton for help?" suggested Oliver.

"That's a good idea," said Reif. They had been so preoccupied with getting the information to Cressida and expecting the centaurs to help they had completely forgotten about the fawns. Dante wasn't so sure, he did not have a good relationship with Langton, but as Oliver pointed out, it wasn't about the relationship between Dante and Langton that mattered, it was the whole kingdom that was at risk. Because of the way Dante and Langton felt about each other Reif said that he would go and ask for help.

Chapter 27
Asking Langton for Help

Langton had been home a few days and had introduced his two sons to their mother. She was still locked away in a cell, he had warned them before he had taken them to visit her, but it was still a highly emotional experience for them all. She had screamed upon seeing their faces and they had backed away as she reached through the bars to touch them. Langton approached the cell and took hold of his wife's hands, she calmed down and he told his sons it was okay to approach. Slowly, they moved closer to the cell, their mother was crying floods of tears. Darius ran forward and put his arms through the bars to reach his mother. Ferdinand stood watching, as the tears flowed down his cheeks, his whole body shook as he sobbed and his legs eventually buckled. He crumpled to the floor besides his father who released his wife's hands and cradled his son. In the blink of an eye, she had grabbed hold of Darius around his neck and tightened her grip. Langton pushed Ferdinand to the floor away from the cell, he removed the flaming torch from the wall and thrust it between the bars at his wife. At first, she would not release Darius, he was choking and turning blue. Again, Langton thrust the flames at his wife. This time, she released Darius and as he fell to the floor, Ferdinand pulled him away, out of reach.

"I am so sorry," said Langton. "I did not expect that, I thought she would be pleased to see you, I thought it would help her to see you." She had withdrawn to the back of the cell and started to scream once more. Langton led his sons up the stairs, leaving the screams behind, it was almost unbearable to think that was their mother. When they had reached the top of the stairs, Langton had closed the door, this helped to muffle the sound.

Darius and Ferdinand had quickly settled back into their lives, all their friends had welcomed them back eagerly, having thought they would never see them again, they all wanted to know everything that had happened to them. They had spent a whole day telling stories about how they arrived at the black mountain, how Arec and Reif who were ogres had taken them in and given them food and shelter and protection, and then the day the humans arrived and everything changed. They had retrieved the crystal egg from the black mountain, how Reif had been transformed from an ogre back into a human and how Arec had died during the transformation. Langton had sat listening to all the stories, he felt particularly sad when they had spoken of Arec, for he had been a good friend of Langton's.

Another day dawned and Reif arrived at the entrance to Langton's home. He called from below, "Is anyone there?"

Langton appeared, "Good morning, Reif. You are up early today."

"I need to speak with you urgently."

"Then you had better come on up." Langton lowered a rope, Reif grabbed hold of the rope with both hands and Langton pulled Reif with ease up the sheer cliff face.

As they entered the cave, Langton asked, "What is it you need to speak about so urgently?"

Reif explained about Eleanor, and Langton listened in silence. "I see," said Langton. "So Cressida and the centaurs won't do anything, and you expect me to help save the kingdom for her?" Reif hadn't thought of it that way before and could understand Langton's point of view. "Why should I risk the lives of my fawns when Cressida sits back and does nothing? Even though she has all those centaurs under her command. I said I will fight alongside Cressida and her centaurs, but I will not fight alone."

Reif's disappointment obviously showed on his face. "I am sorry it has to be this way," said Langton. "Will you have something to eat?"

"Thank you," said Reif. "But I must be going, there is no time to waste, can you lower me back down?"

"Of course," said Langton. "And I hope you are successful with mission." As Reif reached the bottom of the cliff face, he released the rope and sprinted off without saying another word.

Langton watched with a heavy heart as Reif disappeared from view, but he had his own troubles to worry about, and if Cressida was not prepared to fight for her kingdom, then why should he.

Reif made it safely back to the crystal palace a day later. Dante and Oliver had been waiting anxiously. When he arrived, Dante asked, "Well, what did Langton have to say?"

"He will not help us," answered Reif.

"Damn fools the lot of them," moaned Dante.

Oliver asked Reif, "Did you get to see Darius and Ferdinand, are they alright?"

"I'm sorry," said Reif. "I didn't stay long enough to see them, but I am sure they are fine, back with their family."

Dante who had sat down suddenly sprang to his feet, he asked, "Who is at the castle?"

"What do you mean?" asked Oliver.

"Guards," said Dante. "How many guards does Eleanor have?"

A smile spread across Reif's face. "She has none," he said. "Only her servants."

Dante turned to Oliver, "How many royal guards accompany your father?"

"I'm not sure, ten or twelve I think, plus there are five brothers and then there is Stephen and Henry, and of course there is my father and Percival. They are both locked in the dungeon."

"Right," said Dante. "I am ready to leave right now, are you?"

"Of course," said Reif and Oliver together.

They arrived at Eleanor's castle as the evening approached, the suns were beginning to merge as the light faded. Dante had the task of lowering the drawbridge, and Reif had told Dante the way to the tower where Eleanor would be sleeping. While Dante was doing this, Reif and Oliver would find the guards and make their way down to the dungeon to release King Richard and Percival. As Dante flew high above the moat, he couldn't resist dropping a stone into the water. He watched with glee as the monster fish rose to the surface, mouth wide open. "Nothing to eat this time," chuckled Dante. What Dante was unaware of was, by creating such a splash in the water, the giant fish had alerted Eleanor's servants. They looked out from various windows of the castle, scanning the water's surface, nothing, then one of them spotted some movement on the bank opposite. Two human figures, it blinked. As Eleanor lay on her bed with her head feeling as though it had been split in two by an axe, an image suddenly flashed into her brain, she writhed in agony. Dante quickly lowered the drawbridge unchallenged. Another of Eleanor's servants had spotted this, they blinked. Again, the image was received by Eleanor, but she was helpless, unable to move from her bed, paralysed with pain. Reif and Oliver raced across the drawbridge, as Dante headed for the stairs that led to Eleanor, more and more images flashed in her brain, she screamed in agony, Dante had arrived at her door.

Oliver found the guards, the five brothers and Stephen and Henry, sitting in their room having just returned from their evening meal. They were completely taken by surprise as he rushed through the doorway. With no explanation, he said, "Follow me." He led them into the courtyard and said, "Leave, the drawbridge is down."

"What about you?" asked the guards.

"I am going to help rescue my father."

"Then we are coming with you," said the guards. With no time to argue, Oliver raced to the chapel and entered, through the open trap door, the passageway that led to the dungeon. Reif was already there and was being kept away from the cells by four of Eleanor's servants. They each held long spears that glowed white hot. As Oliver and the guards arrived, swords were drawn, and the fighting began. The servants were surprisingly light on their feet, and skilled in the art of fighting. This was not going to be as easy as they had thought, the servants were blinking incessantly. Dante had still not found a way to open the door to Eleanor's tower, but the screams from within had become louder and more frequent. Without warning, the screams stopped and Eleanor's door flew open, she held her staff in her right hand and fired a blast at Dante's chest. He was sent flying down the stairs, unconscious before he hit the bottom. In her left hand, she held the small dainty hand of Nicholas. She slowly made her way down the stairs, stepping over Dante's body, she proceeded to the dungeon. The fighting was fierce, but the guards were winning, two of Eleanor's servants had been slain, only two remained, one had been forced back onto the cell that held King Richard. He had reached through the bars and had his arm around the throat of the servant, it blinked once more sending an image of the dark ceiling to Eleanor, but it did not matter for she stood across from Richard's cell and had seen for herself what had happened. As the last remaining servant perished, the guards all cheered and they retrieved the keys to open the cells. Not one of them had noticed Eleanor's arrival. Only when the cells doors were unlocked did she reveal herself, stepping forward from the shadows. "Congratulations," she said. "You have succeeded in opening the cells, now get inside." A blast from the staff knocked everyone off of their feet and all flew into the cells. Eleanor calmly walked forward, still holding the hand of Nicholas in her left hand. She picked up the keys and locked the cells once more. Richard called to Nicholas, there was no response, he merely looked up at Eleanor with a smile.

"What have you done to my son?" Richard raged.

"He belongs to me now," said Eleanor.

Eleanor triumphantly left the dungeon, leaving Richard and all his men screaming after her. She looked down into the eyes of Nicholas and smiled, without a word being said, Nicholas smiled in return. Meanwhile on the stairs, Dante had recovered, he made his way up to the room at the top of the tower, the door was still wide open, he peered inside, the room was empty. He entered, there was the bed that Eleanor had been lying upon, all dishevelled where she had been writhing in agony. In the centre of the room, there was a large wooden desk, covered in scrolls of paper bound with silk, but that was not what Dante was looking for. He started to search the drawers of the desk, none were locked, but they did not contain what he was looking for either. There was a bookshelf on one wall that covered the wall completely from floor to ceiling, all books on magic, yet, still he could not find the one thing he was looking for. Then he realised in one corner there was a black lace curtain. As he approached, he started to get excited, this had to be it, and when he pulled the curtain to one side, there it was, the crystal egg. He wondered if there were any enchantments to prevent him from taking it, but didn't have time to test it. He plunged his hand toward the velvet cushion and to his surprise, the crystal egg was easily plucked from the cushion. He held it up to the light to admire it when he heard footsteps climbing the stairs. He went to the same large window the harpy always used and jumped into the air. He soared across the moat and landed on the other side. He heard Eleanor screaming from the tower, a smile spread across his face, he knew that she had just discovered the crystal egg missing, she had completely forgotten about Dante. Even climbing the stairs back to the tower, she hadn't registered that his body was missing, now she was standing at the window as she watched Dante heading towards the rainbow forest.

She raced down the stairs and mounted the horse that belonged to Oliver, that was standing in the courtyard. She gave chase across the drawbridge, if only she could catch up with Dante before he reached the rainbow forest. She was gaining fast, but not fast enough. As Dante reached the edge of the forest, a wall of centaurs stepped forth, followed by Cressida wearing the crystal crown. In her haste, Eleanor had forgotten her staff, she turned to ride away but the centaurs had already started to close in, there was no escape. The centaurs parted to allow Cressida through.

"You think you are better than me," said Eleanor. "But I was first born to our father."

"We know you are our half-sister, we have always known," said Cressida. "But a fairy king and a witch do not make a fairy queen."

"I have no desire to be a fairy queen," said Eleanor. "I only wish to rule over this kingdom."

"That is something that you will never do," said Cressida. "Take her," she ordered the centaurs. As the circle of centaurs closed in, from out of the sky a flight of harpies dropped large stones that smashed into the ground, the centaurs backed off, and before anyone of them could fire an arrow, the largest of the harpies had swooped down, and lifted Eleanor from her horse and flew away. Cressida screamed in anger as Eleanor disappeared from sight, although her anger was short lived, for Dante approached his sister and handed her the crystal egg.

"You managed to get it, but how?" asked Cressida.

Dante explained what had happened on the stairs and how Eleanor had left him there to go to the dungeon, and how while she was away he had managed to get the egg. "What about those in the dungeon?" asked Cressida.

"I didn't have time to check on them," said Dante. Cressida gave the command to enter Eleanor's castle. The drawbridge was down, they entered into the courtyard it was completely empty of life.

"Quickly, find the dungeon," she commanded.

Nicholas appeared from the shadows. He seemed dazed and confused. Cressida did not know who he was, having never seen him before.

"Dante, who is this?" she asked.

"This is Prince Nicholas," he said. "He is the one who retrieved the crystal egg from the black mountain."

"I know the way to the dungeon," he said.

"Quickly, follow him," said Cressida. Through the trap door in the chapel and down the narrow passage, Nicholas led the way. As they entered the dungeon, the flame torches on the wall burst into red flame, one last time. The centaurs approached the cells, Richard pointed to where the keys were hanging, the cell doors were unlocked and everyone poured out into the dungeon.

"This way out," said Dante. "Follow me." Richard picked up Nicholas in his arms and followed Dante, as they stepped into the sunlight they shielded their eyes with their hands. It didn't take long for their eyes to become adjusted to the brightness. Cressida greeted them in the courtyard.

"Your Majesty, I cannot thank you and your children enough for what you have done for our kingdom."

"I did nothing but get caught," said Richard. "It is all down to my two sons."

"When you are ready, I can give you safe passage across back to your world." She then turned to Reif, "You are more than welcome to stay if that is what you wish."

"I think I have spent enough time here," said Reif. "I would like to go back home." Richard called his guards together and they approached Dante, who watched them nervously.

"For all your help in returning my sons," said Richard. They poured the bags of gold coins onto the ground at Dante's feet, he was so overwhelmed he didn't know what to say, and ended up saying nothing. Richard turned to Cressida and said, "I think we are ready to go now." They left the courtyard and crossed the drawbridge leaving the castle for the last time.

As they marched towards the boundary between their worlds, Cressida explained, "I can create an opening in the mountain but only for a brief period of time, it will give you enough time to cross, but once closed, it cannot be opened for another ten years."

"I understand," said Richard. Richard then asked, "What about Eleanor and the ogres?" Cressida reassured him now that she had the crystal egg and the crystal crown, there would be no more trouble from Eleanor or the ogres. They would stay within their own lands. The mountain came into view.

"We are here," said Cressida. The mountain looked as solid as any mountain Richard had ever seen, he started to have doubts this was going to work. But before Cressida started, Langton and his twin sons, Darius and Ferdinand, called to Oliver and Nicholas, they raced down the hillside to say goodbye. Stephen and Henry joined in saying farewell, there were tears, but this time they were tears of joy.

"Maybe we will meet again someday," said Oliver.

Cressida placed the crystal egg in its rightful position on top of the crystal crown. Now it was complete, she raised her arms, and gave the command for the mountain to open and grant safe passage. A brilliant white light shot from the crystal egg as the crown glowed, it shone on the mountain and the mountain slowly vanished from sight. "There is the river that lies between our worlds," Cressida said farewell one last time. They started to wade across the river. Prince Nicholas was sitting upon his father's shoulders, even Cressida had a tear in her eyes as she watched them depart as they reached the other side of the river. They started to step out of the water when the boundary began to close. Percival slipped back into the water, Oliver tried to pull him clear but Percival was carried away. Then suddenly, from high in the sky, unnoticed, a giant white eagle swooped down and plucked Nicholas from the shoulders of his father. Richard turned to see the white eagle carrying Nicholas off into the distance, as the boundary closed once more. The last image Richard saw before the mountain fully reappeared was that of Dante and Cressida smiling that sickly smile that Richard knew so well. Percival was also trapped on the other side of the boundary, the river was no longer in sight, just a solid mountain wall. Closed for another ten years. "Nooo," screamed Richard.